RIVER OF DEATH

As he crept inside the barn, Touch the Sky's eyes cut to a few wooden rungs that had been nailed into a support beam, making a crude ladder up into a hayloft.

Hugging the wall, crawling on his knees and elbows, Touch the Sky moved cautiously down to the pile of dirt, eased around it, and abruptly felt a cold stirring in his stomach.

A tunnel entrance yawned before him, a hungry maw calling out to him to enter if he dared.

Why should this bother you? he admonished himself. After all, you knew it was here. You heard Carlson mention it. So why this feeling now as if a dead man had risen before your eyes?

You know perfectly well why that feeling, another voice inside him responded. Because you saw this tunnel long before Carlson mentioned it. You saw it in your dream vision.

Death by water . . .

DESERT MANHUNT

No one even appeared to notice as Big Tree cocked his right arm back and hurled the single-edged knife with lethal accuracy straight toward Touch the Sky.

But one person had noticed. Just as the knife was released, Little Bear's warning roar rose above the din of camp. Hearing it, Honey Eater acted instinctively.

Almost as if it were one long movement, Big Tree tossed the lead line free and leaped onto his pony. Touch the Sky was just in time to recognize his enemy, even as, from the corner of his eye, he saw something hurtling toward him.

An eyeblink later, just as the well-thrown knife should have punctured Touch the Sky's vitals, Honey Eater flew between him and the blade. A feral cry of misery and fear rose from Touch the Sky when he heard the sickening sound of the blade slicing into Honey Eater. Even as the lightning-fast pony raced from camp, bearing Big Tree to freedom, Touch the Sky's wife collapsed in his arms.

CHEYENNE

River of Death/
Desert Manhunt

Judd Cole

LEISURE BOOKS NEW YORK CITY

A LEISURE BOOK®

January 2000

Published by

Dorchester Publishing Co., Inc.
276 Fifth Avenue
New York, NY 10001

ISBN 0-8439-4676-8

River
of
Death

Prologue

Although Matthew Hanchon bore the name given to him by his adopted white parents, he was the son of full-blooded Northern Cheyennes. The lone survivor of a Bluecoat massacre in 1840, the infant was raised by John and Sarah Hanchon in the Wyoming Territory settlement of Bighorn Falls.

His adoptive parents loved him as their own, and at first the youth was happy enough in his limited world. The occasional stares and threats from others meant little—until his sixteenth year and a forbidden love with Kristen, daughter of wealthy rancher Hiram Steele.

Steele's campaign to run Matthew off like a distempered wolf was assisted by Seth Carlson, the jealous, Indian-hating cavalry officer who was in love with Kristen. Carlson delivered a fateful ultimatum: Either Matthew cleared out of Bighorn Falls for good, or Carlson would ruin his parents' contract to supply nearby Fort Bates—and thus ruin their mercantile business.

His heart sad but determined, Matthew set out for the upcountry of the Powder River, Cheyenne territory. Captured by braves from Chief Yellow Bear's tribe, he was declared an Indian spy for the hair-face soldiers and brutally tortured over fire. But only a heartbeat before he was to be scalped and gutted, old Arrow Keeper interceded.

The tribe shaman and protector of the sacred Medicine Arrows, Arrow Keeper had recently experienced an epic vision. This vision foretold that the long-lost son of a great Cheyenne chief would return to his people—and that he would lead them in one last, great victory against their enemies. This youth would be known by the distinctive mark of the warrior, the same birthmark Arrow Keeper spotted buried past this youth's hairline: a mulberry-colored arrowhead.

Arrow Keeper used his influence to spare the youth's life, and ordered that he be allowed to join the tribe and train with the junior warriors. This infuriated two braves especially: the fierce war leader Black Elk and his cunning younger cousin, Wolf Who Hunts Smiling.

Black Elk was jealous of the glances cast at the tall young stranger by Honey Eater, daughter of Chief Yellow Bear. And Wolf Who Hunts Smiling, proudly ambitious despite his youth, hated all whites without exception. This stranger was to him only a make-believe Cheyenne who wore white man's shoes, spoke the paleface tongue, and showed his emotions in his face like the woman-hearted white men.

Arrow Keeper buried the youth's white name forever and gave him a new Cheyenne name: Touch the Sky. But he remained a white man's dog in the eyes of many in the tribe. At first humiliated at every turn, eventually the determined youth mastered the warrior arts. Slowly, as his coup stick filled with enemy scalps, he won the respect of more and more in the tribe.

But with each victory, deceiving appearances triumphed over reality, and the acceptance he so desperately craved eluded him. Worse, his hard-won victories left him with two especially fierce enemies outside the tribe: a Blackfoot called Sis-ki-dee and a Comanche named Big Tree.

As for Black Elk, at first he was hard but fair. When Touch the Sky rode off to save his white parents from outlaws, Honey Eater was convinced that he had deserted her and the tribe forever. She was forced to accept Black Elk's bride-price after her father crossed to the Land of Ghosts. But Touch the Sky returned.

Then, as it became clear to all that Honey Eater loved only Touch the Sky, Black Elk's jealousy drove him to join his younger cousin in plotting against Touch the Sky's life. Finally, Wolf Who Hunts Smiling's treachery forced a crisis: Aiming at Touch the Sky in heavy fog, he instead killed Black Elk. Touch the Sky stood accused of the murder by many in the tribe.

Though it divided the tribe irrevocably, he and Honey Eater performed the squaw-taking ceremony. He had firm allies in his blood brother Little Horse, the youth Two Twists, and Tangle Hair. With Arrow Keeper's mysterious disappearance, Touch the Sky became the tribe's shaman.

But a pretend shaman named Medicine Flute, backed by Touch the Sky's enemies, challenged his authority. And despite his fervent need to stop being the eternal outsider, Touch the Sky was still trapped between two worlds, welcome in neither.

Chapter One

"Tell us a thing, shaman, if you are so wise," Little Horse taunted his tall friend. "For I have noticed something curious."

Little Horse had to speak loudly to be heard above the foaming of the rapids further out in the river. He, Two Twists, and Tangle Hair sat in a little group, watching Touch the Sky's son receive his first swimming lesson. Little Bear, his second winter just behind him, dangled naked between Touch the Sky and Honey Eater. Clearly the river both intrigued and frightened him. His parents held him in up to his navel, and he was still deciding whether to laugh or cry.

"Let *me* tell you a thing, All Behind Him," replied Two Twists, youngest of the Cheyenne braves present. He used the name he had given

Little Horse when the latter began to gain weight. "Here is something very curious. They say a good warrior takes on the traits of his enemies. This Not-So-Little Horse here—he must be a good warrior indeed. See? He is getting a belly pouch like the beer-swilling paleface soldiers."

"Soon," Tangle Hair added, watching the little one decide to laugh with delight, "Little Horse will take to eating beef and mounting his pony from the white man's side."

Even Honey Eater, busy restraining her squirming charge, smiled at the teasing behind them. Usually the braves acted so solemn and taciturn when women and children were around. But this trio, as close as brothers to Touch the Sky, accepted her and the child as trusted equals and let their guards down. Great warriors, she had learned, were often like adolescent boys when among their own. But there were no boys among this group when the war cry sounded.

Little Horse, grinning with the rest, threatened to flay Two Twists' soles. A moment later the two braves were struggling in a wrestling contest, grunting and cursing.

"A new buck knife on Little Horse," Touch the Sky said automatically, for no Indian passed a chance to wager.

Tangle Hair nodded. "A double pipe of white man's tobacco on Two Twists."

"Treachery!" Two Twists shouted in a muffled voice. "The big Indian is sitting on me! Have you seen how swayback all his ponies have become? I am defeated! Take my hair and let me breathe!"

Touch the Sky laughed outright at his companions as he dipped his son even lower, letting the cool mountain runoff rise up under the mite's armpits.

"Brrrr!" Little Bear roared, imitating his mother on a winter morning. His impressive lung power had earned him his name.

This made all of them laugh again. Little Horse and Two Twists quit struggling long enough to admire the little warrior as he dipped his head quickly under the water with no help from either parent.

"Ipewa," Little Horse said, nodding his approval. "Good! Just as the line-back dun always breeds good stock, this Touch the Sky has given our tribe a fighter! Look at him! The entire world knows we Shayienas are not fish-eaters or great swimmers. I have watched good Cheyenne babes of four and five cry in the river. This little tadpole wants to swim right in."

Touch the Sky nodded proudly, though in fact his companions were almost as pleased as he. There was no word for "orphan" in Cheyenne, because every adult was considered a parent to every child. And Touch the Sky had already assured his companions that Little Bear would not exist if not for their vigilance and loyalty in protecting mother and son.

"He wants to wade right in," Touch the Sky agreed. "But he must learn what Arrow Keeper taught me. Search the water first."

Even as he said this, Touch the Sky scooped

one hand into the purling river, just ahead of his floundering son. It emerged holding a jagged-edged object made of metal torn to lethally sharp points and edges. The child had been about to flounder onto it.

Everyone, Little Bear and Honey Eater included, stared at it.

"What in the name of Maiyun is it?" Honey Eater demanded.

The trio on the bank behind them were not as mystified as Honey Eater was. Because any companion of Touch the Sky's was, by necessity, a veteran warrior, they had a better idea what the object was. They were more worried about why it was there.

"It is a shell casing," Touch the Sky replied, now ignoring his son to search the low, rolling banks around them and the scattered clumps of cottonwood. They had picked a secluded spot well upriver from their summer camp. "A shell that has been exploded further upriver and washed down."

He looked at Little Horse. "Buck, you were about to ask me a thing when double-braid here started teasing you. Let me ask that question for you. You are curious about the same thing troubling many of us. The river. We are well into the snowmelt moon, and the freshets have been plentiful. With so much runoff from the mountains, you wonder, why are the Powder and Little Powder Rivers down this season?"

Little Horse stood up, watching Touch the Sky with open admiration.

"Once again, shaman, you have seen with the

14

inner eye. That is the very thing I wonder. Does this"—he nodded toward the twisted scrap in his friend's hand—"somehow explain it?"

Slowly, with Little Bear kicking in spirited protest, Touch the Sky lifted his son and carried him out of the river. Honey Eater followed, her soft doeskin dress wet and clinging to her long legs and the deep, sweeping curves of her hips. Fresh white columbine petals were braided through her hair.

"Explain it?" Touch the Sky repeated, handing the child to Two Twists for a ride on his shoulders. "If so, I do not know how. But these casings are not from explosives used by combat soldiers. They are engineering charges."

Touch the Sky had been forced to use crude Cheyenne equivalents for the paleface words, just as artillery pieces were called big-talking guns. His companions listened to him, but still looked baffled.

"When I grew up among the whites near Fort Bates," Touch the Sky explained, "the soldiers used explosives to level ridges and build bridges or to clear out rocky areas. Engineering charges."

"Like the ones Wolf Who Hunts Smiling and the renegades stole from the blue blouses?" Two Twists asked. "The explosives they used to destroy the path for the iron horse?"

Touch the Sky nodded.

"Brothers, all well and good," Tangle Hair said. "But what do blue flowers have to do with the causes of the wind? Look. See there where the watermark is? Far lower than it should be this time of the season. Where will it be by the time we enter the dry moons? Surely this is bad medicine, not the work of palefaces or Indian renegades with explosives."

This sounded reasonable to each of the Cheyennes, for in their world natural causes took far greater precedence over man-made ones. If the red-speckled cough wiped out your village, it was the work of angry Holy Ones, not an infected blanket.

Touch the Sky respected those natural causes, but his time among whites also taught him respect for man's power to disturb and control nature.

"It is bad medicine," he replied, "no matter the cause. But we have wasted enough words in useless speculation."

He turned to Honey Eater. "Take the little one back to camp. Two Twists and Tangle Hair will ride with you. Little Horse and I are taking a ride upriver to see what can be seen."

No one questioned this, although a troubled light glinted briefly in Honey Eater's eyes. When the rest had left, Touch the Sky and Little Horse caught up their ponies.

"I knew your question before you asked it," Touch the Sky said, "because an omen was placed over my eyes last night in a dream."

"What omen, brother?"

Touch the Sky always tried to be forthright with his band, especially with Little Horse. How many times had they stood back-to-back and cheated death? But this particular omen was so forboding and ominous that speaking of it directly might create powerful bad medicine.

"An omen," the tall warrior replied, swinging up onto his little paint, "that augured trouble by water."

Little Horse was not a brave to show feelings in his face. But this statement, from this highly credible source, shook him to his core. He could read beneath the words. His friend had seen an omen promising death in the water—the worst possible way in the world for an Indian to die. A drowned Indian could never go to the Land of Ghosts. His spirit remained trapped in the water for eternity, cold and lonely, moaning in grief but completely without succor.

Better the bullet, the arrow, the lance, even the deadly Comanche skull-cracker than death in the water.

And because it was bad this time, Little Horse grinned wide and mustered his famous bravado.

"Go forth and bring me the Wendigo," he boasted. "I have no plans to die in my tipi."

Touch the Sky grinned. "Unlike the skinny Medicine Flute, who boasts he can divine the future, I have no foreknowledge of events. But I can tell you this, buck. You will never die in your tipi. Not," he added regretfully, "so long as you cross your lance with mine. Now look sharp, brother. We are about to grab trouble firmly by the tail."

One full sleep's ride west of the Cheyenne camp, in the center of the verdant bottom section white men called Blackford's Valley, an odd coalition had assembled inside a sagging hay barn.

A huge, heavy-jowled man with thick lumps of scar tissue over his eyes spoke to the rest from his perch atop a stack of shoring timbers.

"Men!" shouted Hiram Steele. "It's already starting to rain gold! I called you all together today to make an announcement. Thanks to your efforts so far, I've been able to impress some extremely solvent investors in my Pikestown project. Your wages are guaranteed for the next six months!"

A rousing cheer went up from the twenty men gathered around Hiram. They were all soldiers, though most had removed their blue kersey blouses and were either bare-chested or wore only coarse gray linen undershirts.

Steele lifted a hand to quiet the men.

"Now understand, men. These investors don't know about our little operation here at Salt Lick Creek. I'm keeping it dark from them just the way that you men and Captain Carlson are keeping it dark from your superiors back at Fort Bates."

Hiram had provided a barrel of good grain mash for this occasion. An anonymous trooper, his tongue well oiled with coffin varnish, piped up:

"You ride for Cap'n Carlson, mum's the word! A high private can live like a general in Savvy Seth's platoon! Who *wouldn't* be a soldier!"

Carlson, the only officer in the group and standing closest to Hiram, scowled. "Sew up your lips, Meadows," he growled while the rest of the troopers laughed.

Hiram watched Carlson scowl and forced back a good chuckle. Carlson was crooked as a sidewinder, which made him one of Hiram's most useful business partners here on the frontier. But the West Point graduate and scion of one of the First Families of Virginia had never learned to relax around common men. His men liked serving under him because they could often triple their regular pay by carrying out his and Hiram's schemes. But they had no real respect for him, a fact Carlson was smart enough to grasp but too bullheaded to change.

"Men," Hiram continued, "Pikestown will become a reality, I'm sure of that. Our operation is perfectly brilliant in its simplicity. This barn—" He swept one beefy arm overhead, indicating the building. Behind the knot of men, huge piles of dirt obscured a tunnel opening. "—keeps our operation secret. The initial blasting is almost over and gave us a good operating base. Now the digging makes the change so gradual no one suspects any cause but Mother Nature. Soon Salt Lick Creek is going to undergo one of those 'natural' changes that happen all the time. It's going to shift its course to an old tributary. And once that happens, it means far less water downstream for the blanket-asses living at the Cheyenne camp. Meantime, it also means irrigation water for my— *our*—projected farming community."

Hiram didn't bother adding a technicality that didn't concern Carlson's work crew. Salt Lick Creek was the official treaty boundary of the Northern Cheyenne reservation. Once it jumped its bank to a new tributary, it would cut the reservation in half. Meanwhile, the value of Hiram's new claim at the land office in Register Cliffs was about to increase dramatically. Land now wasted on buffalo range would provide the fertile bottomland for his new community of Pikestown.

All it took was one bend in one good-sized creek. And that bend was being created from underground, using trained military sappers, and by scraping-and-grading crews working after dark.

While the sappers debauched, Hiram got Carlson aside.

"Did your C.O. buy that story about building a cistern near Beaver Creek?"

"Sure," Carlson said. "It's his favorite project. He loves it when the paper-collar boys from the press quote him on how the Army is giving back to the American people."

"You've got a few of your boys working on it?"

Carlson nodded. He was a big, bluff man with wind-blistered cheeks. He still wore his cavalry officer's hat, the brim snapped back to keep his vision clear.

"A small crew. Luckily for us, Colonel Nearhood doesn't know his ass from his elbow when it comes to engineering. He thinks building a rain cistern is a major job. He doesn't realize this is too many men in the field."

Carlson seemed to be listening, but Hiram could tell his mind was somewhere else. And he knew right where it was.

"You're fretting about Hanchon, ain't you?" he said.

Carlson nodded again. "You telling me you're not?"

Hiram frowned. "You think I'd lie to you after all that red bastard's done to us? Man, my own daughter was sweet on that sonofabitch! I caught him up in her bedroom before that whore got wise and ran away from home. I swear it now, I mean to kill him *and* Kristen."

Carlson flushed red to his very earlobes. "You're telling *me* about being shamed by that red nigger and Kristen? Me, who asked her to marry me, only to find out she preferred a flea-bitten, blanket-assed savage over a decent white man?"

"Never mind the shame, soldier blue. Think about the money. We've both put our last red cent into this project. If it works, we're going to die rich with counties named after us. And it *should* work. The brilliance is that all of our work is secret. I can tell you right now, Hanchon *will* be coming, and soon, to check this out. That gives us a chance to kill him. It's also an opportunity to see just how secret our operation is."

Carlson nodded, his features set tight with determination. "He'll be coming. He always does. But we've never been ready for him like we are now. This time, he's riding into a world of hurt."

Chapter Two

"Count upon it," Touch the Sky told his companion. "Back at camp they are celebrating in the Bull Whip dance lodge."

Little Horse nodded. "Celebrating? Brother, they will paint as for war and hold a victory dance! Every time you ride out, they gloat. Your enemies leap atop the stumps and scream: 'See? See how it is? Once again this Touch the Sky rides out without benefit of council! He has gone to play the dog for his hair-face masters!' "

Touch the Sky laughed so hard that he had to slow his pony to a walk. For Little Horse had done an excellent imitation of the whiny-voiced Medicine Flute, pretender to the title of tribal shaman.

The two warriors had ridden perhaps a half sleep's ride up the winding course of the Powder, in no hurry except when exposed too long without cover. Both braves had kept talk to a minimum—this mystery of the receding water level required careful observation to solve it, not endless and pointless discussion.

But now it was time to share a few thoughts. Touch the Sky dropped the paint's buffalo-hair reins, letting them dangle over the horse's ears. Automatically the well-trained pony slowed to a walk, grazing at will on the lush spring bunch-grass covering the river flat.

"The water is down for the entire length," Touch the Sky said.

"As you say." Little Horse produced his clay pipe from a legging sash. He stuffed it with willow-bark tobacco and the two braves smoked to the four directions.

"The water is down," Little Horse repeated, "and going down still more. Look. See that exposed wall of shale there? See the marks? Like rings on a tree. They show each day's level. Brother," Little Horse added, his voice showing concern, "this is no little event. Our tribe is in trouble."

Touch the Sky nodded, his lips pressed in a tight, straight line as they always were when he was baffled or concerned.

"Not little," he agreed. "And if that shell casing we found meant anything, we know pale-faces are involved. Tell me a thing. What else do we know?"

His stout friend met his eye, face impassive. "We know," Little Horse suggested, "that a certain rider left camp soon after we did. But he did not follow us. He merely determined our direction. Then he rode wide to our flank and sped on ahead."

Touch the Sky nodded at all this, well satisfied. Little Horse could find sign where other men saw only bare rock. The dust puffs, appearing soon after they passed their camp, had been faint as wisps of smoke. But both braves had spotted them. Then Touch the Sky had climbed a tree to look.

"A certain rider," Touch the Sky agreed now, "on a pure black pony flying the Bull Whip streamer from its tail. Now tell me another thing. Why did this rider not follow us?"

"Because he knows where we are going. Or better, he knows what we are doing, that we are looking for some cause for this odd trouble with the river."

"As you say." Touch the Sky's eyes slitted against the bright sunlight as they scanned the vast country surrounding them. "And knowing that, where has he gone?"

Little Horse enjoyed this game thoroughly, though his face showed nothing.

"Where else? To warn whoever else he is scheming with that we are coming."

"Better and better," Touch the Sky said. "We have cracked the shell. Now let us expose the meat. Since that rider on the black pony is Wolf Who Hunts Smiling, who is he going to warn?"

"Probably Sis-ki-dee and Big Tree," Little Horse speculated. "Among others. Those three jays are always together for mischief though the Wolf is clever at denying it."

"Those two, certainly," Touch the Sky said. "But the explosives hint that he is also honeying up to his white partners. Hiram Steele is back, brother, all signs point to it. And if Steele comes to the lick, Seth Carlson will come with him."

This talk made both braves a little nervous. Big Tree, Sis-ki-dee, Hiram Steele, Seth Carlson, Wolf Who Hunts Smiling—it was a roster of their most deadly enemies. Any one of them alone could give ten men grief. Together, no man's hell could corral them.

Now Little Horse, too, scanned the surrounding terrain. From long experience, both friends watched for the places that gave marksmen a good bead. They avoided stopping for more than a few seconds. When on the move, they automatically picked up and slowed the pace in the open, making it difficult for a distant rifleman to "lead" them.

"In matters of speculation, shaman," Little Horse said, "you are wrong about as often as the Yellow River runs clear. So Steele is back with a new scheme to make the red man's life a hurting place. What can it be? What is he doing to our river?"

"Ask me where the sun sleeps, while you are at it. That's why we are riding, buck. To see what we can see. For now, know this. Our enemies have no plans to make our mission easy for us. And thanks to Wolf Who Hunts Smiling, they will know we are coming. Is today a good day to die?" Touch the Sky demanded.

Little Horse grinned, sliding his revolving four-barreled scattergun from its rope rigging.

"Not today," he replied. "Today it's one bullet for one enemy!"

"Cheyenne People!" shouted Medicine Flute. "Do you see how it is? Our river is drying up! And now this tall one who once wore white man's shoes has again mysteriously ridden out. He has ridden—"

"—out without benefit of council!" Tangle Hair finished for him. He shouted from a group of Bow String soldiers loyal to Touch the Sky and the tribe's new peace chief, River of Winds. "You sing a familiar litany, bone-blower! And you only sing it when Touch the Sky is gone."

Medicine Flute flushed with rage at the words "bone-blower." This was a reference to his flute, made from the leg bone of a dead Pawnee. He played it constantly, claiming its notes could influence the High Holy Ones. All anyone could verify, however, was that hearing it made infants squall.

"As you say," Medicine Flute said coldly. "I use your own words back on you: 'when Touch the Sky is gone.' I am only suggesting, as shaman, what the average brave has noticed: Touch the Sky only seems to be gone when serious trouble besets this tribe."

"As shaman?" Tangle Hair demanded. He was on his own now, for Two Twists would not leave the site of Touch the Sky's tipi—not with Honey Eater and Little Bear inside, unprotected in this hostile village. "You? Shaman? Not in *this* world, brave imposter. Put all your 'medicine'

26

in an empty parfleche, and you'll have an empty parfleche."

A few of the Bow Strings laughed, supporting Tangle Hair. But a few others were nervous. They trusted Touch the Sky well enough. But this Medicine Flute had often impressed them with his apparent magic. And after all, it was common knowledge that men other than official shamen could possess medicine.

"Brave talk," Medicine Flute responded, "means little once the worm has turned. It matters little who has the official title of shaman. All that matters is the doing. And you may speak up for your leader all you wish. You cannot alter facts. Once again he is gone!"

Medicine Flute had no official right to gather the people in the clearing. But "official" meant little in this tribe divided against itself. For his own safety, Chief River of Winds made very few appearances outside of the regular council meetings. His respect for Touch the Sky, steadfastly maintained even when appearances damned the tall brave, made him a prime target for Touch the Sky's numerous enemies.

"Yes, Touch the Sky is gone," Tangle Hair shouted so all could hear, even those huddled in lodges and tipis. "Any time he seeks to help his people, he must go alone. In the past, every attempt to work through the Council of Forty was thwarted. We all know a burned baby fears the fire. Why should Touch the Sky keep addressing the headmen when they are grouped against him? Never mind Touch the Sky. Wolf Who Hunts Smiling, too, is gone. Neither did *he* seek permission of council. And who will wager that he went out to pick new flowers?"

"I've learned my lesson with Matthew Hanchon," Hiram Steele told the rest of them. "There was a time when I consigned the bastard to the grave without taking his measure. Now I've taken it, and each time I hold up the rule, he's growed. I'll never say that red son is dead until I hold his heart in my hand."

Sis-ki-dee, who knew some English, threw back his close-cropped head and roared with crazy laughter.

"*Hold* his heart?" the renegade Blackfoot warrior scoffed. "I mean to eat it! But you speak straight-arrow when you warn us not to dance yet. That one sheds death like a snake sheds skins."

They huddled in a council circle inside the dilapidated old hay barn: Hiram, Sis-ki-dee, the Comanche terror Big Tree, and Wolf Who Hunts Smiling. Seth Carlson was down in the tunnel under Salt Lick Creek, inspecting progress on the operation to shift the creek's flow. Wolf Who Hunts Smiling had just arrived from his Cheyenne camp with news that the brave he called Woman Face was finally riding their way.

Big Tree, built more like a Mescalero Apache than a Comanche, made a barking sound of contempt. Like most Comanches from the Blanco Canyon country, he was fluent in Spanish and proficient in English. He leveled a sneering gaze on Sis-ki-dee.

"This one speaks with new respect since his

clash with the tall one up in Bloody Bones Canyon."

Sis-ki-dee was not one to show consternation. But this remark made him stare at the ground. Hot shame seeped into his face.

Wolf Who Hunts Smiling only snorted and looked away, for he, too, knew the story well by now. But Hiram was newly returned to the territory.

"What happened up in Bloody Bones Canyon?" he demanded.

Big Tree started to reply—started to say something about how the mighty Sis-ki-dee, known as the Red Peril throughout the Bear Paw country, had actually begged Touch the Sky to spare his life. But the sudden, murderous glint in the Blackfoot warrior's eyes silenced him.

"The same thing happened to me," Sis-ki-dee said stiffly, "that has happened to every man here, more than once. The tall one defeated me."

"You've put the ax right on the haft," Hiram said approvingly. "That arrogant sonofabitch has given all of us a comeuppance. He's due. Way overdue. Any time now, he's going to ride within range of our mounted videttes. That's our first line of defense. Six sharpshooters, and whoever plugs Hanchon gets two thousand dollars in gold double eagles. That motivates a man to aim steady and squeeze slow."

Behind the little circle, sappers operated a hand winch to remove buckets of dirt and muck from below. So far it was being piled inside the barn to disguise the underground operation.

"After the videttes," Hiram continued, "come the sniper stations. Four of them, set up on bluffs overlooking the river. Seth handpicked these men and equipped them with bipods and long-distance Hawken rifles. Fifty-four caliber— the old buffalo ball. You hit a man *anywhere* on his body with that little puppy, he's carrion.

"But let's say our buck decides to defy Cheyenne tradition and move at night." Hiram nodded toward Sis-ki-dee and Big Tree. "Two of the best night fighters on the plains. You two may smell like a whorehouse at low tide, but I'd rather face a grizzly than either one of you after dark."

"Or before it," Big Tree added. Hiram—a big man himself—scowled at this, but said nothing to contradict it.

"Mounted videttes, snipers, you two," Hiram summed up. "But let's just pretend he slips past or through all of it. So what? Unless he gets inside this barn—which we can easily prevent— he will never even guess what the hell is going on. All you see above ground is a big, fast-flowing creek that's shifting its course for 'natural' reasons."

This made the three Indians stare back toward the tunnel. Hiram noticed the apprehensive look on all three faces and grinned. Not only did many red men fear being underwater, they hated even more a confined space—one like this tunnel under the river.

"Care to inspect the operation?" Hiram asked, goading them.

"Would *you* care to hang from your teats by metal hooks for an entire day in a broiling sun?" Wolf Who Hunts Smiling demanded. This was the standard initiation for young Sioux and Cheyenne warriors. "Hair-face," he added, "when you listed all the obstacles Woman Face must defeat, you left one out."

"Which?"

The cunning Cheyenne brave slid his obsidian knife from its sheath. He was small but wiry and strong, with the swift, furtive eyes of one who is constantly on guard for the ever-expected attack.

"You forgot me. Long before any of you vowed to send him over, I stepped between him and the campfire in front of witnesses. To a Cheyenne this is a vow that I mean to kill him. Until I fulfill that vow, I can never truly control the best braves."

Hiram nodded, liking the sound of this. "Plenty of good reasons to kill him. Don't forget, for all I know that filthy red—uhh, Hanchon topped my own daughter. He's also cost me a fortune and got my ass tossed into court. I don't care whose bullet kills him. I just know he needs killing."

Chapter Three

"What is it, shaman?" Little Horse demanded.

The two Cheyenne warriors had stopped and dropped their ponies' halters to let them drink from a backwater of the Powder River. This permitted them to shelter in the thickets rather than risk the open banks.

Touch the Sky had been in the act of peeling loose a sheet of pemmican from the roll in his parfleche, for the warriors had decided to build no cooking fires as they explored the river. Suddenly he looked up and stared toward the distant horizon as if he could hear music there.

But Little Horse, famed for the keenest ears in the tribe, heard nothing. "What?" he demanded again. "What did you hear?"

Touch the Sky shook his head. "It is a feeling, buck, not a noise."

"What manner of feeling? Shaman feelings?"

"Some call me shaman, but many have felt knowledge in their bones. It was a feeling any man might have. It is a warning. A reminder that a man can never be too ready."

Little Horse nodded, understanding. He thought they were being vigilant, but Touch the Sky was saying what must be said. They had faced down much danger in the past, had each come within a hairsbreadth of death more than once. The more a man survived, the more he began to delude himself that he was invincible. And once he believed that, he was worm fodder.

"The country is turning against us now," Touch the Sky said. "We are nearing the spot whites call Blackford's Valley."

"I call it Wendigo," Little Horse declared. "Once before we faced Carlson and Steele in that death trap. Brother, I would follow you into the white man's Hell carrying an empty quiver if you ordered it. But I do not think I would again stay in that stone lodge in Blackford's Valley."

This talk troubled Touch the Sky more than his friend realized. The stone lodge Little Horse meant was the abandoned mill where the Cheyennes had once been forced to take shelter from soldier patrols. Even the stout Little Horse had been reluctant to sleep under a roof; and he had positively quailed when forced to crawl through a short escape tunnel out of the mill.

Natural enough fears in an Indian, thought Touch the Sky. He had once watched a brave

Sioux warrior reduced to quivering fright when confronted with his first flight of stairs. The trouble was, if that omen Touch the Sky had experienced earlier had been correct, Little Horse might indeed have to once again face a confined space. A confined space that just might fill up with water . . .

"The valley offers excellent cover for an enemy," Touch the Sky continued. "Yet we must examine the river through that stretch. Especially the confluence where Salt Lick Creek feeds in. Much of the flow during the warm moons is from the creek. Perhaps there has merely been a huge sawyer formed, and it has turned into a natural dam. That happened once up on the Tongue, recall it? If so, we can bring men back and clear it."

For a few heartbeats Little Horse brightened at this prospect. Then he shook his head.

"Perhaps," he conceded. "But the warning you felt just now would not portend such luck. Time to ride, brother. And I mean to respect that feeling you had, shaman or no. For indeed, no man can be too careful."

Baylis Morningstar unsnapped the rawhide pouch on his sash and removed a pair of brass binoculars. Making sure they would not reflect a stray beam of sunlight, he began a careful study of the terrain where the Powder River entered Blackford's Valley.

The half-breed was a former Army scout who'd fled back to the wilds after killing a sergeant during a gambling match. Captain Seth

Carlson had contacted him by way of an Indian
runner with this job offer. Baylis liked being a
vidette, a mounted sentry. He got to work on
his own. That was when he was at his most ef-
ficient. And after all, he thought, he had killed
eighteen men over the years, each one on his
own and without witnesses. Then the first time
he'd killed a man with witnesses, he'd been
forced to become a fugitive. From now on, he
worked alone. Always.

He elevated and traversed with the binoculars, methodically studying every bit of the terrain. His dun stood well behind him, hobbled
foreleg to rear. Baylis traveled light—his saddle
was merely a sheepskin pad with a leather sur-
cingle and brass stirrups. The entire rig
weighed only three pounds. He had stolen it
from a Papago Indian he'd killed down south
on the Staked Plains of west Texas.

He halted the glasses for a long moment,
studying a point just out from the east rim of
the valley. In the thickets there, he had just seen
a few birds fly up as if startled.

His lips twitched in a little smile. He knew all
about this tall legend called Touch the Sky of
the Northern Cheyenne. Cheyennes . . . no
braves to fool with. Their enemies always re-
ferred to them as "the Fighting Cheyennes."

But he also knew the value of white man's
gold. To most Indians on the Great Plains, it
was still just a glittering yellow rock—good for
decorating one's war vest or a squaw's shawl.
But Baylis had spent time among the hair-face
warriors. He knew how those pretty yellow

coins were more valuable even than fine furs.
They could be traded for fine coffee, good weapons and saddles, the best liquor. Whoever killed
this Touch the Sky would never spend another
hard winter.

Again Baylis patiently studied that spot
where he had seen the birds scatter. He saw
nothing else, but that didn't discourage him.
These braves who would be coming—they were
the best among the best. There would be few
warnings.

While he studied the terrain, Baylis felt his
stomach growl with hunger. He glanced quickly
around. Down near the creek, a fat brown rabbit was nibbling some wild turnip leaves.

The half-breed laid his binoculars aside and
slipped a slingshot from the pouch on his sash.
It was small but powerfully constructed, carved
from bone and strung with buffalo tendon. He
also took a half-ounce lead ball from the pouch
and wrapped the tendon around it as he
stretched it tight.

The shot was ridiculously easy for Baylis,
who could knock a hummingbird out of the air
from 150 yards. Nor was there any question of
a kill—a half-ounce ball could kill a buffalo. The
rabbit suddenly shot straight up in the air,
landed kicking, and then lay still. Later, when
the sun was highest, he would spit it and roast
it further back in the valley so his smoke
couldn't be seen.

He was sure now that he knew where his enemy was. The other videttes might have spotted
him, too. But he had one distinct advantage:

They all killed with firearms. Firearms meant plenty of noise, delays for reloading, and damp powder from dew and humidity.

He, in turn, had learned to kill silently and simply. He could hold ten balls in his left hand and fire them as fast as he could wrap them in the sling. He even knew how to shoot several balls at once for a volley effect.

So *let* them come. For something was coming their way, too: Death, on swift, silent wings of lightning.

Twenty feet beneath the bed of Salt Lick Creek, Seth Carlson's crew of sappers were literally changing the face of the West.

Carlson was damned proud of this idea. True, Hiram was the one financing it, as usual. But this time his military training had provided the perfect cover.

Carlson was a West Point graduate, as were a majority of the officers of that era. No matter what a West Point graduate eventually ended up doing for the Army, all of them received heavy doses of engineering training, both civil and combat. The War Department had first created its Corps of Engineers and Sappers in 1847 in response to the war with Mexico. Captain Robert E. Lee and others had engineered brilliant victories at Cerro Gordo and Chapultepec. Now all officers had some engineering behind them.

And Carlson had used that training to visualize a fortune.

Training his men as sappers—tunnel rats—

had been easy enough. So had the job of convincing Colonel Nearhood that a rainwater cistern must be built to help local farmers and sheepmen. Now his crews had a perfect cover for working in the field.

"Sir," said the trooper named Meadows, approaching Carlson where he stood inspecting the work. "We're runnin' scarce on shoring timbers."

"All right. Take a couple men and go cut some more. But *don't* haul them anywhere near the barn until after dark. Just pile them. If anybody should ask, you're cutting cooking wood for the work party at the cistern."

"Right, sir. Mum's the word."

Both men wore steel helmets with fat candles recessed into the front, miner's hats Hiram had provided. Although gun-cotton torches burned here and there, it was constantly dark in the tunnel. Dark and dank and still dangerous—the shoring was minimal, and the soil around it sometimes unstable.

The plan was simple and already starting to work. Using a tunnel the entire width of the creek as their staging area, they were able to plant underground explosives at key spots where the bed of Salt Lick Creek was already unstable. These were planted in smaller tunnels—called curtains—running off the main tunnel.

The effect of these charges was to change the grade of the bed. This, in turn, slued more and more water off into an old creek bed nearby. This old bed crossed Hiram's land claim. Filled with clear mountain runoff, it would be the best "mother ditch" in Wyoming, perfect for an extensive irrigation system.

But that new creek would do much more than make the two of them big nabobs around here. It would, by becoming the new and official Salt Lick Creek, eliminate a huge portion of the Northern Cheyenne homeland. And just as a rising tide lifts all the boats, a lowering creek would sink that goddamn Matthew Hanchon. Sink the red bastard once and for all.

Hot rage suffused his face as Carlson recalled all the times that damned savage had made a fool of him. The worst of it, of course, was Kristen Steele. That she could actually choose a filthy featherhead over an officer of the U.S. Army was galling enough.

But there was more. Fortunes lost because of Hanchon, promotions passed over, choice assignments given to other men after Hanchon marred his military record.

Oh, the list of offenses was long. Long indeed. And Seth Carlson brooked humiliation from no man.

Carlson relaxed somewhat as he thought about the scene topside, where Salt Lick Creek was starting to overflow its south bank. Soon, as Wolf Who Hunts Smiling liked to say, the worm would turn.

When the insects stop their chorus, then comes trouble.

The words were Arrow Keeper's, and suddenly they snapped in Touch the Sky's memory like burning twigs.

He dropped the paint's reins, halting her, and lifted one hand to stop Little Horse. Holding his finger to his lips to silence his curious friend, Touch the Sky made a careful examination of the area around them.

They had just entered the east side of Blackford's Valley, still tracking the river. The confluence with Salt Lick Creek was still out of sight ahead. Trees and grass and new wildflowers surrounded them here, the cover adequate if not excellent.

First Touch the Sky examined everything with a straight-on inspection. Then he turned sideways to study the same terrain from the corner of his eyes—sometimes that angle revealed things the other could not. He watched for motion, not shape. But nothing alerted him.

He knelt, touched the ground lightly with three fingertips. Nothing. No vibrations.

Finally he stood and smelled deeply of the air, for he had learned to detect the telltale odors of danger—especially white man's horses.

"Nothing," he told his friend finally. "Have I missed anything?"

Little Horse, who had been similarly searching around them, shook his head. "Perhaps an ant crawling on a log, brother, but nothing more."

"Still," Touch the Sky said, musing, "something is wrong."

But what? Jays chattered unconcerned nearby, a badger dug busily at the nearby bank, gray squirrels chased each other from cotton-wood to cottonwood. Nothing to suggest trouble.

The two friends chucked up their ponies and rode on. They eased through a dogleg bend in the river, and abruptly Touch the Sky noticed it: The insect hum had suddenly fallen silent, as abruptly as a door shutting.

He whirled around. Little Horse, sensing nothing, still moved forward toward him.

Touch the Sky felt the nape of his neck tingle, and now it *was* the shaman sense. He reacted without thinking.

Even as he started to roll off his pony's back, he tugged his red-streamered lance from its rigging. He swung the lance hard toward Little Horse, catching him across the chest and sweeping him off his mount. At the same time, as he crashed to the ground, Touch the Sky smacked his paint across the rump, sending him ahead into cover.

"Brother!" Little Horse protested. "What are you—"

There was no gunshot, just a hard, solid *thwack*. A big chunk of wood tore loose from a tree just behind the spot where Touch the Sky's head had been. Still sprawled on the ground, Little Horse turned pale even as more lethal projectiles made both braves roll for better cover.

Chapter Four

Hiram Steele was formidable even when he was in a good mood. But when he was angry, he was truly frightening. His face bloated like an image in a brass knob, his breath came in ragged gasps, and his voice came straight from his barrel chest.

And he was definitely angry now.

"Goddamnit straight to Hell and back!" he roared, his voice scaring some sparrows out of the far corners of the big barn. "It's happening all over again, Seth. In spite of everything, it's happening all over again."

Carlson frowned. He had been sweating like a dog down in the work shaft, and he was in no mood for Steele's tantrums. A streak of clay now matted Carlson's tow hair to one side of his head, and he was pale lately from lack of sleep and sunshine.

"Come down off your hind legs, Hiram," he snapped. "Baylis came here to tell you Hanchon has finally come. He's doing his job. Why kick dirt on his boots?"

"His job was to kill the red bastard, not announce his arrival like the Queen of England was here!"

Carlson sneered. "Hey? How many times have you botched it, Chief? How many times has the Wolf come a cropper trying to do for Hanchon? What about those ugly bastards Siski-dee and Big Tree? You counted their coup feathers? Yet how many times have they aimed at Hanchon and hit only his shadow? And now you're all over Baylis like ugly on a buzzard, all on account that he missed his first shot?"

"Hell," Baylis added deferentially, "that's why we got so many men out there, ain't it, Mr. Steele? You yourself said this one slides through ambushes like grease through a goose."

"That's the straight, Mr. Steele," said Tim Ulrick. He was one of the sharpshooters serving as a sniper at the bluffs overlooking Salt Lick Creek and the valley. "Hell, ol' Baylis here was the first one to spot that tricky sumbitch. He's a good man to have along, even if he is a 'breed."

It was true that Hiram had an explosive temper. But like many volatile men, he could also see the error of his ways—especially when they threatened his profits.

"You boys are right," he conceded. "Baylis, I'd

43

ride the river with you any day. But all of us have got to see this thing right, see it for what it is. *Listen* to me, boys!"

The sudden urgency in Hiram's voice commanded everyone's instant attention. Seth, Baylis, Ulrick, and the rest of the videttes and snipers called to this meeting all watched Steele like hungry cats. Below, a sapper's voice could be heard as he hollered out for a light. The final charges would soon be in place. Tonight or the next night at the latest, they would detonate enough nitroglycerine to finish their task of changing the grade of the creek bed.

"All right, he got past Baylis. Now he's here. Here in the valley, and God knows there's enough places for him and that buck with him to cover down."

"Take my word for it," Carlson said. "I fought Hanchon down on the Staked Plain. He found cover where a lizard couldn't."

Steele nodded. "And he's not afraid to fight at night, like most Injins are. So I figure that's what he'll do. That limits our snipers, obviously. Even so, Tim, I want all four of you to remain up on the bluffs. Hanchon won't sleep *all* day. And a tangle or two with his good buddies Siski-dee and Big Tree will drive him back to daytime attacks. Baylis?"

"Yo?"

"You six videttes are critically important now. Stay in motion. Keep up fixed patterns that will keep Hanchon from surprising the barn. Remember, we can fail at this and we can fail at that. But if he breaches this spot before we can cover the evidence inside, the fat will be in the fire for my Pikestown scheme. I'd like to keep all you men on the payroll, you know that. Pikestown will need good lawmen and whatnot."

"All that," Carlson said, "is true enough. But if Hanchon surprises us in that tunnel . . ."

He did not bother to finish the thought. If even a cornered mouse would fight, what might that savage do in a tunnel?

"I'm not moving from this place," Steele averred. "If he does find that tunnel, Seth boy, it'll be over my dead body."

Carlson said, "The main thing is, we won't need it much longer. Couple more days, then we can seal it off. We'll still need the barn to store tools and live in while we complete the aboveground operation after dark."

Again Hiram nodded, looking a little more optimistic again.

"Okay, boys, get back to it. Don't forget that huge stack of double eagles for the man who lets daylight into Hanchon's soul. We're a team here, and this time we're going to turn our fighting cock into a capon!"

Several times Little Horse had hinted how he would like to know more about the omen vision Touch the Sky had recently reported—the portent of trouble by water. But each time, Touch the Sky only shook his head and said quietly, "Leave it alone, brother."

Little Horse was strong, but Touch the Sky would never tell him or any living man what had been placed over his eyes. Yet he himself was doomed to relive the vision over and over.

It began innocently enough. He, Little Horse, Two Twists, and Tangle Hair had stopped to let their ponies drink from a wide, placid river of clear mountain runoff. The banks were lush, rolling grass, the water sweet and refreshing as they lay on the bank and dipped their heads into it.

Suddenly, Little Horse disappeared into the water, followed by Two Twists and Tangle Hair. Touch the Sky alone remained on the bank. Puzzled, he stood, waded in, looked for his friends, saying, "The joke is over, brothers!" And then his puzzlement quickly turned to a throat-clenching panic when none of them resurfaced.

Each time, the vision was the same. Touch the Sky swallowed air, knifed into the cool current, kicked under. Searching, searching. There, a dark opening of some sort just ahead! When he swam toward it, a wall of bubbles engulfed him. He could see nothing.

Finally breaking clear, he glimpsed a beaded moccasin ahead—his comrades! Desperately Touch the Sky swam forward, reaching, grasping. His hand felt the elkskin moccasin, then an ankle. He tugged, a body rolled over, and abruptly a dead, grinning skull wearing Little Horse's clan feather bumped into Touch the Sky's face!

Each time that happened, Touch the Sky would mercifully start awake. He did so again now, and saw a worried Little Horse staring at him in the moonlight.

"The omen again, shaman?"

Touch the Sky nodded, sitting up. He had slept comfortably, if fitfully, on a dense carpet of pine needles hidden behind a deadfall.

"How is your arm?" he said, changing the subject.

"What, this mosquito bite? I would expect a woman to ask, but not you." When Touch the Sky swept him off his pony during the recent attack, Little Horse had landed on a sharp rock.

Touch the Sky grinned at this insult—Little Horse was in his usual fighting fettle. The tall Cheyenne pulled his Sharps percussion rifle from the buffalo robe protecting it from damp. He made sure a cap was positioned on the nib behind the hammer and the powder in his charger was dry.

"What now?" Little Horse asked. "We scout?"

Touch the Sky nodded. "We scout. So far, brother, we are not even sure *what* we are up against, though we know who must be behind it. We'll move back down to the creek. You take one bank, I the other. Give the owl hoot if you find anything."

Little Horse nodded, slinging his scattergun over one shoulder. Neither brave said a word about it, but Mother Night did not smile on her Indian children when they left the safety of the fire after darkness. And to die at night, away from camp, was to die unclean.

"Brother?" Little Horse said as they headed toward the little clearing where they'd tethered their ponies.

"I have ears, buck."

"If you are killed this night . . ."

47

He paused, and Touch the Sky watched him solemnly, expecting another question about his awful dream vision.

"May I smoke the fine white man's tobacco hidden in your parfleche?"

Touch the Sky felt a grin dividing his face. "Indeed. In fact, you may take it if I am only badly wounded and likely to die." ~

"In that case," Little Horse reasoned, "why not give it to me now, for you must die some day, am I right?"

Touch the Sky laughed outright as he handed it over. "The white man's lawyers could not talk around you! Now give over with all this talk, stout brave, and come earn your tobacco."

The main thing was to find out exactly who they were up against, and then exactly *what* they were up against. So far Touch the Sky had nothing he could place in his parfleche.

The *who* could be surmised, although as that silent slingshot attack proved, there were always new people on Hiram Steele's side. But so far Touch the Sky had no inkling as to the *what*. There was no link between the mystery of the river's shallow level and the presence of his enemies—no link he had discovered, at any rate.

But old Arrow Keeper had spoken straight when he'd said, "The hand that whirls the water in the pool also stirs the quicksand." Proof or no, Touch the Sky's gut hunch and his shaman sense told him the river and Steele were indeed linked. And why attack here, at the edge of Blackford's Valley, unless there was something to hide? There were better spots for killing him. Why here?

"Brother," he had said to Little Horse while they made their preparations for a night scout. "This valley is big. A man might need nine or ten sleeps to explore it well. Where would you start?"

"When we are involved," Little Horse said bluntly, "always start where trouble is the thickest and danger at its worst. Start by staying near the river. I believe your omen. This is trouble by water. When are we shy to meet trouble?"

"Indeed, it comes to us if we don't visit regularly. But you are right, buck. The river. And no better place to start than the confluence where Salt Lick Creek joins the Powder."

So they bore that way now, though keeping well back from the river. They had already seen telltale signs that the river was being patrolled. What bothered Touch the Sky was the fact that they did not see *many* signs. This enemy was good. He recalled an old saying about the Southwest Apaches: "Worry when you see them. Worry even more when you don't."

They had anticipated night fighting when they chose their ponies, avoiding any light markings that would reflect moonlight. The two braves now prepared themselves by wrapping their eyes in blankets—when they finally unwrapped them, their night vision had improved dramatically. They smeared their arms, chests, and faces with dark river clay to cut reflection.

A cloud-obstructed three-quarter moon provided some light, though the canopy of trees overhead often interrupted it. Slowly, stopping often to look and listen and smell, the two braves advanced toward the confluence.

Touch the Sky and Little Horse had connected their wrists with a light sisal rope. Suddenly Touch the Sky felt a sharp tug as Little Horse warned him to halt. He dropped the paint's reins, and she stopped immediately.

Now Touch the Sky noticed what had alerted Little Horse: the faint chinking of bit rings. Riders—white men, probably—down near the river.

More patrollers, Touch the Sky thought grimly. Not necessarily looking for him, but certainly looking for somebody. Or perhaps more accurately, making sure no one discovered something they weren't supposed to discover.

The two warriors remained still, weapons to hand, until the riders had passed by, riding south.

"Glide like a shadow now," Touch the Sky whispered close in his friend's ear. "We are near."

The tall Cheyenne felt his heart hammering; felt, too, the sure knowledge that danger lived in this valley—terrible danger, more than the silence and solitude could prepare one to believe. They had faced death here once before. This time, however, death was back with fresh legions.

The two warriors hobbled their ponies foreleg to rear. Then, moving like stalking cats, they covered the rest of the distance to the confluence on foot. They had to negotiate rough thickets, tangled briars, deadfalls, and boggy backwaters.

They stepped into a small, moonlit clearing. Little Horse pointed ahead. The shadowy mass of an old hay barn, sagging like a swayback mule, loomed off to the right, perhaps a double stone's throw back from the confluence of Salt Lick Creek and the Powder.

Touch the Sky paid little attention to the barn. They had searched it during their last vigil in this valley. It had obviously been abandoned for years, and was pitch black and silent now. He was more concerned with studying the sooty darkness surrounding the confluence. They would have to move in close for any kind of useful examination.

Yet, the nape of his neck throbbed warmly—a familiar sign to Touch the Sky, and one he had learned to heed.

"Brother," he whispered, "call on your medicine now. We're moving closer. But all is not as lonely and quiet as it appears."

Little Horse did touch the medicine pouch on his sash and say a brief, silent prayer. But he also double-checked the mizzen and pan of all four barrels of his scattergun, rotating them to check the action. No sound was worse to a warrior than the fizzle of damp powder at the ultimate moment.

The two moved out, side by side, holding their sisal rope snug for instant, silent communication.

The water brawled noisily, for even low as it was now, the Powder was a good-sized river and Salt Lick Creek had considerable flow this early in the warm moons. They could hear the combined sound out ahead of them, a steady bubbling and sighing.

Abruptly, another noise joined the water sound, subtle at first. So subtle that Touch the Sky strained to verify it in the darkness.

But it was real.

Laughter. Deliberate, mocking laughter. Close by, yet seeming to come from everywhere at once, the airy mocking of ghosts.

Little Horse, too, heard it. And like Touch the Sky, he recovered in an eyeblink and knew full well it was no ghost. They both knew who it was, and it was no discredit to their manhood when a ball of solid ice replaced their stomachs.

"Laughing again, Sis-ki-dee?" Touch the Sky spoke out boldly, knowing it was no use to hold silence now. "I am glad you have become sassy again. You may recall, the last time I saw you, up in Bloody Bones Canyon, you were not laughing. Your face was screwed up like a bawling baby's as you begged me to spare your life. Since, unlike you, I do not kill puling infants, I was forced to let you go."

With a faint whisper of warning, Touch the Sky threw his head back. Something burned his chin, and then he heard a sudden crack as Sis-ki-dee's war lance chunked into a tree beside him.

"Most of what you said just now was lies, Noble Red Man!" came Sis-ki-dee's voice boldly out of the darkness. "Except the part about killing puling babies. You see, that is why I am laughing as I watch you and Horse's Ass crawl through the mud like Big Indians on the warpath. I could have killed both of you long ago. But that would ruin my great joy. For you see, Noble Red Man, you have been lured from your camp so that Big Tree could gut your woman and child!"

Chapter Five

A twig snapped somewhere in the deep darkness surrounding the tipi, and Honey Eater started awake.

She could feel her heart pulsing in her throat. She glanced beside her on the spread-out robes, and saw that Little Bear slept soundly on his belly.

She felt her face tug into a grin, despite her fear, at the sight of the white columbine petal stuck to his chin. Tiny tooth marks on it told her he had tried to eat it.

On the other side of the tipi's center pole, she could hear her aunt, Sharp Nosed Woman, snoring softly. She always stayed with her aunt when Touch the Sky rode out from camp. All seemed well. Especially when she realized that the snapping twig must have been either Tangle

Hair or Two Twists—she could hear both of them outside now, whispering quietly. She knew they were taking turns guarding the tipi.

That knowledge calmed her at first, despite the deep fear she felt for her husband. No one would touch her or her son while those two were on guard.

But though they spoke low, she could not help hearing what they said. And listening to them, Honey Eater tasted the copper bile of fear.

"Did you notice who rode back earlier?" the voice of Two Twists asked.

"I did, double-braid," Tangle Hair answered. "Our tribe's best self-proclaimed 'policeman.' Did you see him cut out two fresh ponies from his string?"

"I did. Wolf Who Hunts Smiling has taken nothing but war mounts. He means to send our comrades under or please the Wendigo trying."

"They are up against it," Tangle Hair agreed. "But never mind the temptation to join them. As much as they must need us, this camp is teetering on the brink of its own grave. If Touch the Sky is killed, the Bull Whips will move instantly here. You know that, don't you?"

"As surely as I know my clan notch," Two Twists said reluctantly. "With those renegades sitting on top of Wendigo Mountain, we are mice with only one hole. They, too, are up to some treachery. There have been smoke and mirror signals between them and Wolf Who Hunts Smiling."

A long silence followed while Honey Eater

felt the nauseous flutter of despair.

"Still," Tangle Hair added, and his words made her face go clammy with sweat, "Touch the Sky's omen of a hard death by water is yet cankering at me."

At Sis-ki-dee's goading words about Honey Eater and Little Bear, Touch the Sky felt a quick spike of panic.

"Steady, shaman," Little Horse whispered beside him even as they ducked for quick cover. "This is their old game. Let them unstring your nerves now, and we are gone beavers. Answer them, buck!"

Touch the Sky knew his stout friend was right again. Sis-ki-dee excelled at finding the single chink in a man's armor, and then pounding away at it.

"Always harping on my woman and child," Touch the Sky called out. Like his friend's, his own eyes desperately searched the thickly wooded and overgrown area surrounding them. But even with their night vision improved, they could see no one. "When you aren't boasting of topping a man's wife, you boast of killing her. No tribe, not even the filthy Diggers, is lower than you 'contrary warriors.' "

"As for your mighty woman-killer named Big Tree," Little Horse put in, leveling his scatter-gun at the darkness, "unless he has eaten pey-ote, he certainly knows better than to enter a Cheyenne camp. Our dogs know the Comanche stink. Big Tree is cowering there with you, Red Peril."

"I am here, Horse's Ass," Big Tree's voice boomed out. "But not cowering. And I will top your mother while you watch."

"And you, Wolf Who Hunts Smiling," Touch the Sky shouted. "Are you enjoying this sport, licker of white feet?"

An arrow whipped by Touch the Sky, passing only inches away from his head.

"It is more interesting than picking lice from my blanket," Wolf Who Hunts Smiling answered boldly. "But as for sport, that has not even begun, Noble Red Man. I play the dog for no white man. I bend them to my purpose. After they help me kill you, I will kill them."

"Yes," Touch the Sky scoffed, trying to purchase time in hopes of spotting their enemies. "Your famous war of extermination. You green-antlered fool! I heard your lackey Medicine Flute swear to the people that the white man's land east of the Great Waters is smaller than a buffalo range! You fools preach they are a small tribe and can be eliminated in one good battle. In truth, there are ten thousand hair-faces for every Indian. You would have better luck stamping out a prairie fire in a windstorm than eliminating the beef-eaters."

A rifle spoke its piece—Sis-ki-dee's North & Savage, Touch the Sky judged from the sharp, precise crack. The slug was several feet off target, and he breathed a little easier. Sis-ki-dee was a good marksmen and wouldn't shoot that wide unless he was guessing at his target.

"The noble savage lectures us!" Big Tree called out sarcastically. "He knows so much about the paleface world because he, too, once worked in the garden like a woman and wore shoes and gorged on beef and pig meat. Now he ruts on an Indian beauty and calls himself a shaman."

Touch the Sky tugged the sisal rope to alert Little Horse. When his friend glanced at him, Touch the Sky rolled his head over his left shoulder, toward the horses behind them. Little Horse nodded, agreeing this was a time to withdraw, not to dig in for their own slaughter.

"I know much indeed about the paleface world," Touch the Sky said. "I know about engineering charges, for instance."

Not one of his enemies said anything to this remark, and Touch the Sky didn't welcome that silence. It confirmed his suspicion that they were teamed up with Steele and probably Carlson. He and Little Horse had not yet gotten close enough to the confluence for a better look, and clearly they would not do so this night.

His enemies chose this moment to open up in earnest. Big Tree and Wolf Who Hunts Smiling unleashed a flurry of arrows, and Sis-ki-dee's North & Savage roared again and again, its sliding magazine letting him fire every few seconds.

"*Now*, brother!" Touch the Sky roared, and Little Horse sent up a virtual wall of buckshot as he fired and rotated, fired and rotated, peppering the trees with four deadly charges.

This formidable firepower sent their enemies scrambling just long enough for the two braves to break from their meager cover and race toward their ponies. But Touch the Sky hardly felt elated by it.

They were safe for the moment, yes. But they knew nothing about the mystery of the disappearing river. All they knew for sure was that every step taken in this valley of death was another step closer to the funeral scaffold.

"We may have hit one of them," Big Tree suggested.

"Are *you* eager to go search the underbrush for proof?" Sis-ki-dee demanded.

"If one was hit, either he was killed or he wasn't," Wolf Who Hunts Smiling said. "If he was killed, his comrade would not leave the body for us to desecrate, count upon it. If he was not killed, then he would never have been deserted by his comrade. These are 'noble' red brothers who cry when a child dies. In short, bucks, either no one is out there or we killed both of them."

All three saw the absurdity of this latter suggestion. Those two Cheyennes would not be killed in a game of shooting-at-rovers. The killing would be hard and the dying important.

The trio was well hidden behind blinds constructed earlier in anticipation of this moment. Behind them, silver-white moonlight gleamed off the swirling waters at the confluence of Salt Lick Creek and the Powder river.

"They have not shown a light from the barn," Big Tree said. "Steele spoke one way when he swore he would not give their presence away. He has staked his sash to the ground, for he means this time to kill the tall one."

"Steele is a Mah-ish-ta-shee-da," Wolf Who Hunts Smiling said, using the ancient Cheyenne name for white men. "And of course he will die with the rest. But he is a good man to have along on any mission to kill Touch the Sky."

Sis-ki-dee's brass nose ring caught a stray shaft of moonlight. "What will they do next?" he asked.

Automatically, the other two waited for Wolf Who Hunts Smiling to answer. After all, he knew their enemy best—had in fact hated him the longest and with the most reason.

"They will complete tonight's mission, which was to examine that confluence. It hardly matters if they do study it—all they will see is Mother Earth getting a slight wrinkle in her skin. They will see that Salt Lick Creek is altering its course into the old tributary it used to follow. It will seem the work of the High Holy Ones, and no Indian will question it."

"We could track them at first light and find their camp," Sis-ki-dee said.

"Have you been skull-struck?" Wolf Who Hunts Smiling demanded. "Would you trail a grizzly into its lair? Besides, they will change their camps often. We are all three excellent at reading sign. But this is no time for stalking. It is a time for luring."

The other two watched him in the imperfect moonlight, unable to decipher his lupine grin. Even now Wolf Who Hunts Smiling's swift-asminnow eyes stayed in constant motion, watching for attack.

"Luring?" Big Tree repeated. "Are you a little girl dropping coy hints in her sewing lodge? Speak it or bury it, Cheyenne. I am in no mood for riddles."

"No riddle, Quohada. Only think. Steele is determined to keep these new intruders away from the huge lodge where his people are sheltered. Naturally they fear any discovery while they are down in their tunnel. But what if I can convince Steele *not* to fill in the tunnel when they finish with it, which they will do within a few sleeps."

Sis-ki-dee's crazy laughter showed that he had caught on—and that he approved. "Leave the tunnel, you mean, and lure Touch the Sky and Little Horse into it?"

Wolf Who Hunts Smiling nodded, grinning. "Lure them into their underwater graves. One charge, exploded after they go in, would both close the tunnel and bring the water rushing in."

A long silence followed this as all three Indians savored the prospect.

"This would be more than revenge," Big Tree finally said. "Knowing that we had trapped Touch the Sky's soul in torment for eternity. Not just revenge—this is a reason to have lived!"

"Never mind gloating now," Wolf Who Hunts Smiling warned them. "Our work this night may not be done. The hair-faces are detonating another underground charge, their last of the underground labor. It may bring our enemies back around."

"Perhaps," Big Tree said. "But I think not. Now that Touch the Sky knows he faces us by night, he may decide that he would rather face videttes and snipers by day. He and Little Horse will return to the confluence, yes. But it will be boldly, in broad daylight."

"They threw everything they had at us," Little Horse boasted, trying to put a good face on their inglorious retreat. "And we made off unscathed. No scalps dangle from our sashes, but at least ours are still in place on our heads."

"As you say, brother," Touch the Sky agreed. "And we have cheated them again as we did on Wendigo Mountain. Too, our mission tonight was no complete waste—at least we learned there must be something worth seeing near that confluence."

The two weary braves had just finished rubbing their ponies down with clumps of sage. Now the horses were tethered in a hidden spot well back from the river, logy with long drinks of cool river water. The Cheyennes themselves had sheltered in a crude wickiup that resembled, from a distance, a tangled deadfall.

Now they eased the gnawing in their bellies with dried fruit and slices of pemmican.

"I will risk a night mission," Touch the Sky said, "if the good of it outweighs the risk of it. But the worst time in the world to face Big Tree or Sis-ki-dee is after sunset. As for Wolf Who Hunts Smiling, *he* is in killing fettle night or day. I counsel for sleeping the rest of this night and riding out by daylight."

Little Horse agreed. "We will make easier targets, but we will also draw easier beads on our enemies. I would rather shoot at a man than at his voice."

Both braves slipped into their own thoughts while the river chuckled and bubbled nearby—the river, source of all life but now the source of much danger. Once or twice, as they lay quiet, Touch the Sky heard a vidette rider down near the water.

But eventually his tense muscles relaxed enough to permit a fitful sleep. Thankfully, Maiyun did not plague him again this night with images of that death-by-water omen.

Uncle Moon owned the sky and was clawing his way toward his zenith, when the earth literally heaved the Indians awake.

It was not a loud, violent explosion. Instead the ground suddenly shifted hard, like a canoe running aground on a sandbar. A brief rumble, like the sound of a distant avalanche, and it was over. Both Cheyennes started to a sitting position, staring at each other in the moonlight.

"Brother?" Little Horse called over. "What happened?"

"How long is a piece of string?" Touch the Sky answered glumly. "But whatever it was, Cheyenne, count upon it: It means a world of hurt for the red man."

Chapter Six

"There it is, Seth boy," Hiram Steele said jubilantly, thumping the grinning soldier hard between the shoulder blades. "There it goddamn is! The gateway to Pikestown and our fortune!"

"Last night's blast did it," Carlson confirmed. "Look at it! I should have been an engineer, not a combat officer! Not one sign that man has been tinkering. All the changes are below, in the slant and thickness of the bed."

Even Wolf Who Hunts Smiling was truly impressed. You could say many things against white men. They always screamed at each other, even when standing close; they showed their emotions in their faces like women; they wore shoes and wasted buffalo meat and built their fires all wrong. But while an Indian was forced to circle around a mountain, the hair-faces simply blew the mountain out of their way, as *this* impressive sight proved.

Dawn threw her first roseate glow over the new day, light enough to see that the former bed of Salt Lick Creek was now virtually dry save for some isolated pools dotting the drying mud. The creek had evidently jumped its old bank and now followed the course of the old tributary that bore due south from here.

"Goddamn dirty shame, ain't it?" Hiram said with mock sympathy. "I mean, my land suddenly water rich, and them poor Northern Cheyennes about to lose most of their summer water."

If he hoped to prick Wolf Who Hunts Smiling with this barb, he failed. Let River of Wind's camp dry up, the renegade's approving eyes proclaimed. He would soon be joining the Comanche and Blackfeet raiders on Wendigo Mountain. Once he did, Hiram Steele and his white brothers would be killed or driven from this territory anyway.

"This is impressive work," the Cheyenne conceded to the palefaces. "We Indians have no medicine like it. But if you wish to remain in the land of the living, I advise both of you to get out of the open. Do you think the tall one is not watching both of you right now through a rifle sight?"

Steele and Carlson were not men to scare easily. But the sense of Wolf Who Hunts Smiling's words struck each of them with the force of a blow. They took cover like the Cheyenne.

"Where's Big Tree and Sis-ki-dee?" Steele demanded.

"Do I look like their dug nurse?" Wolf Who Hunts Smiling retorted. "Presumably they are sleeping—you kept them up all night. What does it matter where they are? Do not count on other men to save your own hair. Touch the Sky has tried more than once to kill me, but each time *I* was ready."

"Yeah, yeah, you're a big Indian," Carlson said with contempt. "Lecturing white men now, is it? He hasn't sent me or Hiram under yet either. I don't need no goddamn lectures from an aboriginal gut-eater too stupid to harness the wheel."

"Both of you come down off your hind legs," Hiram said, though he was still in a good mood. "Our first priority is to kill Hanchon, remember? Once we put paid to him, then we can scrap all we want 'mongst ourselves."

Hiram turned to the officer. "I'll be going into Register Cliffs to sign on some more homesteaders. Do we need the tunnel anymore?"

Seth shook his head. Much of his face was in shadow under the wide brim of his hat.

"All right, then," Hiram said, "have your boys fill it back up."

"That," said Wolf Who Hunts Smiling, "would be foolish."

Both white men were surprised that the Indian had spoken up about this.

"Another damn lecture," Carlson said.

"Unless you got a bone caught in your throat," Steele said, "speak your piece."

"It is foolish to waste the tunnel," Wolf Who Hunts Smiling said. "Of course it must be filled in. But why not fill it up after Touch the Sky and Little Horse find it and go down to explore it?"

Seth looked at Hiram. Hiram suddenly grinned. Seth grinned back.

"Well, now," Carlson said. "You both know goddamn good and well they *will* go into it if they find it. If we let them find it."

"Wolf," Hiram said admiringly, "I'm beginning to realize what a waste it will be if I kill you. You're right, buck. No sense wasting a good grave that's got Hanchon's name on it."

"There they are," Little Horse said bitterly. "Three of our worst enemies in the world. Not one of them exposed to a good shot. If the Wendigo puked up Big Tree and Sis-ki-dee, they would all be congregated in one place. And tomorrow, count upon it, the grass where they stood would be dead."

Touch the Sky nodded. Both braves clung to a dead log out in the middle of the Powder River. They had slipped into the water shortly after sunrise, using reeds to breathe and staying submerged as they drifted along.

Now only their heads protruded out of the streaming current. Their enemy had posted sentries and roaming skirmishers everywhere. But the one place they did not watch well was the river itself.

"Of the three you are looking at now," Touch the Sky said, "it is Wolf Who Hunts Smiling

67

who has set the mark for treachery. True, those two white-eyed pigs are criminals of the lowest kind. But even they are loyal to their own. Yet our wily Wolf has sullied the Medicine Arrows beyond cleansing by shedding blood of his own. And now, only look. Another kind of lifeblood is being bled from our people—our very river."

At least they had finally solved part of the mystery of the receding river level. Salt Lick Creek had evidently leaped its bank, costing the Powder its major feeder between the foothills and the Cheyenne summer camp. The Powder still had plenty of flow right here, but would lose much of this water downriver.

"We may face a drought by the time of the hot moons," Little Horse said. "The entire camp will have to be moved."

Touch the Sky said nothing to this, only watching that unholy trio gloating over their latest triumph. But was it truly their work? What, exactly, did they have to do with it? There was no outward sign of damming or digging.

Little Horse's thoughts, too, wandered in the same direction. "That explosion we heard— why is there no damage here? No dirt heaved out of place?"

"Brother, you ask all the right questions. But I have none of the right answers."

"We signed the talking papers at Fort Laramie," Little Horse said, referring to the latest peace treaty. "That paper forbids the hair-faces from any tampering with the rivers and creeks that cross our land. But first we must have proof they are playing the foxes."

"The talking papers," Touch the Sky repeated, and suddenly heat rushed into his face as he understood the real depth of this new threat.

Little Horse saw the troubled clouds in his friend's dark eyes. "What, brother? What did I say?"

"That same talking paper," Touch the Sky replied grimly, "sets out the boundary of our ranges. It is bounded on the east by 'the deepest point in the channel of Salt Lick Creek.' Do you understand now?"

It took Little Horse only a few heartbeats to comprehend. His face, too, went a few shades paler.

"Yes, I see it, brother. Clear as a blood spoor in new snow I see it. If they succeed in this treachery, we are not just out of water. We will lose over half of our land!"

Touch the Sky nodded. "The half where we hunt the best buffalo herds. The half containing the best graze for our pony herds. The half where we camp, where our women grow their best crops. The half where we gather each spring with the other nine bands of the Cheyenne for the parades and dances."

"The best half of our homeland," Little Horse summed up.

"And would it be a surprise if you learn," Touch the Sky said, "that the land now belongs to Hiram Steele? Belongs, at least, in the eyes of the white man's council."

Now both braves stared at the trio with a new sense of urgency.

"This is the worst trouble in the world," Little

Horse lamented. "We have little enough power in the white man's courts. Even when treaty violations are clear and easily proved, justice can be elusive. How will we defeat whites with no proof of their crime?"

"We won't," Touch the Sky said. "When it comes to justice, all we have is ourselves. We need to discover how they have done this, yes. But only so we can undo it. If we depend on the white-eyes' courts, we will end up on a reservation growing corn and answering roll calls."

"Undo it?" Little Horse repeated doubtfully.

"You heard me, stout buck. Undo it. Either we get Salt Lick Creek back to its old course, or we are a tribe without a home."

The morning passed uneventfully for Tim Ulrick.

He was one of the four sharpshooters Hiram Steele had hired to man the bluffs overlooking the river. It was lonely, boring work, but he didn't mind it. He had a dog tent and a waterproof Mackinaw blanket to protect him if it rained. He had plenty of beans and jerked beef and coffee and whiskey, as well as a stack of sensational dime novels to while away the hours. It beat the living hell out of his last job: riding guard for the Kansas-Pacific Railroad's work crews. Hell, he'd rather be the sniper than the target any damned day.

His rifle, a Hawken .54 buffalo gun, was set up on a bipod overlooking the river and much of Blackford's Valley. From here, when the sun was shining, he could send mirror flashes to the other three snipers.

The morning had been a slow one. Nothing on the river except an old dead log earlier. Just past forenoon the vidette named Baylis Morningstar rode by and shared a smoke with him. He, too, reported no sign of the Cheyennes.

Damn, Ulrick thought. That little breed was death-to-the-devil with that slingshot of his.

Ulrick could see clearly, from this high vantage point, how Salt Lick Creek now followed a new course. He didn't give a plugged peso for the fact that Indians would be displaced by this new project of Steele's, but it was a damn shame to see good rangeland plowed up for a bunch of damned fodder-forkers. And that was exactly what Steele had in mind: turning cattle country into cornfields and sheep pens.

Ulrick's thoughts suddenly dispersed like chaff in the wind as he noticed something below: another damned log, only further downriver this time. But just for a second there, he could have sworn he saw a glimpse of a human head.

He broke out his binoculars and focused them. There was the log, bobbing and weaving. Nothing out of the ordinary—

Wait. What the hell was that?

Ulrick focused even more and squinted.

He saw what looked like a thin reed poking up out of the water—following along on one side of the log.

An ear-to-ear grin split his beard-stubbled face. Ulrick had a sudden vision of that giant stack of gold cartwheels Hiram was paying to the man who did for Matthew Hanchon.

Ulrick scrambled close to his Hawken and took up a prone position behind the weapon. He removed a paper cartridge from his possibles bag and chewed one end off it. He dumped the powder in his charger, inserted the ball and rammed it home, then placed a primer cap on the nib behind the hammer.

Ulrick licked one finger to test the wind. Then he made minor adjustments to his elevation and windage knobs.

Finally ready, he dug a hole with his left elbow until it was comfortable in the dirt. Then, training his sights just below that reed, he inserted his finger behind the trigger guard.

He took a deep breath, relaxed as he let it out. Slowly, squeezing and not jerking, he took up his trigger slack.

Touch the Sky and Little Horse knew they could not return overland to their cold camp in broad daylight. Nor could they float their log against the current without arousing suspicion. So they decided to float well past the confluence and then double back through the trees behind the most heavily patrolled area.

Touch the Sky held on at the back of the big log, Little Horse at the front. Both braves were built very differently, and Touch the Sky had the easier time staying submerged. From time to time he was forced to tap his friend to warn him that he was letting too much of himself show above water.

Out in the channel the river was deep enough to make the going fairly easy. From time to time they encountered a sawyer or other snags, and occasionally fish nibbled at them—an oddly distasteful sensation, considering its harmlessness and the fact that these two braves had faced every demon in the red man's world.

But both realized why it was distasteful. Cheyenne lore included a legend about Indians who died unclean deaths in the water. Their trapped souls were forced to watch while hungry fish nibbled out their dead eyes.

However, Touch the Sky admonished himself to forget such thoughts. The key to survival lay in attending to the present, not in dwelling on thoughts. His wife and son were only one sleep's distance further downriver, their fate too hinging on his success here in the valley.

Again he kicked forward with his right foot, tapping Little Horse. He was letting too much of his reed protrude.

Even as he warned his friend, Touch the Sky felt a sharp prick at his chest—sharper than the curious teeth of fish.

He glanced down and watched a swirl of blood rise up with the bubbles his feet kicked up!

His bear-claw necklace—the one Honey Eater gave him for a wedding gift! One of the claws was gouging into his flesh and muscle!

This was no time to evaluate the sign. Touch the Sky let go of the log, kicked mightily forward, gripped Little Horse around both hips, and tugged his surprised friend down.

73

There was a sharp concussive sound, magnified by the water, as the slug slanted in between both braves, missing each by a finger's breadth. And then both were kicking madly for the far bank, hoping there was only one shooter and praying to Maiyun he now had to reload.

Praying, too, that if they must die, Maiyun would let it be on land.

Chapter Seven

Clearly, Little Bear had gotten over his fear of the water, thought Honey Eater.

She watched her little son splashing and kicking, bravely plunging his head under the water to come up gasping. She shared for a moment in his harmless pleasure, happy for him. Like her, he missed his father. Moments like this helped take both their minds off his absence.

But not for long, Honey Eater thought glumly. A brief glance to either bank would show her the ever-faithful Tangle Hair and Two Twists. They would be at a discreet distance, yet close enough to intervene if there was trouble.

And the river itself . . . She and Little Bear had come down here to cool off, for the day was unseasonably hot by midday. But she had stared in shock. Its depth, already receding, had gone down dramatically, all in one night!

How could such things be, unless the hand of magic was in it? Or the white men with their powerful explosives? And that, of course, meant that Touch the Sky was up against it yet again.

Medicine Flute, the skinny little pretender, was making all kinds of trouble in camp. For Touch the Sky was gone, the river was drying up before their eyes, and the connection seemed obvious enough to her husband's many enemies—Touch the Sky must be causing this trouble.

Fortunately, Chief River of Winds was able to make cooler heads prevail. At the council meeting, he reminded the bickering headmen that Wolf Who Hunts Smiling, too, was out without permission of council. And if a Bull Whip soldier could ride out, he argued, how could one deny this privilege to the tribe's shaman?

But Honey Eater realized how quickly things could change in this unstable camp. Especially if the Powder continued to fall without explanation.

By now the people were terribly concerned. By night the old grandmothers had taken to keening into the early hours, sensing the arrival of some great tragedy. By day they had begun to sew together animal skins for storing water against a coming drought.

But Little Bear sensed none of this. Again his head broke the surface, sleek and shiny, his dark locks plastered to his forehead.

There! Honey Eater saw it clearly in this light when his hair was swept back, the mulberry colored birthmark on his left temple. Just like Touch the Sky, he had the mark of the arrow. He might enjoy his innocence now, she thought. But for him, too, a lifetime of fighting and killing was coming.

Fighting and killing. The very things Touch the Sky was no doubt enmeshed in right now. And Little Horse with him. If any two braves could make it back to camp, they were those two.

But how long? How long could they keep defeating the odds? She watched her healthy, innocent son splashing in the river. Then she glanced again at the clear marks on the banks which told the sad story of a river's disappearance.

Touch the Sky and Little Horse both made it to shore without stopping a slug from the hidden sniper up on the bluff.

"There was only one up there, brother," Touch the Sky said. "That saved us. Few men can recharge a rifle in less than thirty seconds. Good thing he did not have a second piece charged and to hand, for he is a formidable shot."

Little Horse nodded glumly. The two braves had made their way cautiously overland on foot, a distasteful way to travel for Plains warriors. The ground cover was good close to the river, but by now they realized they were surrounded by enemies with eyes like eagles.

So the journey was made cautiously, employing every trick of their warrior training in movement and concealment. In sparsely covered areas, they moved slowly, not quickly, for it was movement and not shape that caught an enemy's eye at a distance.

They were bearing obliquely toward the spot, near the entrance of Blackford's Valley, where they had hidden their ponies.

"Brother," Little Horse said, "when have you seen me sit upon the ground and wail? But this thing would be examined. We are marked for carrion in this valley! If we are unable to move, how can we name their game?"

Even as he spoke, he watched a nearby river bluff carefully. The two braves were easing through a blackberry thicket. It was good cover, but hard to move through.

Touch the Sky nodded. "It comes down to a hard truth, buck. By day we are targets for any who would kill us. By night we face Sis-ki-dee and Big Tree. And no doubt Wolf Who Hunts Smiling."

"The palefaces have the daylight covered," Little Horse said bitterly, "and their cowardly Indian dogs the night. Meantime, our river is drying up! And we may soon even be forced to desert our homeland if Steele goes to the white man's council with his new claim."

"Cheyenne," Touch the Sky admired, "you have cracked the shell and extracted the nut. We know more than we did. Now we must find out how that creek was forced out of its natural course. Once we know that, only then can we try to return things to normal."

"Brother," Little Horse reminded him. "We

have failed to approach that confluence by land. We have just been shot at trying by water. What next? Fly?"

Little Horse had spoken facetiously, but his words evoked a sly grin from Touch the Sky.

"Yes, stout buck. We will fly."

Clearly Little Horse wanted to hear more on this foolish theme. But Touch the Sky nodded toward the bluff again, reminding him it was time to tend to the language of the senses.

Sister Sun was well through the day's journey by the time they had caught up with their ponies and moved them to a new spot. Now it was time to return to their cold camp and retrieve their kits, then move to a new camp. Touch the Sky could feel hunger gnawing at his belly like a rat's incisors.

They showed extra caution as they approached the little copse where they had slept. They were approaching the entrance, a narrow opening in the brush, when Touch the Sky felt it: that graining of his skin that was not caused by fear or cold.

"Hold," he whispered to Little Horse. Both braves dropped to their knees, examining the area around them carefully.

Little Horse gripped his friend's shoulder and pointed. Touch the Sky sighted along his companion's finger and saw a tangled vine just out ahead of them. It appeared, at first glance, to belong to the natural confusion of brush carpeting the ground.

"It is too green and fresh," Little Horse whispered. "It was broken off and placed there for some reason. The rest of the vines are all old and dead, see?"

Touch the Sky nodded. He reached to one side and pulled a long stick up from the dead brush. Then he moved forward and gave it a thrust toward the vine.

It tripped the hidden deadfall trap immediately. A bent sapling, hidden behind bigger trees, suddenly whipped straight, taking its empty net of vines with it.

Touch the Sky recognized Cheyenne handiwork here. And he knew the trap had not been erected simply to annoy them. The moment the vine net cleared the treetops, an arrow whipped through it. Moments later came the drum of escaping hooves.

Little Horse retrieved the shaft.

"Look," he said, pointing to the chipped flint point. "Made by our tribe. Are you surprised?"

"Wolf Who Hunts Smiling," Touch the Sky said grimly, his lips pressed into a straight, determined slit. "He had it all set up, then found a good spot to wait."

It made both of them nervous that he had been able to track down this camp. After all, it had been used only one night. Would they now have to change camps every few hours?

Touch the Sky glanced around at the surrounding valley walls in the waning light. This was a place of great natural beauty. But for them it had become a death trap. Those walls seemed to be pressing in on them, and it was only a matter of time before they would be caught, then crushed.

"Never mind," he said. "The fight goes forward. We will move to a new spot. Then, after the sun goes to her rest, we will return to that confluence."

"Yes," Little Horse said skeptically. "And we will be 'flying' there as you promised, right?"

"Like two jays."

"Shaman tricks?" Little Horse pressed.

"Only Medicine Flute will tell you he can truly fly," Touch the Sky said. "No shaman tricks this time. You will see. Now move quickly, brother, and keep both eyes to the sides."

"Gentlemen," Hiram Steele told the men gathered around him at the bar, "the sun travels west, and so does opportunity. This new Homestead Act gives all of you a nice parcel of ground, and all you have to do is prove it up a little and it's yours."

"Nice parcel, my sweet aunt," groused a man with a heavy Swedish accent. "A hunnert and forty-four acres is a big farm back East, ya sure. But this ground out here, why, she's dry as a year-old cow chip! You can't farm it. She's only good for ranching, and you can't ranch on less than ten times that much land."

"Correction, my friend," Hiram said, pouring the man out another shot of good grain mash. "The ground *was* dry as a year-old cow chip. Not anymore. It will soon be well irrigated."

"Ahuh," said another man. "And the Queen of England will sing 'Lulu Girl' at the mining camp on Bear Creek!"

"Friend, I speak straight-arrow. You've heard

that Salt Lick Creek has jumped its bank? That it follows an old bed south from its old route?"

"Ya sure," said the Swede. "Goddamnedest thing it was, too. But fella, that's not government ground it goes through. That's Injin land."

"It was," Hiram assured him. "But the boundary was determined by the old course of the creek. Fact is, that new feeder goes right across *my* grantland. And now the plots around it are up for grabs. All you need to do is get your butts into Register Cliffs and sign up. We'll soon have corn and oats and barley fields flourishing hereabouts. And the cream of it is, there won't be any Cheyenne Indian problem left around here."

"Sounds too good to be true," said the man. "But I'm all for it. It's a damn shame, that good land going to waste so buffalo can ruin it. The gum'ment had no right to set it aside for the savages."

Hiram's big, bluff face was divided by a grin. "That's my point. Now Mother Nature has come to the aid of the white man. You boys get on out there and stake you out a tomahawk claim. What the paper collars in Washington have given to the red arabs we're taking back for the white man!"

Little Horse soon learned what his friend meant by "flying." And the idea made him nervous.

"We should travel through the trees?" he said doubtfully. "Brother, have you visited the Peyote Soldiers?"

"No peyote dream," his friend assured him. "Look yourself. Between this new camp and the confluence, the trees are thick and close. See how the tops weave together like fingers? Big Tree and Sis-ki-dee will watch by river and ground, but never up into the trees. It will be slow, but we can get right out over the confluence."

Little Horse didn't like it, but offered no more objections. Like most Indians, the Cheyennes climbed trees only to get a good view in new territory. Their main use for trees, besides harvesting nuts, was for the bark—not only to make many things, but as food for their ponies during the winters. But Little Horse agreed they were up against it this time. They had to try something.

Surprisingly, it went much better than either brave anticipated. Many of the trees were massive oaks or birch, with sturdy and plentiful limbs. A bright moon and unclouded sky assisted their trek—especially through the birch trees, for their silver bark reflected well and showed sturdy limbs easily.

There were tense moments. Long jumps between limbs, for one thing. And occasionally they were forced to climb down briefly to reach another good tree. This left them exposed on the ground. But before too long, both of them were creeping out onto a massive limb overlooking the confluence of Salt Lick Creek and the Powder River.

And what they finally discovered there made the journey well worth it.

Wordlessly, hanging above them like bats, the friends watched the paleface work crew working with shovels and graders. They worked in the moonlight, making little noise above the purling of the water. As best as Touch the Sky could guess, they seemed to be reinforcing the new turn in the creek, heaping gravel and dirt on the bank.

However, this seemed minor to Touch the Sky, hardly the kind of work that could alter a huge creek's flow so drastically.

He found out why when he saw a familiar face ease into the moonlight to supervise the work.

Captain Seth Carlson! The two Cheyennes exchanged a long glance.

"How's it going, Meadows?" Touch the Sky heard him say.

"Hunky-dory, Cap'n. That last nitro blast done good work. Thanks to that tunnel, we got the bed sloped perfect now. It won't be nothing to shape things up topside."

"Good man. Work for about another hour tonight, then secure all the tools in the barn."

"Right, sir. You want us to ride back to the fort?"

"No. Colonel Nearhood has got a bug up his ass to visit the rainwater cistern we're supposed to be working on over at Beaver Creek. Take the men and report to the camp there. By the way, have all of you taken your gear out of the barn?"

"Yessir."

"All right. Remember, from now on stay clear

of the barn except when you're storing or getting tools."

"You got it, sir."

Touch the Sky and Little Horse watched the officer speak to a few more men before swinging up onto his cavalry sorrel and riding off.

The barn. Touch the Sky could see it from here, its shake roof looming up from the trees surrounding it. He had paid it little attention. But Carlson's remarks made it clear that structure was somehow important to this infernal project. Important for more than just storing tools.

Thanks to that tunnel. What tunnel?

Whatever that hair-face soldier had meant, the very word "tunnel" immediately jolted Touch the Sky. For it was a tunnel that he and Little Horse had faced in that awful death vision.

Chapter Eight

"I tell you this much, Quohada," Sis-ki-dee told Big Tree. "They are near. You may place my words in your parfleche, for they have substance. They are near."

The two renegades stood in the deep shadows under the canopy of trees that crowded the confluence of Salt Lick Creek and the Powder. Uncle Moon had clawed his way high into the sky. They could see the paleface work crew from here, putting the finishing touches on their mischief.

"They are near," the big Comanche agreed. He had removed his bone breastplate to avoid reflecting moonlight. Both braves wore vermilion to cut reflection from their skin. But this was not a scouting mission, it was a blood hunt, and both were heavily armed.

"Near," Big Tree continued, "but 'near' is not a target when you are eager to close for the kill. How many times has the tall Bear Caller been 'near' us? And how many times has he slipped away like water through a net?"

Big Tree had used the nickname given to Touch the Sky by Pawnees after, they claimed, he'd used magic to summon a grizzly bear to his aid.

"How many times?" Sis-ki-dee said bitterly. "Better to ask how many ways can a man be played for a green-antlered fool? But never forget, Quohada, true it is, he still wears his plew. But so do we wear ours! How many times has he tried to kill *us* and failed? I spent most of one night on that iron horse with him and those Wendigo-spawned white orphans. He searched, and though he got his blade into me, he could not stop me from gutting one of the children."

"No. But he stopped us from ransoming the rest of them. Just as he has stopped us from every scheme that might acquire gold for our new Renegade Nation. Just as he will stop this scheme of the hair-faces if we are not successful this time."

"If we fail this time," Sis-ki-dee said, "then I will finally believe that the tall one is indeed protected by big medicine. Even as we speak, the Wolf Who Hunts Smiling is making their world a hurting place. Hiram Steele and Seth Carlson have made a pact between them to kill Touch the Sky. Have you seen the hatred in their white eyes? By day and night this area crawls with greedy white men eager to earn gold for the tall one's scalp. Every sense tells me they have finally ridden to the Last River."

Both braves fell silent and again listened for any sounds that did not belong to the night. But all seemed well. Only the steady scraping of tools, the hooting of owls, the rhythmic rise and fall of the insect hum that was always loud near water could be heard.

While Wolf Who Hunts Smiling searched the backwaters and adjacent meadows for the enemy's ponies, the two renegades had covered the valley floor. But neither the water nor the game traces nearby had yielded any clues to the intruders' whereabouts.

Either brave could find sign on bare rock. Just as either brave could move with such silence and stealth that he could steal a sleeping woman from her husband's bed without waking either. Yet all their skill and cunning were now as useless as a spavined horse.

"I know they are close," Sis-ki-dee insisted again. "I can smell their Cheyenne stink as clear as bear grease in a Crow woman's hair."

Big Tree was about to reply when something dropped down the back of his neck and lodged between his foxskin quiver and his shoulder.

He reached up and pulled it out. A piece of bark.

Bark? Why?

He showed it to Sis-ki-dee, then pointed up into the trees above them.

Neither brave said a word. Nor were they convinced it meant anything. The bark could easily have been loosened by a nocturnal animal.

But *this* was the spot where their enemies wanted to be. And they were nowhere else around. Why not overhead?

"You must be wrong," Big Tree said loudly, flashing a caution sign to his friend. "There is no sign of them. I say they have gone back to their summer camp to rest and recruit new ponies. We will not see them this night."

At first, intent only on eavesdropping on the work crew, Touch the Sky and Little Horse were not aware that their enemies had wandered under the very tree in which they were hidden.

However, soon the sound of their voices drifted up to them. The sound, but not the precise words.

Touch the Sky's first reaction was one of numb fear. He and Little Horse had been able to carry only their sash knives for this climb. Knives against Sis-ki-dee and Big Tree would be as pathetic as a sisal whip against a raging she-bear.

But then the humor of it occurred to both hidden braves. After all, there was no reason to think even these two expert stalkers would ever decide to search every tree on Maiyun's green earth. If they stayed quiet, they were safe.

Little Horse nudged his friend, thinking the same thing. Hugging a fat limb, both braves enjoyed a brief grin in the darkness.

Speaking very quietly, Touch the Sky said, "Now we know where they are. If we watch where they go when they leave, we will not need to stay in the trees."

Little Horse nodded, anticipating a relatively easy journey back to their cold camp. Like his companion he was sleepy and hungry.

The steady drone of voices rose to identify the speaker: Big Tree.

"There is no sign of them. I say they have gone back to their summer camp to rest and recruit new ponies. We will not see them this night."

Little Horse nudged his friend again. "Thus the great red hunters," he whispered. "Were we any closer, they would be wearing us for war bonnets."

Despite the humor of the moment, Touch the Sky could not help feeling a little nubbin of anger and resentment. For a long time now it had festered within him like a slug festering in pus. Thanks to those two below, every day for him and those foolish enough to love him was like a brutal initiation rite. Other men could lie in peace with their women. But for him and those who followed him, "peace" was an illusion. One created by the Wendigo to drive men mad—as elusive as the fabled white buffalo whose birth would mark the coming epoch of the Red Nations.

But he forced himself to shake off such thoughts. For now they must only be patient and wait for their enemies to leave.

"Yes, Quohada, you speak straight words," Sis-ki-dee said. "We will not spot our fighting Cheyennes this night. They have eluded us yet again."

As both braves appeared to be carrying on a

mundane conversation, a secret plan was going forward. Sis-ki-dee produced two paper cartridges and chewed them open, ramming the double charge of powder down the muzzle of his North & Savage. This was to produce extra muzzle flash.

While he thumbed a primer cap into place behind the hammer, he motioned to Big Tree. The Comanche shrugged his osage-wood bow from his shoulder and pulled a handful of arrows from his quiver, notching one and holding the rest ready in his left hand. Big Tree could string and launch up to twenty arrows in the time it took a soldier to charge his rifle once.

Big Tree understood the plan immediately. In the darkness, a double-charged muzzle flash would produce excellent light. He must stare overhead and hope for a target, saturating the area with arrows. After all, even one brief glimpse would orient him—he had once skewered a Pawnee through the vitals thanks to a flicker of lightning.

"Yes, buck," Sis-ki-dee said, raising his voice as he moved into position. "As you say, his squaw Honey Eater is a fine little tidbit. In a tribe known for beauties she stands out. I mean to top her while the Bear Caller looks on. That is, if he is still alive to witness my prowess as a lover."

Touch the Sky was growing apprehensive.

It had sounded like the two renegades were about to depart. Now he could hear them talking some more.

91

This time it was Sis-ki-dee's voice that rose in volume. When Touch the Sky heard the usual filth about Honey Eater he frowned deeply—not from anger, for the vile trash spoken by these two had long ago ceased to prick his thick hide.

No. What troubled him was the fact that Sis-ki-dee was speaking the words as if to goad. Did that mean . . . ?

Alarm tingled his nape.

"Brother!" Touch the Sky whispered. "They have—"

KA-WHUMPF!

The double-charged roar of the North & Savage seemed like the loudest noise on earth. The ball whistled harmlessly past them and snapped off a limb. But for an eyeblink's time, Touch the Sky could see every limb and leaf around them in the intense muzzle flash.

Fwip! Fwip! Fwip! Big Tree loosed a mad flurry of fire-hardened arrows at their spot. Luckily the thick limb took most of them, loud thwacks sounding all around them. Touch the Sky felt a burning line of pain as one creased his elbow. Another nicked his heel.

But though they survived that initial volley, their position was known. Even now Sis-ki-dee was ramming another charge home, planning to illuminate them again. And this time Big Tree would be even better oriented to control his shots.

"Brother!" Touch the Sky said. "Nothing else for it! Dive into the river, then stay under the surface and swim hard!"

As loath as his companion was to submerge in that bad-death river, there was indeed nothing else for it. Both braves lowered themselves until they were hanging; then, even as Sis-ki-dee's rifle spat fire again, they plummeted into the channel of the river. The loud splashes announced their move.

"There!" Touch the Sky heard Sis-ki-dee shout. "In the water!"

Arrows sliced into the river all around them, but both braves kicked furiously even as they hugged the bottom. The river was down considerably now, thanks to the paleface treachery. But it was still, thank Maiyun, fairly deep and swift in the middle. Soon they had left the deadly confluence well behind them.

Chests heaving with the exertion, both braves waded ashore and immediately took cover in the thickets.

"Will they follow us?" Little Horse wondered.

"I doubt it," Touch the Sky said. "Big Tree wears two quivers. But he must have emptied both of them by now. Still, this is no place to stand and discuss the causes of the wind. They are too close. Move quick, brother, but attend to your senses. This valley is filled with starving curs, and we are the red meat they crave."

But even as they moved back to the treeline, Touch the Sky was thinking about how they were going to get inside that barn.

Wolf Who Hunts Smiling worked patiently and proficiently in the darkness.

He did not truly expect to find Touch the Sky

and Little Horse, not when they did not wish to be found. Nor was he eager to do so. Closing with either one of those two was a bloody task for ten men. Both together would be a match for a Bluecoat regiment.

But Indians without ponies were soon dead Indians. So far, he had decided, his two tribal enemies had been sneaking around on foot. Soon, however, they would need horses to make their escape.

Good places to hide horses were plentiful in Blackford's Valley. But Wolf Who Hunts Smiling knew they would want their ponies near to hand. Therefore he limited his search, at first, to the best places within a reasonable distance of the confluence.

He also knew a thing those two were not aware he knew. Little Horse had trained his pony to respond to a soft, warbling whistle like a thrush. Hearing it, the little cayuse would immediately come to his master.

Wolf Who Hunts Smiling combed the thickets and copses and hidden meadows, patiently repeating the whistle.

He flinched when he heard the familiar report of Sis-ki-dee's rifle. A wide, lupine grin divided his face. The Blackfoot was a bullet hoarder—if he fired his rifle, it meant he had a sure target. It boomed a second time. One for Little Horse, too?

Again Wolf Who Hunts Smiling made the warbling whistle. And this time a soft nickering responded. Moments later, Little Horse's cayuse and Touch the Sky's paint were greeting him fondly, reassured by the familiar Cheyenne smell.

It was a moment's work to throat-slash both of them. At first, before they buckled on their forelegs, there was an eerie trumpeting sound as air rushed through their gaping throats.

Elation hummed in Wolf Who Hunts Smiling's blood. Sis-ki-dee and Big Tree giving them hurt at the confluence, their ponies dying— Touch the Sky and Little Horse were trapped. They had no place to run, and no way to run there if they did.

"The worm has finally turned, Woman Face!" he announced into the black maw of the night. Then Wolf Who Hunts Smiling disappeared into the darkness.

Chapter Nine

"That's all we goddamn need!" Hiram Steele raged, his face bloating from the intensity of his anger and frustration. "See it? See it, Seth? What did I tell you? It's happening all over a-goddamn-gain!"

"Hiram, for Christ sakes, simmer down—"

"Simmer a cat's tail, you blockhead! You heard what the buck just told us. That red bastard Hanchon *heard* you talking to Meadows. He spied on you. All the men I'm paying, and they still got through."

"If I was you," Carlson warned quietly, eyes sliding to the two renegades beside them, "I'd put a stopper on the 'red bastard' talk, if you catch my drift. These two aren't exactly as sweet as scrubbed angels."

Despite his seething anger, Steele did indeed

catch Carlson's drift. One good look at Sis-ki-dee in broad daylight could humble a man, his eyes were so insane and mocking and clearly on the verge of violence. Big Tree, in turn, was so battle-scarred he put a panther-clawed war horse to shame.

"There," Carlson said. "I'll say this for you, Hiram. You've got a hair-trigger temper, but you calm down quick and start talking sense. Now here's some sense for you. You only *figure* that Hanchon heard me and Meadows. I don't even remember what we said. It might have been nothing."

"It's not so much his hearing you," Hiram conceded. "Hell, we *want* to lure him in the barn now anyway, right? It's just the idea that those red bas—uhh, bucks can slip past all of us at will, no matter what we throw up against them."

Wolf Who Hunts Smiling, too, was present at this meeting. Nearby, some cursory work went forward on the rainwater cistern the soldiers were building near Beaver Creek—their excuse for being in the field these days. Now Wolf Who Hunts Smiling laughed with sharp scorn.

"Let them slip around all they want to. It has cost them their ponies. Besides, why do white men sit upon the ground and wail like women over the past? It is too dead to skin! I do not whine when my last shot misses. I concentrate on killing with the next. My plan to lure them into your tunnel is the best one yet. You must be ready, for they may enter that barn as soon as the night arrives."

The two white men exchanged glances. Though they despised this arrogant, lice-infested savage, he was cunning—and this time he was right.

"We'll be ready," Steele assured him. He sent a high sign to Carlson, and the two white men walked off a few paces.

"Your commanding officer still planning on coming out here?"

Carlson nodded. "Supposed to be an inspection. Mainly, though, he's just grabbing some glory. There's an ink-slinger from the *Register-Gazette* coming out with him. They plan to make a big stirring and to-do over how the Army is making life sweet for the homesteaders. Pure crock."

"It's a pain in the ass," Steele agreed. "But unavoidable. Besides, if I just happen to be passing by, we can get some free promotion for our Pikestown project."

Carlson brightened a little at that prospect.

Steele said, "I contacted a lawyer in Laramie. Spelled out the situation here with the new course of Salt Lick Creek and asked him if I calculated my boundary right. He said it looks jake to him. We're going to Territorial Court, it's already on the docket. This lawyer claims that no Indians yet have won a case in the white man's court. Won't be long, Seth boy, we'll be swimming in gold cartwheels."

Carlson's face registered nothing as he watched Sis-ki-dee and Big Tree hunker in the dirt for a smoke with Wolf Who Hunts Smiling.

"It's not the courts I'm worried about,

Hiram," he finally said. "Seems to me you're hitching the cart before the horse, old son. It's Matt Hanchon we have to kill, and pretty damn quick, or our cake is dough."

"We will kill him," Hiram vowed. "Run Meadows and the rest of the men through the plan one more time. We've got snipers and videttes on him by day, a trap in the tunnel by night. So far Hanchon's clover has been deep. But luck can't last a lifetime unless a man dies young."

Touch the Sky did not mind a sacrifice when the cause was clear and just. But his bitterness upon discovering his throat-slashed pony was increased by the murky nature of this mission.

"They have killed our horses before," he finally said, resigned to the inevitable, "and they will again. We must accept that and deal with the practical question. How do we replace our mounts? True, we must work on foot much. But surely ponies will be crucial at some point, at least to escape."

Little Horse nodded. "Clearly, hiding them will be a problem. But I would breathe easier knowing I had a horse."

"We will have horses," Touch the Sky vowed. "And soon. It must have been the work of our wily Wolf. The renegades were well behind us."

Both braves sat with their backs to a solid stone wall, for they had found a small limestone cave, its entrance hidden by a huge tangle of hawthorn. Their weapons lay to hand beside them.

"Brother," Touch the Sky said carefully, "I

would speak with you. It is about my dream vision."

Even in the dimness of the cave, Little Horse paled noticeably.

"Well?" he demanded with a great show of bravado. "Is there a bone caught in your throat?"

"You could not understand what I heard last night," Touch the Sky said. "Do you know that big lodge near the confluence?"

"The one that sags like an old mule?"

"That one. Yes. We must go inside it. Evidently, our industrious paleface land-grabbers are using it as part of their treachery."

Little Horse shrugged. This was not so bad, after all. True, no Plains Indian liked going into confined places when a fight was brewing, but he had gone into smaller ones.

"And inside that lodge," Touch the Sky continued, "we may well find a tunnel, and it will have to be explored."

He used a crude Cheyenne translation for "tunnel," something like "big worm hole." But Little Horse understood.

"What men have done, men will do," Little Horse said bravely. "Who stood back to back at Buffalo Creek and defeated a score of hiders? *We* did, buck! The kill light was in our eyes, and no man spoke to us of surrender. But only tell me a thing, how do we get into this lodge? Look at us now, forced to hole up like badgers."

"How?" Touch the Sky shrugged. "Ask me where the shadows go. We will find a way even as we make it. First we rest, then we eat. Then we must replace our ponies."

"How? Brother, even if it were safe and the current swift, the Powder would not get us back to camp for at least two sleeps. It would take about that long on foot, too."

Touch the Sky nodded. "As you say. But Beaver Creek is much closer, straight-arrow?"

"Straight-arrow," Little Horse said. "What is there?"

"More talk I overheard. The soldiers are there, building a huge water trap."

Little Horse understood. "And where there are soldiers, there are horses."

"Not the best, surely. Too big, too spoiled, too spirit-broken for good combat mounts. But good enough until we can get to our pony strings back in the common corral."

"And then," Little Horse said causally, "that tunnel?"

"Soon," Touch the Sky agreed, "the tunnel."

Colonel Raymond Nearhood was a career soldier whose distinguished service had mostly been east of the Mississippi in administrative work. He was middling honest, as officers of his day went, his greed tempered by a strong dose of Methodist piety. But he was well past fifty years of age and strongly set in his ways. Rather than learn the million and one things a man needed to learn on the frontier, he counted on his subordinates to make him look good.

Captain Seth Carlson had proven indispensable, if sometimes mysteriously independent. Now the colonel praised him lavishly for the benefit of Cyrus Bergman, a reporter for the *Register-Gazette*.

"Here's the very man right here, Mr. Bergman," the colonel said, introducing the two men. "Captain Carlson not only came up with the idea of a cistern for the local citizens, he did the necessary research to master the engineering. All on his own. This man is a cavalry officer by training, and a crackerjack one, too."

Carlson beamed. "That's an O in the last syllable of my name."

"Yes, Captain, I know your name already," the reporter commented. "Weren't you involved in some kind of scandal under the former C.O.? Something about trying to swindle Northern Cheyennes out of some trade goods?"

Carlson flushed and Colonel Nearhood, who knew none of this, frowned so deeply his silver eyebrows touched.

"Must have been someone else," Carlson muttered. He gave the high sign to Hiram Steele. But Hiram, hearing the reporter's remark, had already withdrawn. This Indian lover was no reporter to talk to about Pikestown.

"When this cistern is completed," Nearhood said hastily, pointing over the huge concave digging, "not only can mother ditches be run off it for irrigation, but it will serve as a stock pond, too."

"Interesting," said Bergman, who did not seem too impressed by the project.

The soldiers working on the project were now dressed in clean fatigue clothes and lined up for inspection. There was a slight commotion from the rope corral where their stock was kept. Carlson glanced in that direction, but saw nothing.

Just a snake, he told himself. Or maybe they'd whiffed a bear. Horses hated the smell of bear.

"Colonel," the reporter said, "what do you think about the situation at Salt Lick Creek?"

"What situation is that, sir?"

"You haven't heard? The creek jumped its bank and now feeds into an old bed that goes south by southwest. The Powder now has no major feeders in this area. It's drastically down."

"Yes, of course," Nearhood said, scowling at Carlson for not telling him this. "I am aware of that situation. What can we say, Mr. Bergman? Man proposes, but God disposes."

He beamed when the reporter jotted that into his pad.

"By the way, Colonel," Bergman added. "Any chance of seeing the Coal Torpedo before I leave?"

"Of course, of course," Nearhood said, injecting great joviality into his tone. The Coal Torpedo was his pride and joy, a magnificent black pacer that had been presented to him by Winfield Scott himself. The horse was valued at a thousand dollars in a land where fifty dollars bought a damned good cow pony.

Carlson, Nearhood, and Bergman headed toward the rope corral, Hiram staying back out of the way.

"The Coal Torpedo is trained to hate the Indian smell," Nearhood boasted. "If an Indian even gets fifty feet downwind of him, he'll attack."

"I'll be damned," Carlson muttered. "The rope on the east side is down. We could have lost some . . ."

He trailed off, a sickening churn deep in his belly reminding him of that commotion he had just seen.

"Where in God's name is my horse?" Nearhood demanded.

"The same place," Carlson answered grimly, "as my sorrel. Look!"

He pointed at a low ridge to their west. Two horses, their riders' single braids flying out behind them, were just disappearing over the ridge.

Chapter Ten

"We must, as one tribe, bring this traitor to justice!" Wolf Who Hunts Smiling fumed. "Every great tribe falls, and falls hard, once there is a loss of manly will to punish tribal lawbreakers."

Wolf Who Hunts Smiling had returned to his summer camp after killing Touch the Sky's and Little Horse's ponies. So far as he knew, they were still stranded afoot—if they were even alive. The net in Blackford's Valley was closing quickly, yes. But Wolf Who Hunts Smiling had seen victory snatched from his very jaws too often before.

Every campaign against Touch the Sky had to be a cunning and brilliant stratagem. Now, when it appeared the tall one and Little Horse could not possibly emerge alive from that valley, was the time to prepare for their death in camp.

No letup, no quarter, until the plains were soaked with the tainted blood of Touch the Sky, who had caused the Council of Forty to strip Wolf Who Hunts Smiling of his coup feathers. He valued nothing so much as his war honors, and many would live to regret that decision.

Medicine Flute stepped forward to toss his views into the hotchpot. The clearing was slowly filling with curious braves, more and more of them wondering why Touch the Sky was still gone from camp.

"When he killed our former war leader," Medicine Flute shouted, referring to Black Elk, "Woman Face put the putrid stink of the murderer on this entire tribe! But it doesn't stop there. Have you seen how he openly defies our councils, and even Chief River of Winds says little or nothing? If another brave behaved thus, he would hang from a pole."

"And now," Wolf Who Hunts Smiling said, taking over, nudging his lackey back, "I have seen him huddling with white men at the place where they have stolen our river! Why, unless somehow he has pitched into their game?"

Not every brave gathered believed all of this. The gleam of ambition in Wolf Who Hunts Smiling's eyes was plain to all but a soft-brain. But unfortunately for Touch the Sky and his dwindling supporters, neither Tangle Hair nor Two Twists were present to control this gathering and defend their leader.

"We have been warned about the Southern

Cheyenne Dog Soldiers," Wolf Who Hunts Smiling said. "But how is *our* tall renegade any less danger than Roman Nose? Roman Nose, at least, was born among us."

"What does it take to remove the blinders from your eyes?" Medicine Flute demanded in a voice that still cracked like an adolescent's. "How far will even the most skeptical among us stretch the notion of coincidence? When Woman Face goes on a hunt with us, we find no buffalo; when Woman Face wanders down to the river early in the morning, our war leader is slain; when Woman Face deals with white traders on 'our behalf,' we end up with smallpox blankets!"

This was well done, thought Wolf Who Hunts Smiling. Tonight Medicine Flute had the gift of speaking. The wily warrior moved back away from the dancing flames of a clan fire, letting his lickspittle weave lies like truth.

"Indeed, red brothers," Medicine Flute called out. "Touch the Sky is far more dangerous than Roman Nose and the Dog Soldiers. And more cowardly. Roman Nose announces his rebel's status openly and boldly! They say he first snapped the common pipe, then he and his followers rode out in open defiance of the Headmen.

"Yet only look at our 'Dog Soldier.' He rides out, claiming only he is mighty enough to 'save' our river. Yet have you seen it? Our river is down more than ever since Touch the Sky left. And our own best Bull Whip trooper has seen him hunkering in the dirt with the Mah-ish-ta-shee-da who pox us!"

This was sophistry at its finest, and several braves muttered their approval.

"Brother," Wolf Who Hunts Smiling said to his pretend shaman in a whisper, "they say I can talk tears out of a dead man. But no tongue is more honeyed this night than yours."

However, an older brave named Trains the Hawk called out, "Medicine Flute!"

"I have ears."

"Yes, but is there a brain between them? Did I just now hear you call Touch the Sky a coward? Touch the Sky, who counted first coup at Tongue River?"

"Touch the Sky, who defeated the sellers of strong water?" shouted someone else.

"Touch the Sky, who got our women back from the Comancheros?" called out another. "A coward? Say what you will about the tall one who arrived among us wearing shoes and letting his feelings show in his face. Say he is a traitor, if you must. Call him a murderer. But call him a coward, and you would speak more sense to call a grizzly a flea."

"Nor would that word be used near Touch the Sky's name," shouted a young Bow String trooper, "if he were with us to hear it."

Medicine Flute bristled. He was about to demand more respect, as shaman-by-right. But Wolf Who Hunts Smiling silenced him with a warning nudge.

"Medicine Flute spoke in the flush of emotion, bucks, as we all do now and again. But never forget that bravery alone does not preclude treachery. I will concede that Touch the Sky is one of the best—perhaps *the* best—warrior on the Plains. But the Pawnees who stole our Medicine Arrows were brave, too! Yet, look how much suffering it cost this tribe before we got them back. A good warrior may still be a pretend Cheyenne!

"This Touch the Sky is a Bluecoat spy. He lives with us, but serves his beef-eater masters. He ruts on our women, but carries the paleface stink. He earns gold every time a red man dies! The sooner we send him under, the safer all of us will be!"

Touch the Sky and Little Horse had found it easier than rolling off a log to lighten the Army corral by two good horses. And since all good warriors gave the blade a "Spanish twist" once it was in, they made it a point to take the horses of the two highest-ranking soldiers present.

But though it was easy to steal them, they knew it would be the Wendigo's own work to move through the valley by daylight on their new trophies. So rather than risk exposure to snipers, they immediately broke for the tableland beyond the valley.

Carlson knew them well enough by now not to bother sending anyone to chase them. Cheyennes specialized in fighting running battles, and Bluecoats hated to chase them since it was impossible to know when the brave fleeing before you might suddenly reverse his pony and charge.

"Carlson is no coward," Touch the Sky said during their first break to water the lathered mounts. "But it is his nature to humiliate and break a man before he kills him. The clean, quick kill of the true warrior does not satisfy his bloodlust to master a man. Failing that, he prefers the ambush with heavy firepower."

Little Horse nodded, watching the magnificent black pacer drink. Doubt clouded his eyes. This was a pretty horse, and Little Horse did not trust pretty mounts. Also, it was huge, easily seventeen hands, as was Carlson's sorrel. Both Indians were used to sturdy, slightly ungainly-looking animals of only fourteen hands.

"Brother," he said as Touch the Sky pulled himself atop a boulder to study the terrain around this little runoff rill. "I can abide the saddle, but I confess, I get dizzy on top of that huge animal."

"Yes, buck, but admit it, have you ever moved so fast at such an easy pace?"

Little Horse grinned, for it was true. This magnificent beast never broke into a gallop. Yet it matched the sorrel for speed. And so smoothly that a man could crimp a shell without losing a grain of powder.

"See anything?" Little Horse asked.

Touch the Sky shook his head, taking care not to raise his head above the skyline. "No dust puffs. Do you feel pursuit?"

Little Horse knelt and placed three fingertips on the ground. "Nothing."

"Good enough. We will spend the rest of this daylight learning these horses. Face it, we have no time to break them, so we must let them break us. I confess, Carlson has a better horse than he deserves. This one seems to have a good nature—not so spirit-broken as most of the Army mounts."

"This Spanish giant, too," Little Horse admitted, "is good horseflesh. I may keep him for my string."

Touch the Sky dropped back to the ground. He flopped on his belly and took a long, cool drink from the rill. Then, somewhat reluctantly, he stood up again. It had felt good to lie there, and it reminded him how little sleep he had gotten lately.

"When Sister Sun goes to her rest," he decided, "we will search out a place to shelter the horses. Either Tangle Hair or Two Twists sent smoke earlier—you saw it?"

Little Horse, busy peeling pemmican from a roll with his knife, nodded. "The Wolf rode back earlier. Meaning he will not be prowling this night, looking for horses to kill."

"No guarantee," Touch the Sky said, "that Siski-dee or Big Tree will not hunt them out. But we must take the risk. We hide the horses, then we scout that barn."

Little Horse knew this was coming, of course, and only nodded. He said in his usual practical tone of battle preparation, "How do we approach it? Land or river? I take it you will not send us back into the trees?"

"One of us by river," Touch the Sky replied, "the other by foot on land. Both from opposite directions. One man is a smaller target, and by separating we have a better chance that one of us will get a look at that barn. And that is *all* we are doing, at first—a quick look to establish what is in there. It was Arrow Keeper who always told me it is best to look before wading in. This stinks like a trap. That is why we are also going to make a diversion. A good one."

Little Horse perked up a bit at this, for it smacked of good sport. Stealing the white men's best horses had reminded him how much he enjoyed bedeviling his enemies.

"What manner of diversion?" Little Horse asked.

"Have you noticed," Touch the Sky said casually, "the dry patch of Johnson grass in the middle of the valley?"

Little Horse grinned. "Hip-high? A good-sized meadow of it, exposed to the wind?"

Touch the Sky grinned right back. Setting fires as a diversion was a common Indian trick—all the more common because it was so effective. Whites seemed obsessed with rushing to a fire and putting it out, whereas most Indians chose to get out of the way.

"It will probably not draw all of our enemies off," Touch the Sky conceded. "But it will distract them, break their concentration on us. If they are trying to lure us into the barn, perhaps they mean to kill us there. Or perhaps they will spring the trap just outside it.

"But listen now, brother, for we must get it right the first time. Whichever of us reaches that barn first must mark the entrance when he leaves so the other will know it has been entered. Since I have no clan, we will both use your clan notch, agreed?"

Little Horse nodded. Touch the Sky meant the distinctive cut that each clan wore in its feathers.

"Mark it when you leave," Touch the Sky emphasized. Little Horse knew that mark served a second, more urgent function. If it was *not* there, it meant that one of them might be inside—still exploring, trapped, or dead.

"Tonight we get the lay of the place," Touch the Sky said. "Then we make our plan. And may the High Holy Ones ride with us."

Chapter Eleven

"Whatever you do," Carlson warned Meadows, "don't try to engage him in a fight. I know that Indian better than any other white man alive—any who've fought him, anyhow. Lay low and avoid a fight."

Meadows winked at the two other enlisted men with them up in the loft of the old barn.

"Hell," he said in his hillman's twang, "this child didn't join the Army so's he could fight. Ain't no heroes here, Cap'n,'cept for you. Ain't that the straight, Dakota?"

Dakota Jones, operator of the ten-barrel Gatling gun mounted on a bipod behind them, grinned and shrugged. "Cheyennes ain't no tribe to fool with. But ain't none of 'em coming up in this loft, you can take that to the bank."

Carlson nodded. "It'll be a sort of pincers ma-

neuver," he explained. "I know Hanchon. I don't
think he'll come up here right off the bat—not
if he discovers that tunnel first, which he will."

The officer paused to glance below them into
the big, dilapidated old barn. The tunnel opening was plainly exposed behind a huge pile of
displaced earth.

"Hanchon *might* throw a quick peek from the
ladder into the loft," Carlson mused. "If so, don't
risk shooting at him. The gun will be well hidden in a stack of hay, plus it'll likely be dark up
here. Only shoot at him if it's absolutely assured
you will score hits."

" 'At's right," Meadows said, chuckling. He
held up a metal box with a wire trailing from it.
The wire was hidden under straw, then routed
out of sight in the walls and floor. The box was
a galvanic-charger device linked to a series of
keg bombs planted near the tunnel.

"Leave him to me," Meadows said. "I push
this little plunger, and ka-boom!"

Carlson nodded. "Very little solid earth sep-
arates that tunnel from the river flowing over it.
Those bombs will bring water sucking into that
tunnel. If the explosion doesn't kill him, he'll
drown."

"Like routin' a prairie pup out of his hole,"
Meadows said.

"But do *not*," his platoon leader admonished,
"blow that tunnel until you know he's well into
it. Don't forget, we've got twenty feet or so of
entrance shaft that doesn't run under the river.
Give him time. If he goes in, he'll explore it all
the way to the main gallery. Give him at least

three minutes down there before you hit that charger."

"Sir?" Dakota said. "When you think he'll come?"

"He's come a cropper too many times trying to move around by daylight. Besides, there'll be near a full moon tonight, and Hanchon will know that. It'll be tonight."

"You be here, sir?"

"I'd trade a year's pay if I could be. But I have a staff meeting with Colonel Nearhood. After just losing his prize horse to savages, the Old Man's not exactly in a chipper mood. I'm counting on you men. Do I need to remind you about Hiram's two-thousand-dollar bonus if you kill Hanchon?"

"Oh, sir," Meadows said with mock indignation, "we are not interested in no dirty blood money! Why, sir! We're here to make the West safe for women and children."

"You've got a mouth on you, Meadows," Carlson said. "But you're a good man when the weather turns rough. You two just lay low and keep a tight asshole. You've got the best chance yet of killing Hanchon. You do that, and I guarantee there'll be no more hog and hominy on *your* plates."

Touch the Sky and Little Horse followed their plan. What light remained for that day was spent in learning their new mounts. So far this mission had not required horses. But a good horse was like a good gun. A hundred of them were useless if not instantly to hand when

116

needed, while one was enough if it was available at the right moment.

Then, carefully avoiding vidette riders and those river bluffs where the snipers were stationed, they sneaked back into the valley. They made sure to water the horses well and let them graze a few hours, eliminating the need to tether them close to the river or creek.

Since these horses could not be counted upon to maintain silence, the two Cheyennes reluctantly decided to muzzle them with strips of rawhide. It was a miserable way to treat horses, but they could not afford to lose these mounts.

"Draw a reed," Touch the Sky instructed his friend, holding his right hand out to him. "The shortest one will go by land. He will thus have the task of setting that Johnson grass on fire. The other heads in by water."

Little Horse nodded. He didn't notice a third piece of reed tucked up under Touch the Sky's curled fingers—the shortest piece of all. When Little Horse drew the losing piece, Touch the Sky performed a quick sleight-of-hand.

"I lose," he announced. "You take the river."

Touch the Sky had considered this deception carefully before duping his friend. But clearly, the Cheyenne who went by land would arrive first, even with the delay to start a fire. The river route was almost twice as long.

It was not a question of Little Horse's bravery or competence. Touch the Sky was convinced that Little Horse was the finest warrior in the Cheyenne nation. But Little Horse was all Cheyenne, from birth on, whereas Touch the Sky

117

had been raised among white men. The fear of entering that barn, especially at night, was naturally far stronger for Little Horse—especially since there might also be a tunnel in that barn, a second source of supreme terror for an Indian.

Besides all that, Touch the Sky thought, was the matter of justice. It was hatred of Matthew Hanchon that brought these two white enemies into the Cheyenne homeland like some murderous plague. Yet how many times had Little Horse or Tangle Hair or Two Twists suffered at their hands?

Little Horse did not argue. Gambling was a standard way of settling such questions, and no Indian questioned the outcome of chance.

"Remember," Touch the Sky said. "Just a quick look this night. Then we counsel and make our plan. But just to be safe . . ."

He removed a small piece of charcoal from his possibles bag and marked first his, then Little Horse's face with it. Black, to a Cheyenne, symbolized joy at the death of an enemy.

"I have marked us," Touch the Sky told his friend solemnly. "And the color that is on us is death. We may fall this night, brother. No shame in dying. But if you must fall, land on the bones of an enemy!"

Touch the Sky moved out shortly after sunset, leaving his rifle behind and taking his sash knife and his bow and quiver.

He made good time, mainly because he was reckless and violated much of his training. He moved openly through patches of shimmering moonlight, seldom checked his back-trail, and seldom stopped to listen, feel, and smell.

Once he barely leaped under a bush in time to avoid a vidette. He had a clear shot at the man, and might have dropped him quietly with an arrow. Yet he held back reluctantly. It was bad enough that he violated the Cheyenne way by going out from camp at night. He was sworn, by honor and duty, to restrict all killing to pure self-defense.

He wondered how Little Horse was doing. At least there had been no shots so far. But then Touch the Sky recalled that deadly slingshot master. In this valley, death could sneak up quietly on light paws.

Soon enough the Johnson grass was brushing his thighs and hips. Touch the Sky always carried crumbled bark in his possibles bag for use as kindling. He scooped some out now along with his flint and steel.

He made a little mound from the bark, then tore up some handfuls of grass to lay over it. He struck downward a few times with his steel, sending sparks leaping into the kindling. Soon there was a little orange glow that he carefully blew on until a tiny finger of flame leaped up.

That finger quickly became a long arm. Then, as a stiff breeze picked up, flames began snapping and sparking.

Touch the Sky quickly receded out of the light, resuming his trek.

*   *   *

Little Horse, too, had thrown caution to the wind.

He might have lost the draw, but he had no intention of letting his friend arrive first if he could help it. Despite his great fear of that barn, Little Horse's every instinct urged him to protect Touch the Sky. A warrior fought for many things. But one of the most important reasons was to spare his companions.

For one thing, Touch the Sky was Keeper of the Arrows. He was also the tribe's shaman and, in Little Horse's opinion, the best warrior west of the Great Waters. On top of all that was Arrow Keeper's great vision at Medicine Lake. A vision which told of Touch the Sky's great importance to the survival of the Shaiyena tribe.

So now he did not travel underwater, breathing through a reed while he clung to a slow-moving log. Instead, he swam boldly on the surface, holding onto a log, yes, but kicking hard behind it. In this way he made much better time.

He breathed a little easier after he spotted the burnt-orange glow of a good-sized fire further into the interior of the valley. And just as Touch the Sky had predicted, it drew whites the way magnets drew iron filings—he could hear the vidette riders shouting to each other as they galloped to see what was happening.

Still kicking, Little Horse felt the night-chilled water gliding around him. The log began to bob erratically, warning him that a blockage of some sort lay ahead. He craned his neck and spotted a huge sawyer blocking the channel.

But this could not be. He and Touch the Sky had only recently floated through this spot with no trouble. Sawyers did not form so rapidly . . . not by themselves.

Before he could grasp the true meaning of that thought, Little Horse heard sinister, insane laughter from the nearby bank.

Sis-ki-dee!

Desperately, Little Horse craned his neck again for a look ahead toward that rapidly approaching sawyer—just in time to spot Big Tree, hunched down in the midst of it with a knife in his teeth!

Little Horse had the best ears in his tribe. Above the rush of water, he heard the decisive metallic click when Sis-ki-dee thumbed back his hammer.

There was nothing else for it. Against two other men Little Horse would not hesitate to fight. But *these* two were at least one too many for any man born of woman.

With Sis-ki-dee to his right, Big Tree ahead, and the current pushing at him relentlessly from behind, Little Horse had only one escape route and he took it.

He gave the log a mighty heave forward toward Big Tree even as he tucked and rolled to avoid Sis-ki-dee's shot. Then he scrambled up the opposite bank and into the trees.

There was no chance of his reaching that barn, and Little Horse knew it. He would be lucky to last this night. Now he must go into hiding and only hope the gods would smile on Touch the Sky.

*   *   *

Touch the Sky had enough weighing on his mind as he approached the looming, shadowy mass of the old barn, but adding fuel to his worry was the precise crack of Sis-ki-dee's rifle, coming from the river.

Little Horse!

Had he, after all, sent his best friend to his death?

But Touch the Sky was too disciplined to reason thus for very long. He was a warrior and so was Little Horse. They knew the rules, and even more important, they knew the odds. Both of them had eluded death too many times not to realize that they were living on Maiyun's grace—what the white men called "borrowed time."

Perhaps, once again, Little Horse had thwarted the Black Warrior called Death. If not, he had died as every warrior prayed he might die, in the middle of dangerous action.

For now, Touch the Sky knew he must shut down all thought, for thought would kill him. Now he must only attend to his survival senses.

It was a relatively easy matter to ensure that no sentinels were in the immediate area. The barn itself, while close to the confluence of creek and river, sat on a small knoll with no trees around it.

He circled it several times, studying it, listening, looking, carefully sniffing the air. With help from Arrow Keeper and Little Horse, he had trained his nose to pick up odors white men seldom thought about: liquor, the stinking liniments they used, the heavy bay rum tonic all soldiers wore after a trip to the post barber.

Nothing lingered outside the barn. Deciding this part was secure, he planned his entrance.

There were two easy ways in—the front and back doors, still intact but standing ajar. But he skipped those and opted for a spot in the middle of the barn where several boards had fallen away, leaving a small entrance between the joists.

He hesitated after crouching in front of the hole. For a long moment he felt it: a cold tingling in his nape, his shaman sense warning him that some manner of danger lay within.

But despite the cold ball of ice in his stomach, he had to go in. He had to see if there was indeed a tunnel entrance in that dark, forboding building. A tunnel, or any clue as to what the hair-faces had done to steal the Powder River's water. The Cheyennes could not begin to fight this thing until they knew more about what they were up against. The effect of the treachery was clear—now he must find the cause.

Touch the Sky briefly touched his medicine pouch, drawing ancestral strength and courage from the badger claws he carried within. Then, gripping a rotting four-by-four, he scuttled under the wall of the big barn.

It was a moment's easy work to get inside, listening as he squatted near the south wall. Somewhere in a back corner an owl hooted, but he heard nothing else. Just the sounds of the nearby water.

Nor could he see anything too threatening in the generous moonwash pouring inside. Most conspicuous was a huge pile of dirt about half-way along the wall.

Touch the Sky's eyes cut to a few wooden rungs that had been nailed into a support beam, making a crude ladder up into a hayloft.

He should secure the top, he realized. But it was more logical to look around down here first. Anyone hiding up there would be bound to make noise coming down. He was safe from surprise attack from up there, so long as he didn't offer a clear target.

Hugging the wall, crawling low on his knees and elbows, he moved cautiously down to the pile of dirt. As he eased around it, he abruptly felt a cold stirring in his stomach.

A tunnel entrance yawned before him, a hungry maw calling out to him to enter if he dared.

After all, he admonished himself, you knew it was here. You heard Carlson mention it. So why this feeling now as if a dead man had risen and asked for a hump steak?

You know perfectly well why, another voice inside him responded. Because you saw this tunnel long before Carlson mentioned it. You saw it in your dream vision.

Death by water.

For a long moment Touch the Sky debated going into the tunnel. But then he recalled his own strict orders to Little Horse. Tonight they would only make sure it existed. Then they would make their plan.

Besides, that tingling was back in his nape. There was a time for plunging recklessly forward, consequences be damned. But this was not that time.

Touch the Sky crawled back outside. Before he left, he slipped around front and made a lop-sided V notch about halfway up the door frame—Little Horse's clan notch. If his friend had survived, and if he arrived here, he would know that Touch the Sky had already been inside and left.

For a long moment before he left, Touch the Sky stared up toward that loft. He could have sworn he heard a hoarse whisper from up there. But perhaps, after all, it was only a rat.

Now, it was time to return to the cold camp and see if his best friend in all the world still belonged to the living.

Chapter Twelve

"We're not going to get icy boots," Hiram Steele insisted. "That's what those two blanket-asses are counting on, that we'll start to unstring under the pressure."

"Pressure, my sweet aunt," Carlson scoffed. "All they've done is steal two horses and manage to keep giving us the slip. All right, granted, Colonel Nearhood's pacer was a nice little coup for them. But how many dead and wounded we got this time? Not a one. Considering all that's at stake here for me and you, Hiram, this has been a pretty good showing so far. And the best is yet to come."

"That's what I need to hear," Steele agreed. The two men sat under the fly of Carlson's tent, discussing Meadows's report on the events at the barn. Carlson's unit was camped on a little rise near the cistern project at Beaver Creek.

"Where's the Wolf?" Steele complained, craning his neck to study the camp. "Everybody else is here and waiting on him."

"My scouts said he's close," Carlson replied. "He'll be here by the time we finish our coffee. You just simmer down and remember, don't rile the renegades, any of them. Any one of them would gut his own mother for a chaw."

"Why should I rile them? Hell, how many whites I got on the payroll? None of them has come through either. Only one thing will pull us through this, Seth boy—teamwork. From here on out, we've all got to think like one man, one man bent on one target. We're a team, and if any one of us fails, he drags the whole team into the mud."

Carlson nodded. "The thing last night with Hanchon and the tunnel. He *will* go into that tunnel, Hiram, you know he will. But that bastard is not only savage as a meat axe, he's cunning. Guile and deception come natural to him. He suspected a trap. But eventually, he'll go in."

Steele said, "I hope to hell he does. But we can't assume he will. A mouse that has only one hole is quickly taken. That's why we're having this meeting. This is no time to start praying Hanchon takes the bait at the barn. You've seen how a wolverine attacks: fast, savage, unrelenting, never letting up even for a breath until its prey is stone dead. That's how we're going to be. Every place Hanchon goes, we have to make that a hurting place."

Steele gazed out across the distant mountain

peaks of the Wyoming Territory. His gray eyes were determined, but something else, too. They held hard little points of fear and uncertainty.

"Seth," he said quietly. "How bad do you want Hanchon dead?"

Carlson, his sunburned face half in shadow under the brim of his black cavalry hat, was some time answering this.

"I want that red son cold as a wagon wheel," he finally said. "I want it worse than hell-thirst. I want him so mother-loving bad that I'd gladly die too if I knew I was taking him with me. He came between me and your daughter, you know that. She'd've married me if that cunning son-ofabitch hadn't used his lies and guile on her."

Hiram only nodded, encouraging Carlson in his delusion. Hiram knew far better. His daughter had detested Seth Carlson from the first day, and she would have even without Matthew Hanchon's influence.

"Well, soldier blue, multiply your need to kill him by five, and that's how bad *I* want him. But understand this. This project of ours is far beyond the need for revenge. I've got all my savings invested in our irrigation plan. Plus I've made promises to a lot of men around here. If Hanchon whips us this time, I'll do more than eat crow. I might end up, at my age, a bagline bum."

"My bacon's in the fire too," Carlson reminded him. "So far we've given my men plenty of whiskey. But they also expect a nice ration of the profits once Pikestown is up and running. We short them, it could get nasty. I've had a few men in the past file depositions."

"Teamwork," Steele repeated. Impatiently, he slid his watch from his fob pocket and thumbed back the cover. "Where the *hell* is that goddamn Wolf Who Hunts Smiling?"

"Here he comes," Little Horse said triumphantly. "Just as you said he would, brother."

Touch the Sky, too, watched Wolf Who Hunts Smiling approaching along the old game trace that followed the Powder River toward Blackford's Valley.

"He has come to serve his white masters," Touch the Sky said. "I knew he would ride back to camp briefly to plant more lies about what we are up to. Also, by appearing there now and again, he throws off some suspicion."

"While we," Little Horse said, "by staying gone create the impression of greater treachery."

"As you say." Touch the Sky's jaw tensed as he studied his worst tribal enemy's approach. The only good news lately was the discovery of that tunnel and finding out that Little Horse had survived Sis-ki-dee's attack.

"If he is coming back," Touch the Sky mused out loud, "no doubt there is to be a council of our enemies."

He looked at Little Horse. "Buck, has there been enough sport for you on this mission?"

Little Horse grinned, sensing mischief aplenty. "Sport? None at all. Just target-shooting, with us the targets."

Touch the Sky nodded. "Your thoughts fly

with mine. Our enemies are feeling far too cocky by now. They have made the rules all along. So look to your battle rig! We have plans to make about that barn. But first, we are going to follow our wily Wolf. And then we are going to make life warm at this important council."

"Ulrick?"

"Yo!"

"I want you and the rest of the snipers," Hiram Steele said, "to take up new positions. By now Hanchon has spotted all of you."

"You waste your time," Big Tree said, his voice heavy with contempt. "The Bear Caller will not be taken by a sniper."

"He bleeds, too," Steele said. "I've seen him. Don't matter what the Apaches say about this Geronimo who bullets can't find. Bullets can find Hanchon."

"Only if the marksman can find him first," Sis-ki-dee said. "No one finds the tall one until he wants to be found."

Wolf Who Hunts Smiling, too, joined his fellow renegades in this revolt. "It will not be a paleface who kills him," he insisted. "It will be I, Sis-ki-dee, or Big Tree. These paid killers of yours, they are capable men and good shots. But 'capable' and 'good' are not enough to kill Touch the Sky."

"Get it, Tim?" Baylis Morningstar said to Ulrick, scorn poison-tipping his voice. "It'll need some real by-God men to kill Hanchon. Only these Innuns can get 'er done. The rest of us are still on ma's milk, but they're full-growed and about as rough!"

Hiram angrily started to interrupt this battle-in-progress. But Carlson suddenly stood up.

"I'll be a sonofabitch," he said slowly. "Look!"

He pointed toward a long, tree-covered slope about two hundred yards beyond the cistern. Everyone followed his finger.

"Well, I'll be," Hiram said, for there, grazing peacefully, was Colonel Nearhood's magnificent pacer.

"It's draggin' a lead line," Ulrick said.

"Must've got loose," Carlson said, a wide, ear-to-ear smile dividing his face. He had been in trouble with Nearhood since the Cheyennes had stolen that animal from the C.O. Getting it back would make life easier around the post.

"There's your big bad Indian," Hiram scoffed. "Best goddamn horse he ever put his filthy hands on, and he can't even keep it tied."

However, Wolf Who Hunts Smiling, Big Tree, and Sis-ki-dee had exchanged knowing glances. All three braves discreetly hunkered down. They realized they were about to enjoy a good show.

"I'll ride up and get him," Carlson said. "He's not a spooky animal by nature, but the Indian smell might still have him nerved. You two," he said, nodding at Morningstar and Ulrick, "take up my flanks. He bolts, squeeze him in toward me and I'll try to drop a loop on him."

"All of you, hurry it the hell up," Hiram groused. "I want to get this damned meeting over pronto."

131

Carlson caught up his new mount, a good coyote dun, and swung up into leather, shaking out a loop. Baylis and Ulrick took up spots to the right and left of him, fanning out perhaps thirty yards. The rest of the men watched with moderate interest, glad for some diversion.

They were perhaps fifty yards from the pacer and closing, when the mild diversion suddenly turned into a Wild West show.

A rifle shot rang out, and Morningstar's horse dropped clean, trapping its rider's leg under him. A flurry of arrows soon protruded from Carlson's dun and Ulrick's claybank, both men barely getting their legs out of the stirrups before their horses went down.

It was over in a matter of seconds. Carlson, dazed, was still trying to fumble his service revolver from its holster when the rapid drumbeat of shod hooves emerged from the trees. His own sorrel came charging out, Touch the Sky and Little Horse riding double.

They both unleashed more stinging arrows as they rode. A man went down screaming, an arrow pushing something pink and glistening through his ribcage. Carlson, too, unleashed a banshee roar of pain as a flint arrow point sliced a big piece of meat away from his left buttock.

Carlson leaped behind his dead horse. But Hanchon and his stout little partner ignored the three white men cowering on the ground. They raced toward the pacer. Hanchon made a magnificent leap, at full gallop, and bounced into the saddle of the surprised horse.

And a few eyeblinks later, the two gutsy Cheyennes were charging the rest of the meeting!

Hiram and most of the snipers and videttes wore side arms. Their rifles were propped against trees nearby, but there was no time to get them.

Hiram shouted something incoherent and dived behind a boulder, jerking his Colt Navy from its big chamois holster. The weapon bucked in his fist as the other men opened fire.

In the heat of this surprise attack, their enemy did just what Touch the Sky hoped they would: They foolishly aimed for the Indians first, instead of their mounts. Had they shot at horses, they might have grounded the riders and then killed them at will.

Nor had the defenders counted on Little Horse's formidable revolving four-barrel flintlock shotgun. It was heavy and unwieldy, and often Little Horse's companions teased him for carrying it. But now, close in like this, it showed its effectiveness.

While Touch the Sky unleashed arrow after arrow, Little Horse revolved and blasted, revolved and blasted, sending out a virtual wall of buckshot. Even as Hiram watched, one of the sniper's faces was reduced to a red smear. Another caught a full load in the abdomen, his vitals bursting out his back in a colorful spray that made Hiram's gorge rise.

Not that the whites did not get off many shots. Bullets nipped at their attackers' ears and flew past with a blowfly drone. But courage kept them sure in the saddle, and moments after it had begun, the attack was over.

The two gutsy Cheyennes were retreating into the scrub pines of the east, leaving behind dead and wounded horses and men.

"Hii-ya!" Touch the Sky taunted them, shrieking the shrill Cheyenne war cry. "Hii-ya, hii-*ya!*"

In a final gesture of supreme contempt, both warriors paused and spun their mounts around, rising in the stirrups to lift their clouts. Hiram Steele and the rest of the white men gathered there knew full well what that gesture meant: *Kiss my red ass, white fools!*

Chapter Thirteen

It was the Indian way to boast after a good raid. When Beaver Creek was well behind them, and no pursuers were in sight, the two Cheyennes halted to rest and water their ponies at a natural sink in the Crying Horse Hills. This was in the midst of Sioux ranges, and thus relatively safe for any Northern Cheyenne, cousins to the Sioux.

"Brother!" Little Horse exclaimed, elation still clear in his face. "I am becoming a traitor to mountain ponies! These 'American' horses performed like seasoned warriors! Carlson's sorrel even took a bullet graze without bolting."

Touch the Sky, too, shared in his friend's exuberance. True it was, they'd faced nearly insurmountable odds in a seemingly impossible task. But, oh, how his blood was singing to finally taste a bit of the pony warrior's life again!

"I did my job," he said frankly. "But this time, Little Horse, it was you and your scattergun who made the grass run red with blood. It was a charge to be sung about in the lodges! A charge to be painted by the elders in the winter-count that is the history of our tribe. Nor was it murder, as these palefaces are trying to do against us. They sent out the first soldier, we only sent out the second. Too bad for them that the second soldier was Little Horse of the Northern Cheyenne!"

Soon, however, bleak reality set in. Still watching their back-trail for dust puffs, Little Horse said, "What next, shaman? We have served notice we are not hair-face playthings. We have found the spot where the whites have worked Wendigo tricks on Salt Lick Creek. We even know where their worm hole is, as well as the identity of our major enemies. Just now we sent two of their lickspittles across the divide. We have accomplished some work, but left much undone. So what next?"

"Two things," Touch the Sky answered promptly, for he was not one to stand and wring his hands where the road was washed out. "We are going to see Firetop, and through him, Tom Riley. And only then will you and I go back into that worm hole the whites call a tunnel."

Little Horse considered this. "Firetop" was the Cheyenne name for redheaded Corey Robinson, the paleface who had grown up with Touch the Sky when he lived in Bighorn Falls under the name Matthew Hanchon. Firetop had once helped save the Cheyennes from a savage attack by Pawnees. To this day he carried a blue feather that guaranteed safe passage among any tribes friendly to the Cheyennes.

"I am always glad to thump Firetop on the back," Little Horse said. "But you would not pick this time for a friendly smoke. How can Firetop help?"

"His only part in it," Touch the Sky said, "will be to bring Tom Riley back from the soldier town. It is Riley we must talk to, brother. We are up against the white man's devil called engineering and demolitions. Tom knows something about such things."

Tom Riley was a cavalry officer at Fort Bates, and was unquestionably Seth Carlson's chief nemesis there. True, Riley was a "mustanger," a former enlisted man who had not attended West Point, as had Carlson. But Tom's brother Caleb was a successful miner in the Sans Arcs range. Tom had helped him from time to time in such projects as blowing out bluffs to build a spur-line railroad.

Little Horse nodded at the sense of this. If a man wanted to learn how to fish, he did not go to a Paiute in the desert. He went to a mountain Ute who loved trout.

"If we must crawl into that worm hole," Little Horse admitted, "by all means, we must parley with Tom Riley. I will die if I must, shaman, but I hope to someday bounce a son on my knee. I want the best odds at living!"

* * *

137

"So *that* explains it," Tom Riley said. "I knew that yellow-bellied Carlson had to be up to no good. But he's managed to wangle it so I'm stuck on post these days inventorying every piece of gear that belongs to the Fourth Cavalry. I heard about Salt Lick Creek, of course, from my Indian scouts. But I never figured Carlson and Steele for it. I should have."

The four of them sat around a crude deal table in Corey's split-log cabin: Touch the Sky, Corey Robinson, Captain Tom Riley in fatigue clothes, and Little Horse. From time to time Touch the Sky translated something for Little Horse.

"You didn't actually see any blasts?" Riley asked.

Touch the Sky shook his head. "We heard at least one. It was at night, and sounded muffled. As if perhaps it was underground."

"It was," Riley said with conviction. "I'm no engineer, but I know some sappers and miners and I've helped my brother Caleb with several blasts. What Carlson's men did is called hydraulic angle blasting. It's done to change the grade or slope of riverbeds. They've also probably built up the bed with rocks and gravel, sort of a riprap."

"How the hell can they work *under* a river?" Corey demanded. "I understand the tunnel. But wouldn't the water come rushing into it when they set bombs off?"

"The main tunnel is called the gallery," Tom explained. "You don't detonate explosives in the gallery. You run smaller tunnels, called curtains, off the gallery. That plants the explosive very near the water. Then the curtain is filled back up before the bomb is detonated by galvanic charge. Sounds to me like they're done now. What Touch the Sky probably found was the entrance to the gallery. But why didn't they fill it up, I'm wondering. It's stupid to leave evidence."

"They may still be working down there," Corey suggested.

"That," Touch the Sky said, watching his companion Little Horse even though he spoke English, "is why we have to go into it. If the creek's flow was changed from that gallery, then it's only from the gallery that it can be restored to its original course."

Riley nodded. "There's a bit of good news in all this. As with most things, it should be easier to destroy their work than it was to alter that creek's flow. I can maybe help you with advice and equipment. But no way can I leave the post right now—Carlson's got his toadies on me like dark on night. I can ride south, toward Bighorn Falls, and they ignore me. But if I aim toward Blackford's Valley, Colonel Nearhood will know about it. And I'll be digging four-holers."

Touch the Sky asked, "What do you need from me?"

"Your powers of observation, partner. I've known you to make maps and diagrams in your head that are better than ones on paper. You'll have to *look* at that gallery, look close. Look for tools, gabions—containers for dirt—or explosives. If it's incriminating enough, I'll somehow convince Colonel Nearhood to examine it. We could put Steele and Carlson's necks in the wringer, with a little luck. Nearhood has his faults, including a vast ignorance of Indians and the frontier. But he's a rule-book commander, and he abides by the treaties."

But alter that luck just a hair, Touch the Sky thought, and he and Little Horse would be descending into their graves.

"Meaning," he said, "that if the tunnel is just that—an empty tunnel—it will not be evidence enough that they turned the creek?"

Tom shook his head. " 'Fraid not. Not when it's a white man's word against Indians. *We* know they did it. But proof is elusive in the white man's courts."

"Yes," Touch the Sky agreed. "We know they did it. So if the proof is lacking, we won't worry about the courts."

"Hell, this ain't so awful goddamn bad," said Dakota Jones, stretching out in the hayloft and lacing his fingers behind his head. "It's boring, but what in the Army ain't? Long as the cap'n keeps bringin' us some chewin's now and then, and makings for a few smokes, hell, it ain't so bad at all."

Meadows nodded. He was seated behind the loft's south window, watching down toward the Powder and Salt Lick Creek.

"Long as you got that gun pointed at the top of the ladder," he said, "we got nothing to worry about. Ain't nobody getting up here through a wall of lead."

The Gatling was well concealed in a mound of straw.

"Two hunnert fifty rounds a minute," Jones bragged. "A damn fly couldn't squeak through."

"You just remember," Meadows cautioned. "Don't shoot the moment you see a feather. Wait until he actually climbs up into the loft. For one thing, it might not be Hanchon that peeks up here. Might be that short pard of his. We won't be able to see real good in the dark."

"Say," Jones said as something occurred to him. "If Hanchon goes into the gallery like Carlson thinks he will, and you push that button, will *we* get caught in the blast?"

Meadows, who knew more about those hidden keg mines, shook his his head. "It'll be like the first circle of Hell down below, chappie. But all we'll get up here is a little shook up."

Jones started to say something else, but Meadows suddenly hushed him by raising one hand. "Shush it, boy!"

He moved closer to the window and looked carefully outside into the late afternoon light.

"What?" Jones demanded, knocking some hay aside to check the action of the Gatling.

"Somebody coming," Meadows told him. "And whoever it is is riding hell-bent for election! Hear them hooves?"

Moments later Meadows whistled out loud.

"Well, lick my left one! It's our Innuns, Dakota! They ain't waitin' for dark. Quick, get down behind that Gatling. Not a peep! All they got to do is go into that tunnel long enough, and

I'll blow both their red asses to the happy hunting grounds."

It had been Touch the Sky's suggestion, quickly approved by Little Horse. Why wait until after dark, he had asked, to explore that tunnel? The whites were expecting them to do just that.

Better, Touch the Sky argued, to move now while the hair-faces were still rattled from the lightning raid earlier that morning.

Of course, that presented the problem of snipers and videttes. But for one thing, two of them had been felled by Little Horse's shotgun. And of course, they needed good targets. So the two Cheyennes had simply raced to the barn at a full gallop, never once letting up. They also avoided straight lines, not allowing their enemies to "lead" them with their sights.

Even so, several marksmen had taken shots at them along the way, one shot ripping through Touch the Sky's kit. But finally there it was— the barn, looming up before them.

"We must work quickly, brother," he told Little Horse as they swung down from their purloined mounts. "Take your horse right inside the barn and hobble him after we secure the building. Those snipers have mirrors. They will signal to someone that we have come here. We quickly study the tunnel, and then we leave."

Little Horse's eyes were distant with worry. Touch the Sky's death omen was strong on his mind, as was the Cheyenne fear of enclosed places and death by water.

A quick search of the main floor showed the barn was empty.

"Brother," Little Horse whispered, pointing toward the ladder.

Touch the Sky nodded. He knew Little Horse could not go up there—he had never climbed a ladder in his life, and indeed, only once had he faced a set of stairs.

Touch the Sky tested the first rung. Then, pulse thudding in his temples, he eased up to the level of the loft and peered into it.

Nothing. Just mounds of old straw everywhere. But why, as he gazed around, did he feel sweat break out on his back? Perhaps he should climb up all the way and poke into the straw a little?

He decided that was a good idea. Touch the Sky started to haul himself up into the loft.

"Brother," Little Horse called from below, his voice pitched high with nervousness. "If we are crawling into that worm hole, let us do it now while my courage holds. I would get this over with one way or another."

Touch the Sky abandoned his plan to search the loft and began climbing down again. "Do you have the torch?"

Little Horse, staring toward the dark maw of the tunnel entrance, brandished a short limb wrapped with tow that had been soaked in coal oil at Corey's place.

The two braves exchanged a long look.

"Let us go get ourselves killed," Little Horse said, pumping himself up with bravado to mask a nearly crippling fear. "I have no desire to die in my sleep of old age."

143

Chapter Fourteen

Every fiber of Touch the Sky's being rebelled against descending into that tunnel.

Questions plagued him. Why, if Steele and Carlson had finished their treacherous work, had it been left here to incriminate them? True, whites could treat Indian rights with impunity here in the Wyoming Territory. But Steele had already lost one battle in court, out in Kansas, when he'd tried to swindle Cherokees. Once burned, twice shy. Common sense told Touch the Sky he should have sealed this tunnel.

Unless it were intended as some kind of trap?

Yet what else was there for it? If he ignored that tunnel, he stood no chance of proving white treachery—or at least, of correcting it on his own.

Besides, as Arrow Keeper had taught him, a

144

man did not always avoid a thing simply because it frightened him. If all Cheyennes behaved that way, their tribe would have been wiped out long before this.

There was one final persuasion: his dream vision. Despite the warning that came with it, the vision was clearly meant to tell him he must enter that tunnel.

Now, as he sparked his torch with his flint and steel, he looked at his companion's whey-faced fear.

"Brother," Touch the Sky said casually, "I would feel better if one of us stayed on guard up here."

Little Horse knew exactly what his companion was doing.

"Fine," he answered. "Give me the torch. I will go down while you keep watch."

Despite the tension of the moment, Touch the Sky mustered a nervy little grin. "Cheyenne," he said fondly, "you were not born in the woods to be scared by an owl. Stay close to me, but cast plenty of glances back toward this entrance to see if we've been followed in. We are going to move quickly. The longer we are down there, the better our chances of staying down there forever. We need to make a mind picture, then talk to Tom Riley again."

"Don't worry," Little Horse said. "I have no plans to whittle a lance while I'm down there."

Each brave made one last check of his weapons and then started into the tunnel entrance.

It was tall enough that they could walk upright, and perhaps as wide across as a wagon lane. As the tunnel descended from the barn, it sloped gradually until at perhaps fifteen or twenty feet it leveled out again.

This exploration would have been impossible without the long-burning torch. It was as dark as new tar down below. Yellow-orange splashes of light revealed the rammed-earth walls and regularly spaced supports of thick logs.

"This explains all the signs of woodcutting we've seen around here lately," Touch the Sky said grimly.

So far, however, they were disappointed in their search for any incriminating evidence. There was no sign of any excavating tools. As far as the white man's law was concerned, there was no more connection between this tunnel and the new route of Salt Lick Creek than there was between the moon and the color of rainbows.

Fear held both braves by the throat. Constantly, Little Horse searched the receding dimness behind them as they moved forward. They could hear the steady flow of the water, very near by. That reminded them both of that horrible death omen.

Touch the Sky slowly rounded a bend in the tunnel. Suddenly, something scurried across his foot and he shouted out. A moment later, feeling like a woman-hearted fool, he watched a huge black rat race out of the glow of the torch.

Abruptly, the tunnel, which Riley had called a gallery, simply ended. Close examination of the walls did indeed reveal the "curtains" Tom had also mentioned, smaller tunnels that had been run off of this one and then filled back in. Presumably, to insert explosives out into the middle of the creek bed.

But these did not constitute proof either.

"Brother," he said to Little Horse, disappointment seeping into his tone, "we have not found the evidence that might have brought the law into this matter. We will describe what we found to Tom Riley, but I don't see how it can help much."

Little Horse, by now so nervous that sweat glistened on his forehead, said, "Shaman, let us cry about our bad luck later. If there is nothing down here, then why are we? I will not breathe easy until this place is smoke behind us."

"As you say. But we will not rush out of here like prairie dogs being smoked from their hole. We might have missed something we will spot on the way back."

"Do it, Meadows!" Dakota Jones urged in a harsh whisper. "Christ sakes, man, *do* it. Blow 'em damn Innuns to hell!"

Jones still hunched down in the straw behind his Gatling gun. Meadows had crept to the very edge of the loft, the galvanic detonator clutched in his right hand.

"Can't" he answered tersely. "Cap'n said to wait at least three minutes. We got one more minute, then I smoke their red asses."

"Now," Jones urged. "Do it now!"

Stubbornly, Meadows shook his head. "One more minute, chappie. There's two thousand dollars in bright yaller boys hanging on this. We got to do it right. This ain't just some blanket ass that's jumped from the rez. Both of them featherheads are mean as a badger in a barrel. If we bollix this up, our hair'll be hanging off their sashes."

They had just begun their return to the barn when Touch the Sky's sharp eyes noticed it in the flickering light: a tiny gleam of wire, protruding from the dirt wall.

Detonating wire. He might not know how to use it, but he could certainly recognize it.

Working quickly and carefully, he followed it with one finger, pulling it gently out of the dirt behind which it was packed.

"Brother," Little Horse urged, "quickly!"

Touch the Sky ignored his friend, for his exploring fingers had just made contact with something hard and cool. He knocked loose some dirt. Bright yellow letters were exposed:

NGER: HIGH EXPLO

His time in the white man's school saved him, for he knew instantly what those partial words said: DANGER: HIGH EXPLOSIVES!

Left over from the plan to divert the river?

No, whispered an urgent voice at the back of his mind. *Not left over. Planted here to kill you and Little Horse!*

"Out, brother!" he abruptly exclaimed, giving his stout little companion a mighty shove toward the entrance. "Fly like the Wendigo is after you!"

*   *   *

"Now, goddamnit!" Jones urged Meadows. "Katy Christ, Jim, *now!* It's been a minute!"

Meadows grinned and nodded. "Fire in the hole, partner," he said softly, removing the cotter key that kept the detonator points from making contact.

He had placed his thumb on the plunger key and was about to depress it when, all of a sudden, the two Cheyennes burst out of the tunnel, chests heaving.

"Hell and corruption," cursed Meadows, leaping back from the edge of the loft.

Still cursing silently, he watched the braves quickly untie their stolen horses' hobbles and lead them out of the barn. A moment later both soldiers heard the sound of two thousand dollars getting away at a full gallop.

"Aw, damn," Dakota Jones muttered. "Hiram Steele ain't going to like this. He ain't goin' to like it one little bit."

"Sounds like keg mines," Tom Riley said when Touch the Sky had explained their little adventure in the tunnel. "And there's no way they were left there by accident. Carlson has to play hell to get his hands on demolitions. He's not about to leave them behind. They were planted there to kill you, I'd stake my commission on it."

"So how's come they're still alive?" Corey demanded from across the table.

Touch the Sky answered this one. "Because we went in the daylight," he suggested. "And our enemy is looking for us by night."

"Could be," Tom agreed. "The main thing is, you made it out."

"With no proof," Touch the Sky said bitterly.

"With no proof," Tom agreed. "But assuming you've got the stones to go back down there, your problems may be over."

Touch the Sky watched his friend closely. "Well, do I have to beg for more?"

Tom's mouth twisted into a grin. "You don't see it? A keg mine—even better, a few of them—delivers one hell of a wallop. Planted where they are, they won't disturb the new grade of the riverbed. But if you and Little Horse were to dig out one of those old curtains, you could stuff the mines in one of them—much closer to the water. You'd need some kind of detonating device, but we could rig that. With luck, you could blow Salt Lick Creek right back into its former route."

Just thinking about going back down in that death hole made Touch the Sky's skin go clammy. But Tom was right. This was a chance—perhaps the only chance—to beat Carlson and Steele at their own game.

"True," Riley added, "Steele and Carlson will get off unpunished. But not really. By now, can you imagine how much work and money they've stuck into this project?"

"Yeah," Corey said. "But, hey? What keeps those two from doing it all over again?"

Tom shook his head. "Can't happen. Near-hood knows now about the creek changing its bed. Even a man like him, with his head stuck up his sitter half the time, would snap wise if the creek jumped back to its old bed and then—wham—jumped out of it *again*. Hell, carrot-top, even you ain't that consarn stupid."

By now Touch the Sky had debated all he needed to.

"Tom's right," he said. "It's the only hope. And the longer we wait, the less our chance of blowing that tunnel before they fill it back in."

"I can tell you how to detonate those mines," Tom said. "And I can probably manage to get you some blasting fuse. A remote detonator would be best, but I can't lay hands on one. It's risky, Touch the Sky, I won't kid you."

Touch the Sky nodded but said nothing. He was well aware of the risk—and well aware that he still had to translate all of this for Little Horse. That stout warrior had been so happy to get out of that tunnel that he had scattered his white man's tobacco—the tobacco he wrangled from Touch the Sky—to the winds as a thank-you to the holy ones. How would he take it when he learned they were going back down that "worm hole"?

But what was the alternative? To let Hiram Steele and Seth Carlson not only dry up their most important river, but steal their best Cheyenne hunting ranges as well?

"Start talking, soldier blue," Touch the Sky told Riley.

Dakota Jones had been wrong. Hiram Steele was surprisingly philosophical about the bad news from the barn.

"Never mind, Seth boy," Steele told Carlson

151

as they sat in the soldier's bell tent, sipping good rye whiskey. "Just never mind. It's like you said yesterday. We haven't killed Hanchon this time either. But here's the difference. That red son-ofabitch has failed to stop us, for once! *Let* the bastard live! Actually, that's even better. Now he'll have to bear witness while his 'proud and noble people' starve and go naked!"

Carlson's glum face slowly settled in a smile. "By God, Hiram, you're right. We've been so obsessed with killing Hanchon we haven't considered any alternatives. Once their buffalo ranges are plowed under with barley and oats and corn, the Cheyenne will be reduced to begging and growing gardens. Just like the Poncas, the tribe they're always scorning as dirt-scatterers."

Hiram nodded. "Then it's settled. Have a work crew fill that tunnel in as soon as possible. Pard, we got an irrigation project to get started on."

Carlson grinned. "You know, Hiram? In a way, we succeeded after all. For a man as proud as Matthew Hanchon, watching his people go under *will* kill him."

Chapter Fifteen

"I always wanted a long life," Sharp Nosed Woman said sadly. "Even with all the grief this tribe has faced, I wanted to live a long time and see the little ones dance the Animal Dance as I did in my youth. But *this* makes me wish I had died a-borning, rather than live to see it."

Honey Eater's aunt, not one to cry at trifles, now turned suddenly from the rest to hide the crystal teardrops spilling over her lashes.

"Our Powder River!" she cried. "Well over forty winters now have I returned here with the rest of my people. I have felt the lush new grass under my bare feet, smelled the clean, sweet smell of prairie and river. Down there, Honey Eater, around that little cottonwood island at the turn, that is where your bride lodge was built! Oh, how the young girls sang your love when you and Touch the Sky exchanged the squaw-taking vows."

Honey Eater, busy helping her aunt fashion a travois from sapling poles and buffalo-hair ropes, was near tears herself.

Watching them vigilantly from opposite flanks were Tangle Hair and Two Twists. Now Honey Eater held Tangle Hair's eyes as she replied.

"*You* remember my bride lodge, Aunt? Good. Then how must it reign in my mind? Never will I forget the words of this one here"—she pointed at the shy Tangle Hair—"as we were about to enter. He told Touch the Sky, 'We made the entrance tall, brother, because we knew you would be passing through it. And none taller than the woman on your arm.'"

Tangle Hair flushed and looked across the dwindling river, trying to hold his face passive as warriors must. He loved Honey Eater like the sister he'd never had, but it would not do to show womanly feelings.

"He said that?" Sharp Nosed Woman exclaimed, new tears springing to her eyes. "Our Tangle Hair is a poet, and a fine one."

Two Twists secretly agreed that Tangle Hair, a stout warrior indeed, was also a man whose well of inner feeling was deep—and he admired him greatly for this. Nonetheless, he could not resist teasing him a bit.

"Oh, Tangle Hair," he called out, "yesterday I saw a hawk kill a mouse. Please sing the mouse's eulogy in phrases that will make my eyes leak!"

"You beast," Sharp Nosed Woman said, though with no real rancor, for she considered Two Twists one of the tribe's best young men—if a bit mouthy.

All this levity, however, could not erase the horrible reality now pressing on Honey Eater: Because of the disappearing river, they were packing up their camp and moving to a new summer camp.

River! That was like calling a burial mound a mountain. Just look at it. The only thing left now was a narrow, sluggish channel surrounded by scabrous, drying mud.

She, too, had known no summer camp but this one. Despite all they had suffered here—pestilence, raids, near-starvation—this was her home. And it was the tribe's ancestral home. The Powder River for summer camps, the Tongue River for winter camps. Since the days when the Shaiyena were driven from the woodlands now called Minnesota, that had been the pattern.

But tragic as it was to be forced to move, that was not the end of her troubles. For understandable reasons, notably Touch the Sky's long, unexplained absence from camp, the collective anger of the tribe had focused on her.

Little Bear was playing nearby, weaving a necklace of flower stems. She watched her son for a few moments, enjoying his blessed innocence. Oh, sacred Maiyun, what trouble was destined for that little mite once he wore a warrior's shield! But for now, so far anyway, his

155

was a world in which he was loved and cared for and secure.

Now what was in store for him? Especially with the tribe's anger focused on his mother and father?

"You three," she suddenly said to her aunt and their two guardians. "You do well at pretending I am not the outcast of this tribe. But for your own safety, perhaps you had better spend less time around me."

Honey Eater was not being overly dramatic. She had indeed become an outcast. No one in her clan would touch a utensil she had touched. Though course no Cheyenne, even a murderer, was ever starved by the tribe, her meat rations were always piled separately during the hunt distribution.

"And perhaps *you* had best control your tongue before I box your ears," her aunt said sharply. "We three know where your man is. He is out risking his scalp to solve the mystery of this disappearing river. As for those two"—she nodded toward Tangle Hair and Two Twists— "they have no ears for such talk."

"Indeed, sister," Two Twists said, "you are perhaps a new outcast. But Tangle Hair here and I have been taboo since we crossed our lances with that of Touch the Sky. Where would we go if we didn't guard you? They don't want us."

"Never mind," Two Twists added. "Arrow Keeper said once that if one man knows better than the Council of Forty, that man is a majority of one. Touch the Sky, too, is a majority of one. And count upon it, the majority *will* rule."

"Hii-ya!" Little Bear suddenly shrilled, imitating the war cry. Hearing it, Two Twists and Tangle Hair both grinned proudly.

Honey Eater and Sharp Nosed Woman, however, exchanged long, sad glances. Glances women understood and men never noticed.

"Best face it like men," Touch the Sky told Corey, after saying the same thing to Little Horse in Cheyenne. "There's a good chance that whoever sets up the blast will get killed before it's ready. That means, since Corey will be on sentry duty outside the barn, Little Horse will have to know the procedure too."

The three friends had decided on a dawn raid, a straight ride from the rim of Blackford's Valley to the barn and the confluence. By choosing dawn, they had covered their ride through the valley in darkness, yet arrived with enough light to scout the barn.

Corey had insisted on coming along this time. Though Touch the Sky was deeply reluctant to risk his friend, he admitted he desperately needed the help. Corey, a fair to middling hand with his sixteen-shot Henry, was to dig a rifle pit in good cover within range of the barn.

Now all three hunkered behind some blackberry brambles while Touch the Sky laid a coil of fuse and a cylindrical metal object in the grass.

"I saw more than one mine," Touch the Sky said. "I'm not sure how many. But all of them should be shoved into the curtain just to be sure we get the job done. Only one mine needs to be wired—the others will go off if they're close enough."

"These little worm holes you call curtains," Little Horse said. "They are full of dirt."

"Loose dirt," Touch the Sky said. He nodded to a spade protruding from the boot of Corey's saddle. "Tom says it will come out fast and easy. This hard thing is a blasting cap. You crimp the fuse to it like this. Then the blasting cap is inserted into a hole—Tom called it a cap well—on top of the mines. Do you have the sulfur matches Corey gave us?"

Little Horse nodded, feeling in his parfleche to make sure.

"Ready?" he said in Cheyenne to Little Horse. His friend nodded.

"Ready?" he said to Corey.

"Hell, no," Corey said. "You boys're the big warriors. Me, I'm just a humble carpenter. But yeah, let's go. Hiram Steele once sent that bastard Abbot Fontaine to play thump-thump on me. You remember?"

Touch the Sky nodded. "How could I forget? Your face was bruised so purple it looked like a bunch of grapes."

Corey grinned. "Yeah, but it don't matter. Cuz ol' Little Horse done for Abbot's butt. Done for him good."

"Tether our horses here," Touch the Sky decided. "We can get to the barn on foot in maybe ten minutes. That way we can listen better as we approach."

His decision turned out to be crucial. The

stealthy trio were about to break out of the last line of trees when they heard the snuffling of horses and the chinking of bit rings.

Touch the Sky threw up a quick hand, halting his companions. He moved forward a few paces, knelt, and cleared some brush with one hand.

A paleface work crew was assembling just outside the barn—a work crew equipped with shovels and wheelbarrows! A crew obviously intending to fill in that tunnel.

The cold bile of fear erupted up Touch the Sky's throat. He motioned for his friends to come forward and join him. He wanted them to see it too. The palefaces were about to seal off the Cheyennes' only chance to revive their river and save their homeland.

The sturdy Little Horse, a stranger to panic, could not keep his eyes from bulging like wet, white marbles.

"Brother," he whispered. "There are three of us and at least fifteen of them. They all have carbines. I am willing to risk it. But do we ask Firetop to face these odds? This is not his homeland stand, but ours."

"As you say," Touch the Sky agreed. "Therefore we even the odds. Look, coming out the door of the barn."

Little Horse did look. A soldier lugging a huge gun with legs on it was emerging into the new dawn light. He set the gun down outside the door and wiped the straw off his uniform.

"A Gatling," Touch the Sky whispered. "I know the gun. Tom showed me how to fire it up in the Sans Arcs. Is your shotgun loaded—all four barrels?"

"Is a Comanche as ugly as a buzzard?"

"Good. I have a plan. A plan more crazy than brave. Corey stays here, potshotting as many as he can. You slip over to their right and rain pellets on them with the scattergun. As soon as all four loads are spent, switch to your bow. But first target of all—kill that hair-face who carried the gun out and is still standing beside it. I am taking over that gun, and I mean to sweep these locusts back."

It was a crazy plan indeed, Little Horse saw, likely to kill both of them, and thus, already his blood was up for the challenge.

Touch the Sky translated for Corey. "You will be critical once Little Horse and I go inside the barn," Touch the Sky assured him. "I'm going to drive them back for a while with the Gatling. But they'll get their courage back after we go inside. It's up to you to discourage them. But stay covered. I'm used to looking at your ugly face."

"Well, yours still scares hell out of me every time I see it," Corey assured him, masking his fear. "Now quit the damned speechifying, and let's make some crooked soldiers earn their pay for a change."

Corey moved slightly to one side and quickly dug out a wallow, using one half of his bull's-eye canteen. Touch the Sky waited until he had shells ready to hand and had dug his sighting elbow in good.

"Now, brother," he whispered to Little Horse.

"Move quick but quiet. See that wide oak over there? Get behind it, then open fire. At the first shotgun blast, I take off for the Gatling."

"Brother?" Little Horse said, hesitating.

"What, buck? Time is wasting."

Little Horse grinned. "Good chance you'll be killed. If so, may I have the licorice drops you have been hoarding in your legging sash?"

"Why not?" Touch the Sky said, grinning back. "After all, I stole them from your parfleche."

He slapped his friend hard on the rump, and Little Horse took off at a crouch. He leapfrogged from tree to bush, easily evading the whites in the grainy half-light. They were busy breaking out their tools and getting torches ready.

Touch the Sky waited until Little Horse was in position. Then he glanced back over his shoulder to make eye contact with Corey.

The redhead nodded.

Touch the Sky touched his medicine pouch and said a brief battle prayer. Then, every muscle tensed to spring, he gave the nod to Little Horse.

Chapter Sixteen

Tim Ulrick was up before dawn, and heard the noise when a trio of horses headed toward the confluence. He imitated the sound of a loon, and soon Baylis Morningstar joined him at Ulrick's new camp closer to the river.

"I heard it," Morningstar informed him even before Ulrick could ask. "That was the sound of money, Tim."

"One thousand apiece," Ulrick suggested, "if we was to team up on him. I see now it'll take two with *that* one."

Morningstar's hip pouch bulged with steel balls for his powerful sling. He considered Ulrick's suggestion, and decided the man was right. Baylis had never had more than thirty dollars at once in his whole damn life. One thousand, two thousand . . . down in Old Mexico a man could buy a town for one thousand, and all the women in it, too.

"It's a deal, pard," the half-breed agreed. "Now catch up your horse. If we mean to kill those two Cheyennes, we best get it done fast. There's others in line."

All three renegades spotted it just as dawn painted the eastern horizon in copper flames. It was clearly visible in the sky over a distant mountain peak, almost aflame as the new sun backlit it.

For a long time Wolf Who Hunts Smiling, Sis-ki-dee, and Big Tree stared at it in absolute silence. All three were painted for battle, their war kits readied.

Below the spot they occupied on a limestone ridge, Morningstar and Ulrick raced by, heading toward the confluence. Sis-ki-dee looked at them. Then, again, he stared at the object floating in the sky over that distant mountain.

"Big Tree," Sis-ki-dee remarked casually. "I have been considering a thing. I think it is time to visit our men on Wendigo Mountain before they drink our cache of good liquor. I left Scalp Cane in charge, but you know how he can be his own man."

Slowly Big Tree nodded. "As you say. I have new horses to break, too. How about you, buck?" Big Tree added, quartering his horse around to look at Wolf Who Hunts Smiling.

At first, looking at that cloud formation with the others, Wolf Who Hunts Smiling had felt a bitter anger and disappointment. But there were some men whom bees refused to sting, and this Wolf was one of them. He shook off his disappointment, for determination had ousted it.

"What about me?" he responded. "I am with my renegade brothers! White men may charge in to a certain death, but we three are of one mind: Fight only when we can win! *That*"—he pointed toward the horizon—"tells us our part in the fight is over for now, if we are wise. But mark me. Though this is not the time, a time is indeed coming—a time when we three will dance in his guts and smear our bodies with his blood!"

All three Indians crossed their lances as one. And as one, they took a final awed glance at that remarkable cloud over the mountain: a cloud shaped precisely like an arrowhead, the mark of the warrior, the mark visible in Touch the Sky's hair when it was wet and plastered back.

Wolf Who Hunts Smiling thought of something. "Carlson is at the fort, but do we warn Steele? He is with the soldier work crew."

"Would he warn you?" Big Tree shot back.

All three shared a grin, then headed out of Blackford's Valley.

Little Horse had taken up his position behind the oak and was just starting to slip his finger inside the trigger guard. Abruptly, the rapid drumbeat of approaching hooves from behind warned him.

He spun around just as Ulrick and Mornings-tar rounded a turn. Little Horse cursed at having to waste one of four valuable shots, but there was no alternative. Aiming carefully between the two riders, turning the choke to spray wide, he squeezed off a load of buckshot and blew both men from their saddles.

That first blast was still reverberating over the river when Touch the Sky burst toward the soldier lugging the Gatling. A trooper aimed his carbine at Touch the Sky and, behind the Cheyenne, Corey's Henry barked. There was a loud thwap as the slug punched into the soldier's breastbone, evoking a spray of blood and a scream of agony as he collapsed.

Little Horse, meantime, braved almost certain death as he dashed forward. He had to make sure he was close enough to kill the soldier with the Gatling, yet avoid damaging the gun.

Touch the Sky raced in from the south, Little Horse from the north, and their only allies were surprise and Corey Robinson's busy Henry. Little Horse's scattergun exploded again, Dakota Jones slammed back into the wall of the barn, and within moments Touch the Sky was frantically re-attaching the hopper full of shells, which had fallen off when the trooper dropped the gun.

Little Horse used his remaining two shells to good advantage, forcing the frightened soldiers to take cover while Touch the Sky readied the Gatling.

But when Little Horse's hammer clicked uselessly, Hiram Steele was up and charging with a roar like a bull.

"Now, boys!" he screamed. "Now, kill them! The shotgun is spent! Now! Now, do it, goddamnit, *do* it!"

Hiram was so agitated that he was pulling his own shots wildly, the slugs taking chunks out of the barn behind Touch the Sky. But some of the soldiers, already in a prone position, were starting to draw a better bead on him.

"No hurry, brother," Little Horse said with feigned boredom even as the bullets flew past his ears like angry hornets. "These are only white men."

Now Hiram was dangerously close, and Little Horse took the risk of pulling his sash knife and rising to his knees, ready to throw.

"Down, fool!" Touch the Sky ordered, knocking his friend aside with one hand. A moment later the Gatling gun was bucking on its bipod, barrels clicking with precision as Touch the Sky revolved the crank.

A line of snake holes was stitched across Steele's thighs and he cried out in agony, collapsing in the grass. Behind him, several soldiers dropped like sacks of grain before the rest bolted and ran for the woods behind them.

"Hurry, you two!" Corey screamed from his rifle pit. "Hurry! Get in there and blow that goddamn tunnel! The soldiers will be back when they regroup. I'll hold the line as long as I can. But you two better damn hurry!"

Little Horse scrambled to his feet as Touch the Sky pulled the coil of fuse and the blasting cap from his parfleche. They exchanged one final look, and Touch the Sky knew his friend was thinking of the same thing he was: an omen of bad death—bad death by water.

Touch the Sky found a total of three keg mines buried in the wall of the main gallery. If there were more, he didn't worry about them. Tom said three would do it.

While Touch the Sky dug the mines out, Little Horse frantically went to work with the spade, clearing out one of the curtains or smaller side tunnels. These ran close to the water, but stopped a few feet short. Close enough, both Indians hoped, that one good blast would undo the paleface treachery.

Each keg mine was awkward to carry and perhaps as heavy as a small man. Touch the Sky wrestled them down, then helped Little Horse in the frantic effort to clear a side tunnel.

Faintly, they heard shots above them.

"Soldiers coming back," Touch the Sky said grimly. "Hold on, Corey, hold on!"

"Firetop will hold or die in the attempt," Little Horse said, even as the two friends wrestled the first mine into the tunnel.

It would have been a hard job for big men who were well rested. It was agony for these sleep-starved, exhausted warriors. Especially confined in such a small place with enemies somewhere behind them, liable to come down at any moment.

"Take this," Touch the Sky said, gasping for breath. He handed the coil of fuse to Little Horse. "Wind it out toward the gallery. I am going to rig the cap."

Little Horse was more than happy to head

back. Sweat pouring from him, every limb trembling from the cramp and effort, he began squirming back.

Touch the Sky, willing his fingers steady, crimped one end of the fuse to the blasting cap. It contained enough black powder to explode the mines, once inserted into the vertical wells on top.

When all was ready, Touch the Sky joined his friend in flight from the curtain. Little Horse had already snapped off the fuse right where it emerged into the gallery. That should give them plenty of time to get back above ground before the explosion.

Touch the Sky removed a sulfur match and scratched it on the rough sole of his elkskin moccasin. The fuse sparked to life. But shots continued to sound outside, and they knew this battle was far from over.

A moment later, however, and they heard a very welcome sound: Corey's shout of triumph as the Gatling barked into action again. He had made a dash for the gun and now commanded the entire front of the barn! Within moments the sound of opposing guns was silenced.

Both braves whooped in triumph. Just before they broke for the sloping tunnel that led above ground, Touch the Sky made one final check of the fuse.

Even as he glanced down the narrow tunnel, a big clot of loose dirt plopped down onto the fuse, snuffing it out about fifteen feet from the keg mines.

His heart leaped into his throat. Little Horse

saw it, too. He was about to leap into the tunnel when Touch the Sky reluctantly applied one of his white man's skills. He threw a hard upper-cut and knocked his friend partially unconscious.

Corey couldn't hold out forever. Touch the Sky scrambled madly into the tunnel. He found the fuse, pulled it out of the dirt, and somehow got it lit again. Once he was sure it was burning, he began the mad scramble to safety. But he would never make it, never—

"Little Horse!" he screamed, for he could see his friend waiting for him now, guarding the entrance with knife in hand. "Get out! Get out! Now!"

His friend ignored him. Touch the Sky was squirming to get out of the last few feet of the tunnel when strong hands gripped him, tugging. Little Horse had almost pulled him free when the world suddenly came apart.

Never, as each brave was picked up and heaved like so much river-tossed wreckage, had they heard anything so loud. First came a powerful concussion like a mule kick to the skull. Then a huge wall of dirt, followed by a welling juggernaut of water.

It washed over them, tumbling them, heaving, bouncing, and there was no way to get out from under it. The dirt and the water formed instant mud, tons of it, and they were wildly scrambling to get clear of it.

Sticky clay filled their ears and noses and throats, blinded them, held their limbs like tight ropes. Still they struggled, fought, squirmed to-

ward the safety above ground. Fighting thus for
their own lives, they could not see how the main
brunt of the powerful explosion was churning
a huge spray of rocks and water out over the
confluence, altering it.

Touch the Sky, choking so bad he couldn't
even sing his death song, suddenly felt something slap his face. He grasped for it and felt a
rope! He clung desperately with one hand, the
other searching the river of mud for Little
Horse. He found a wrist and clung to it.

Corey, his face white as moonstone, was just
outside the barn with one of the saddled soldier
mounts. Expertly, he dallied the rope around
the saddlehorn and whacked the horse on the
rump hard. It surged forward, and Corey
watched two Indians—so covered with mud
you couldn't tell them apart if you were their
mother—come oozing out of the flowing muck.

"Still not full, but it is rising," Honey Eater
said happily almost one full moon after the battle in Blackford's Valley. "And rising well. Soon,
we will have our river back. The Council of
Forty has ceased all talk of moving to a new
camp."

Touch the Sky nodded. He sat with his
woman on the rolling bank of the Powder. Little
Bear was actually swimming now, in short
bursts, showing off for his proud parents.

The tall warrior had learned by now to take
happiness like he took food and sleep, in broken
doses, snatched when he could. He felt the joy
of this moment all the more keenly because of

the trouble he knew was coming—was always coming, for the red man.

Hiram Steele, he'd heard, was bitter and ruined, nothing but a common drunk picking barroom fights in Register Cliffs. But Steele was like the red-speckled cough or the yellow vomit that wiped out tribes: a parasite that would always return when least expected, bent on the destruction of the red man.

Yes, trouble clouds were blowing close. But for now Touch the Sky threw back his head and tasted the great love for his woman and child, for this time with them and the beauty of Mother Earth.

Desert
Manhunt

GET YOUR 4
FREE* BOOKS NOW—
A VALUE BETWEEN
$16 AND $20

Mail the Free* Book Certificate Today!

FREE* BOOKS
CERTIFICATE!

YES! I want to subscribe to the Leisure Western
Book Club. Please send me my 4 FREE* BOOKS. Then,
each month, I'll receive the four newest Leisure Western
Selections to preview FREE* for 10 days. If I decide to
keep them, I will pay the Special Member's Only dis-
counted price of just $3.36 each, a total of $13.44 ($14.50
US in Canada). This saves me between $3 and $6 off the
bookstore price. There are no shipping, handling or other
charges.* There is no minimum number of books I must
buy and I may cancel the program at any time. In any
case, the 4 FREE* BOOKS are mine to keep—at a value
of between $17 and $20!

*In Canada, add $5.00 Canadian shipping and handling
per order for first shipment. For all subsequent shipments
to Canada the cost of membership in the Book Club is
$14.50 US, which includes $7.50 shipping and handling
per month. All payments must be made in US currency.

Name _____

Address _____

City_____ State_____ Country_____

Zip_____ Telephone_____

Tear here and mail your FREE* book card today!

Get Four Books Totally
F R E E* —
A Value between
$16 and $20

PLEASE RUSH
MY FOUR FREE*
BOOKS TO ME
RIGHT AWAY!

LeisureWestern Book Club
P.O. Box 6613
Edison, NJ 08818-6613

AFFIX
STAMP
HERE

Prologue

Although Matthew Hanchon bore the name given to him by his adopted white parents, he was the son of full-blooded Northern Cheyennes. The lone survivor of a bluecoat massacre in 1840, the infant was raised by John and Sarah Hanchon in the Wyoming Territory settlement of Bighorn Falls.

His parents loved him as their own, and at first the youth was happy enough in his limited world. The occasional stares and threats from others meant little—until his sixteenth year and a forbidden love with Kristen, daughter of the wealthy rancher Hiram Steele.

Steele's campaign to run Matthew off like a distempered wolf was assisted by Seth Carlson, the jealous, Indian-hating cavalry officer who was in love with Kristen. Carlson delivered a fateful ultimatum: Either Matthew cleared out of Bighorn

Falls for good, or Carlson would ruin his parents' contract to supply nearby Fort Bates—and thus ruin their mercantile business.

His heart sad but determined, Matthew set out for the upcountry of the Powder River, Cheyenne territory. Captured by braves from Chief Yellow Bear's tribe, he was declared an Indian spy for the hair-face soldiers and was brutally tortured over fire. But only a heartbeat before he was to be scalped and gutted, old Arrow Keeper interceded.

The tribe shaman and protector of the sacred Medicine Arrows, Arrow Keeper had recently experienced an epic vision. This vision foretold that the long-lost son of a great Cheyenne chief would return to his people—and that he would lead them in one last, great victory against their enemies. This youth would be known by the distinctive mark of the warrior, the same birthmark Arrow Keeper spotted buried past this youth's hairline: a mulberry-colored arrowhead.

Arrow Keeper used his influence to spare the youth's life. He also ordered that he be allowed to join the tribe, training with the junior warriors. This infuriated two braves especially: the fierce war leader, Black Elk, and his cunning younger cousin, Wolf Who Hunts Smiling.

Black Elk was jealous of the glances cast at the tall young stranger by Honey Eater, daughter of Chief Yellow Bear. And Wolf Who Hunts Smiling, proudly ambitious despite his youth, hated all whites without exception. This stranger was, to him, only a make-believe Cheyenne who wore white man's shoes, spoke the paleface tongue, and showed his emotions in his face like the woman-hearted white men.

Arrow Keeper buried the stranger's white name forever and gave him a new Cheyenne name: Touch the Sky. But he remained a white man's dog in the eyes of many in the tribe. At first humiliated at every turn, eventually the determined youth mastered the warrior arts. Slowly, as his coup stick filled with enemy scalps, he won the respect of more and more in the tribe.

But with each victory, deceiving appearances triumphed over reality, and the acceptance he so desperately craved eluded him. Worse, his hard-won victories left him with two especially fierce enemies outside the tribe: a Blackfoot called Siski-dee and a Comanche named Big Tree.

As for Black Elk, at first he was hard but fair. When Touch the Sky rode off to save his white parents from outlaws, Honey Eater was convinced that he had deserted her and the tribe forever. She was forced to accept Black Elk's bride-price after her father crossed to the Land of Ghosts. But Touch the Sky returned.

Then, as it became clear to all that Honey Eater loved only Touch the Sky, Black Elk's jealousy drove him to join his younger cousin in plotting against Touch the Sky's life. Finally, Wolf Who Hunts Smiling's treachery forced a crisis: Aiming at Touch the Sky in heavy fog, he instead killed Black Elk. Now Touch the Sky stood accused of the murder in the eyes of many.

Though it divided the tribe irrevocably, he and Honey Eater performed the squaw-taking ceremony. He had firm allies in his blood brother Little Horse, the youth Two Twists, and Tangle Hair. Following Arrow Keeper's mysterious disappearance, Touch the Sky became the tribe shaman.

But a pretend shaman named Medicine Flute, backed by Touch the Sky's enemies, challenged his authority. And despite his fervent need to stop being the eternal outsider, Touch the Sky was still trapped between two worlds, welcome in neither.

Chapter One

"Brother," Little Horse said, "there may be hope for this tribe yet."

These unexpected words made the tall, broad-shouldered warrior called Touch the Sky pull up short. The two Cheyenne braves were walking across the central camp clearing toward the common corral.

"Buck," Touch the Sky said, "some in this tribe call me White Man Runs Him, but others call me Shaman. Yet you are the one speaking riddles. Old Arrow Keeper taught me there is *always* hope in the breast of a warrior. I never questioned that you are indeed a warrior, and none better between where we stand now and the Marias River. So give tongue to this hope of yours. I would gladly hear of it."

Little Horse nodded. All around them, the lush

11

new grass of the snow-melt moons was springing up. The winter-starved ponies, gaunt and weak from gnawing on cottonwood bark all winter, were putting meat on their bones. Bright-colored wildflowers dotted the meadows, and the ice-locked valleys were once again rich with wild game.

"I do not suggest," Little Horse said, "that we are not still a tribe dangerously divided against itself. We are. The Bullwhip soldiers swear allegiance to Wolf Who Hunts Smiling and his pretend shaman, the cowardly Medicine Flute. The Bowstring soldiers are loyal to Chief River of Winds and you. We are still a powder keg, and it could go off anytime."

Touch the Sky's lips tilted into a grim smile. He wore his hair in long, loose locks except where it was cut short over his eyes to clear his vision. Little Horse, in contrast, wore his hair in a single braid tied with red strings.

"As you say, we are a powder keg," Touch the Sky agreed. "So why sing of hope?"

They had resumed walking. All around them the women and children scurried, for the finishing touches were being added to the Northern Cheyenne summer camp at the confluence of the Powder and Little Powder rivers. Tipis had been erected in clan circles, with their entrances all facing east toward the birthplace of Sister Sun. But the meat racks still had to be built in preparation for the spring hunt.

"Only notice something, brother," Little Horse said. "True, you can look down toward the river and see all our enemies congregated around Medicine Flute's tipi. But have you looked closely at them?"

Touch the Sky did just that. Then he said, "Crack the nut and expose the meat. I still see no clear signs of hope."

Indeed, even as he spoke, one of those around Medicine Flute's tipi caught his eye: a small but muscle-hardened warrior with swift, furtive eyes— eyes that remained constantly in motion, on guard for the ever-expected attack. But they slowed down now long enough to beam pure hatred at Touch the Sky.

Wolf Who Hunts Smiling. But his name fell short of his treachery, for Touch the Sky knew from bitter experience there was no evil deed beyond this Wolf's doing.

"You do not see it?" said an incredulous Little Horse. "You, who can find sign on a hardpan canyon floor? Brother, there is something very different. Look at them. They are gambling, whittling arrow points, drinking corn beer. See Hawk Trainer over there? He is playing with his bird. What are they usually up to when they congregate after the cold moons?"

Slowly his friend's point sank home. Touch the Sky nodded, for he knew quite well what his enemies were usually up to.

"By custom," he answered, "they should be huddled in council. Scheming. Plotting the overthrow of this camp."

Little Horse nodded. "As you say. Notice how few of them are bothering to watch our movements. Usually they stay on you, me, Tangle Hair, and Two Twists like vultures on carrion. And earlier today, when Two Twists rode out on herd guard—none of the Whips harassed him as they usually do."

Touch the Sky considered all this. By now the two braves had reached the buffalo-hair rope corral. It held only the favorite mounts of the braves, for each man had as many as ten ponies on his string, and the rest were allowed to range free under a herd guard.

"And consider Wendigo Mountain," Little Horse continued. "You heard the word-bringer from Red Shale. Since your bluecoat friend Tom Riley led his pony soldiers against the renegades camped on Wendigo Mountain, Big Tree's Comanches and Sis-ki-dee's Blackfoot marauders have been routed from their bastion. No one has seen them for several moons."

"Yes," Touch the Sky said quietly. "No one has seen them."

Something in his tone gave Little Horse pause. But the short, stoutly muscled warrior went on. "And with the renegades routed, Wolf Who Hunts Smiling is afraid to strike. He needs his allies to ensure the fight here in camp. All these reasons, shaman, seem to me fodder for hope."

Touch the Sky always listened closely when Little Horse spoke, for his friend was a man of few words. It was Little Horse's way to pay attention only to things that mattered.

"You could be right, stout fighter," the tall brave conceded. He gave a sharp whistle, and a powerfully muscled coyote dun broke from the rest of the ponies, trotting over to greet him by nuzzling his shoulder.

Desert Manhunt

Little Horse recognized the doubt in his friend's voice. "I could be, you are saying, but you do not think so?"

"No, brother, I do not. First of all, as to *those* jays"—Touch the Sky nodded across toward the Bullwhips—"they are distracted now, in an especially good mood, because our trade goods are due to arrive soon."

Little Horse nodded, for he had forgotten this point. Every year the Far West Mining Company sent a huge shipment of trade goods by pack train to the Northern Cheyenne camp. This was the annual payment, arranged by Touch the Sky, for Cheyenne permission to haul the miners' gold ore across Cheyenne ranges. The arrival of the goods was always a festive occasion rivaling the Spring Dance.

"As for our enemies on Wendigo Mountain," Touch the Sky went on, "I was almost happier when we knew where they were. When it comes to that bunch, you are in trouble when you see them and in greater trouble when you don't."

All of this sobered Little Horse. His friend was right, and he knew it. Touch the Sky quickly inspected his dun's hooves while Little Horse leaped onto his bay and ran him around the corral a few laps to work out the kinks.

Touch the Sky tweaked the dun's ears fondly while glancing back toward camp. A small group of children were playing war near the river. Touch the Sky watched the boys counting coup on each other with willow branches and realized, his pride mixed with sadness, that they were not playing at

15

all. This was the vital early training in warfare that would continue until they were well beyond their fortieth winter—assuming they survived that long.

One of the boys, younger than the rest but sturdy and fast, suddenly roared with ferocious triumph as he counted coup. Touch the Sky felt an ear-to-ear smile stretch his face, and pride swelled his throat. It was that roar that had earned his son his first name in life: Little Bear—the name given to him by his parents, the name that would be replaced once more in life when he earned his warrior's name.

Absorbed in watching his son, Touch the Sky did not realize that his friend had returned quietly to his side.

"You are watching your boy," Little Horse said. "And thinking of that boy's mother. That is why you find it so much harder to find hope. I have no child to bounce on my knee, or woman to feed. My world is an easier place than yours."

Touch the Sky shook his head. "Your world *could* be easier. You could live free and easy, and top any woman who was for the taking. Instead, you fight my battles with me, and Maiyun knows I have battles enough for ten men. Yes, my world is a hard place. But I am not moaning." He met his friend's eye. "Not moaning," he repeated. "Just worried. Arrow Keeper appeared to me in a dream last night."

Little Horse's copper skin paled a shade. No one could say for sure if Arrow Keeper, tribe shaman before Touch the Sky, was in the Land of Ghosts.

He had simply disappeared one day. But it was sure—sure as death itself—that he never appeared to Touch the Sky unless serious trouble was in the wind.

Little Horse had to lick his lips before he could speak. His words were almost a whisper. "What did he say?"

Only now, when Touch the Sky finally answered, did Little Horse fully comprehend his friend's despondency.

"He told me," Touch the Sky replied tonelessly, "that the worst hurt in the world is coming for me."

The Wyoming Territory river-bend settlement called Bighorn Falls was located one day's hard ride south of the Cheyenne summer camp. Treaties signed earlier at Fort Laramie had established an uneasy peace between white settlers and the local tribes, among whom the Sioux and their Cheyenne cousins dominated in this area.

But "peace" was a word written on water. Both sides had shown bad faith. White miners, forbidden by treaty from prospecting the sacred Black Hills, had gone in anyway. Renegade Indians, in turn, had attacked whites and stolen their property.

All this tumbled through his thoughts as the grizzled former mountain man called Old Knobby watched the pack train below him.

The old trapper had known, as soon as he spotted the long line of sweating bull-whackers, who they were. Bearing north, horses and mules and even a few oxen yoked Mexican fashion were all loaded high with trade goods.

"Heap big doin's up Powder River way," he informed his horse, a big claybank mare grazing behind him on a grassy ridge overlooking Bighorn Falls. "Them goods is for Matthew's tribe."

New calico cloth, he thought. Powder, lead, and balls for the upcoming hunts. Steel knives, sulfur matches, mirrors, combs, flour, sugar, coffee—after a winter of pemmican and yarrow tea, those goods would be like rain to dry earth. All because Matthew had put his bacon in the fire once again for his people. Yet the red men didn't want him any more than the white men did.

"It's a goddamn pisspot of a world," Knobby informed his mare. The old man was somewhat ashamed of riding a mare in this wild country where only women and children would be seen on one. But the claybank had endless stamina and a gentle gait that was easy on Old Knobby's rheumatism. Like all former mountain men, he talked to his animals as if they were people.

Knobby watched the long pack train snake its way across the wide gravel ford just north of town. Curious onlookers had gathered to watch them, though the bull-whackers were such a rough crowd of half-breeds and hard cases that women were hustling the younger boys away.

Old Knobby chuckled at the sight. He could hear the teamsters cussing even from here. They reminded him of the old Green River Rendezvous days. One of the heavily burdened mules had managed to lie down. That meant it had to be un-packed again so that it could stand.

Knobby shook his head again as the cussed irony of it hit him. Matthew or Touch the Sky or whatever the hell you called him, that red son had grown up here in the Falls. The Hanchons raised him like their own blood, and he loved them back the same. Only one full day's ride between them, but it might as well be the entire Pacific Ocean.

The Hanchons had been good to Knobby after he proved his loyalty to their adopted boy. When his fondness for wagon-yard whiskey cost him his job as hostler in town, John and Sarah Hanchon took him on at their mustang spread. He was too damned old and stove up for the hard work. But Knobby had proven invaluable to the younger hands, showing them how to break green horses to leather. He was also a good line guard when the horses were up in their summer pastures as they were now.

The old man was about to turn away and ride back to his shack to boil some coffee. But just then something caught his eye below.

Knobby squinted, studying the scene even more closely. The old man removed his flap hat, revealing the silver-dollar-size raw spot on his crown—a Cheyenne warrior had started to scalp him until the trapper let daylight into his soul with a pepperbox pistol.

"Well, cuss my coup," he said finally, convinced. His hearing was starting to go, he was sprung in the knees, and he was growing long in the tooth. But Old Knobby could still see like a young eagle.

19

Judd Cole

And he had definitely gotten a good look when that last bull-whacker paused at the river, removed his wide felt hat, and mopped the sweat from his face.

His Injun face, Knobby thought.

That in itself was not unusual. Many of the teamsters were 'breeds, and plenty of Indians hired on with white freighting companies. But Knobby was sure he had recognized this Indian—recognized his broad, homely Comanche features and short hair parted exactly in the middle.

"Hellfire and corruption," he swore softly to his mare. "We got a herring in the pickle barrel, Fireaway. That ain't no freighter. That's that sneaky Comanche bastard Big Tree, and I'll be et fir a tater if he ain't planning to send Matthew across the great divide!"

Knobby didn't stop to wonder how in hell the renegade got mixed in with the freighters. Hell, maybe Hiram Steele arranged it. That hidebound son of a bitch had had blood in his eye for Matthew ever since the youth had the audacity to fall in love with Steele's daughter, Kristen.

The why of it didn't matter now. Knobby knew he had to get word to Matthew somehow. The best man to send would be Corey Robinson, Matt's old boyhood chum. But Corey was laid up with that leg he busted in a fall from his horse.

"Looks like it's me and you, girl," Knobby said to his mare. He didn't look forward to such a long ride to the upcountry of the Powder. But he could be spared, and besides, an old coot on a mare was beneath the dignity of most warriors—he stood a good chance of crossing Indian ranges unmo-

20

lested, especially as he spoke Sioux and knew sign talk.

"Let's go shake the oat bag," he told his claybank. "One good feed, girl, then we got us a hard ride. There's trouble on the spit."

Chapter Two

"The pack train is closer!" shouted an old grand-mother of the Antelope Eaters Clan. She had run down to the river to spread the word. "The Lakota at Medicine Bend Creek have sent mirror flashes. It passed there."

"The moccasin telegraph is quick," Two Twists said bitterly to Touch the Sky, looking toward the Bullwhip lodge. "When you made medicine with the white miners, the Whips and their lick-spittles called you White Man Runs Him and a traitor. They still use that as fodder when they are singing the litany of your supposed sins. But look now! They plan to be first in line when the goods are distributed. These mighty warriors have mighty mouths! They talk one way, but be-have many."

Touch the Sky nodded, for all of it was spoken

straight arrow. He, Honey Eater, and Little Bear, surrounded by Touch the Sky's loyal band of three, sat near the water. Honey Eater's aunt, Sharp Nosed Woman, had joined them. Little Bear, just shy of his fourth winter now, frolicked in the water, using a log for a canoe. The two women were shelling wild peas into a battered metal pot. The men filed arrow points and crimped shells or worked on cleaning and repairing their weapons.

"They are bald hypocrites," Touch the Sky agreed. "But each item they add to their hoard makes it harder for them to paint the white settlers black. Let them speak two ways, so long as they confine their 'boldness' to their words."

Tangle Hair, who rivaled Little Horse in taciturnity, nodded at this. "I am indifferent to most of the goods," he boasted, though he added as an afterthought, "Except for the sugar and coffee. But only look up at the camp. Touch the Sky has created another annual festival for the Shaiyena tribe."

It was true. A festival spirit dominated camp. The women had put on their best cloth dresses, adorned with all manner of jewelry and feathers and bright coins, including Presidential Medals with engravings of the Great White Father.

"Yes," Touch the Sky said, watching his wife and child. "It has brought a little peace, if only for a time."

Honey Eater knew the custom, of course, and would never have spoken to join a conversation of men. But her eyes met her husband's, and he saw that she, too, shared in his belief.

Again Touch the Sky felt it, even after years of living with this woman: that stirring of belly flies inside at the power of her beauty. The skin flawless and smooth as wild honey; the big, obsidian eyes shaped like wing tips; the beautiful, glossy mass of her hair, white columbine petals threaded through it. In a tribe famous for its beauties, still this one stood out.

But again his mind returned to the memory of Arrow Keeper, like a tongue returning to a broken tooth. *The worst hurt in the world is coming.* The wording was important. Arrow Keeper did not say "trouble." He said "hurt." Touch the Sky had learned a long time ago that, for him and those fool enough to follow him, the end of one battle only marked the beginning of the next. Suffering and pain had become close companions.

But the strongest man in the world was soft somewhere, he thought, glancing at his wife and child. He found some comfort when he reminded himself that they should be safe. No man had truer friends, or better fighters for companions, than he did. Every man in his band would unhesitatingly die to save Honey Eater or Little Bear.

"Brother," Little Horse said, as if divining his friend's thoughts from his troubled eyes, "I recalled a thing this morning. I recalled how Seth Carlson and Hiram Steele once used the pack train to slip an infected blanket into this camp. You will be serving as interpreter. May I suggest a thing? Before we touch any of the goods, make sure the freighters will also touch them."

Touch the Sky nodded, grinning. "I will,

brother. And the first who refuses will watch the camp dogs eat his entrails."

Touch the Sky had run through the list of his enemies—the leaders of the pack, at any rate. Seth Carlson, the bluecoat pony soldier who was convinced Touch the Sky had stolen Kristen Steele from him; Hiram Steele himself, obsessed with the false idea that his daughter had been topped by a red man; Big Tree, the Comanche terror from the Blanco Canyon; Sis-ki-dee, the Blackfoot madman known widely as the Red Peril; and closest to home, the cunning and ambitious Wolf Who Hunts Smiling.

He had faced each of them separately, and all of them at once, and still they had not killed him. But neither had he lessened their numbers. He had killed their white gunslicks and red toadies, but the five remained—all of them, poised to strike at any time.

"Hii-ya! Hii-*ya*!"

The Cheyenne war cry. Hearing it startled Touch the Sky out of his reverie. Everyone on the bank stared out toward the river.

Little Bear had come up with a "spear" somewhere, a stick with a blunt point at one end. As the rest watched, he again shouted the war cry as he leaped from his canoe, attempting to spear a trout.

The clumsy little mite missed by a stone's throw. But his serious war face and the energy of his attempt impressed the men on the bank, who all loosed a mighty cheer of admiration. Even the women suspended modesty and joined the cheer.

Again Touch the Sky's eyes met those of his wife. She smiled at him, a smile that encouraged him to take hope.

Hope. He tried to school himself in that thought. But the sere, cracked, wind-rawed face of Arrow Keeper stayed with him. So did the whispered word, sinister and foreboding: *hurt.*

Old Knobby's spirits were in far better shape than his sitter.

He had taken a great chance and ridden north all through the night, knowing the slower pack train would make camp at sunset. Since he had a comfortable jump on them, the old trapper held his claybank to nothing faster than an easy trot. Assisted by a generous moon and an explosion of stars, he followed the Old Lakota Trace, which he had not ridden in twenty years.

God-in-whirlwinds! he thought. The West, while still far from tame, was already starting to simmer down from the wild-and-woolly days he remembered. Hell, there was a way station up on Beaver Creek now—part of the new short-line stage service from Laramie and Register Cliffs. And homesteaders on the old buffalo ranges! Why, the damned hoe-men were even putting up fences to protect their crops.

"Damn tarnal foolishness, Fireaway," Knobby assured the claybank mare as they came up out of a cutbank. "It's got so's a man can't eat good meat 'less he pays a goddamn tax on it."

Old Knobby never thought it would come to this: to actually feeling *sorry* the old dangers were gone. But the old dangers had always been exaggerated—it was the old freedoms he missed. From the Cumberland Gap to South Pass, only the names changed—the desire for freedom was constant. Men pushed on west to get away from cussed "syphilization." From its foolish laws and cowardly restrictions and womanish fussing.

The claybank abruptly stopped and crow-hopped slightly off the trail. Knobby was instantly alert, searching the moonlit darkness around him.

But it was only some settler's hound dog, and a friendly one at that. Knobby could count its ribs—evidently it had strayed too far from home.

Feeling sorry for it, he drew a cold corn dodger from the fiber sack tied to his saddle horn.

"Wrap your teeth around that, old campaigner," he said, tossing the food to the hound.

Why, hell, Knobby thought again as he pressured the mare with his knees, resuming the journey north to the Powder River country of the Cheyennes. A damned dog! Used to was, a man might meet up with a silvertip bear hereabouts.

Still . . . this easy journey meant a timely warning for Matthew and his tribe. Knobby knew that was most important. And right now, he was way ahead of that two-faced, back-stabbing, conniving Comanche devil Big Tree. Knobby would be in plenty of time to warn Matthew.

Was it the whole damned shebang? Knobby wondered. Were they *all* in on it—the entire pack train? Were they all going to strike once inside the camp? That didn't seem likely. Among tribes renowned for making fierce stands in their very camps, Cheyennes were second to none. Even the women and children would pitch into the fight. Besides, they'd be ready.

No. The old man shook his head, digging at a tick in his beard. No—Big Tree was sneaking in to kill one Indian, and that Indian was Matt Hanchon, better known these days as Touch the Sky of the Northern Cheyenne.

While he rode, the old trailsman let his mind roam free, recalling his days and nights in the awesome Great Stony Mountains, now called the Rockies by greenhorns. Funny how making this ride brought back all the old ways and lore. He even remembered his first lesson in survival, taught by the legendary Caleb Greenwood himself: "When it's cold, walk in the shade. When it's hot, walk in the sun. That way you'll never meet a snake."

The claybank shied and again crow-hopped sideways.

"Gee up there, girl," Knobby scoffed at his mount. "It's just 'at ol' hound, following our back trail."

Knobby figured to get word to Matthew, rest up a few hours while his horse grazed, and then return before John Hanchon missed him. John and Sarah already had grief enough, worrying about their adopted boy. Lord knows they saw him seldom enough. Sarah, especially, would take it hard if Knobby had to explain that Big Tree was out for Matt's hair—Big Tree, the same red devil who had planted an arrow in Sarah's back.

"H'ar now!" the old man grumbled when the claybank again started fighting him. "We got to git, Fireaway!"

Desert Manhunt

It was that damned hound. Knobby had two guns in his twin saddle boots—the old Kentucky over-and-under he called Patsy Plumb and a weak scattergun loaded with buckshot, used mainly for close-in defense when he was surprised.

It wasn't his way to waste a shot. But this trip was turning into a Sunday stroll, so he could afford it. He had to scare off that hound, or the mare would be fidgety the whole damn way. Besides, the buckshot wouldn't seriously hurt at this range—only sting and scare.

Knobby halted his mare, slid the gun from its boot, grunting with the effort as he slewed around in the saddle. Aiming to one side of the hound's shadowy form, he squeezed off the load.

The exploding gun sent the dog scrambling and made the claybank jump a bit. "There, you damned nancy," Old Knobby said, turning back around. "Now, git—"

A sudden orange flash exploded inside Knobby's skull, pain made him cry out, and the force of the surprise blow knocked the old man out of his saddle. He had enough presence of mind and strength left to grab his rigging as he slid down, breaking his fall.

Knobby balanced on the feather edge of awareness, pain thudding in his skull like tom-toms. He lay half on the ground, his legs caught in the twisted stirrups and latigos. His flap hat slid away from his eyes, and he saw them peering down at him, one holding the mare's bridle: Indians!

They laughed in scorn, one pointing at his horse. What kind of man would ride a mare?

He recognized them as Digger Indians from

29

their filthy hides and tangled, dirty hair. The notorious thieves from the Missouri River country, pushed west by land-hungry whites. Maybe he could palaver with them, make medicine. Maybe—

One of the Diggers again slammed the stout tree branch into the old man's head, and Knobby's world closed down to pain and darkness.

When the camp crier announced that the pack train had crossed Weeping Woman Ridge, Touch the Sky and his comrades went into action.

The Bullwhips and the Bowstrings, the tribe's two soldier societies, were its official policemen. It was their job to be on guard when any outsiders entered camp. And Touch the Sky knew outsiders were expected, especially the Bowstrings, who were mostly loyal to Chief River of Winds and the Law-ways, as well as the Council of Forty.

But the Bullwhips, most of them lickspittles of Wolf Who Hunts Smiling, could not be trusted. Yes, they would have their weapons to hand—but who knew which side they would join if fighting broke out? To counter that possibility, Touch the Sky and his band—the equal of any forty men— would be ready to assist the Bowstrings.

Honey Eater did not need to be told how critical this time was. She would hang back, keeping Little Bear with her, until Touch the Sky had made his initial inspection of the arriving party. Only then would she and the rest of the women and children and elders be called out by the camp crier.

The soldiers cleared the camp clearing of ex-

cited Indians, the Bullwhips occasionally resort-
ing to their dreaded whips when someone lagged
behind.

Eventually the clearing was empty except for
the armed braves. They watched the long pack
train snake its way down the ridge outside camp,
flying a white truce flag. Cheyennes kept many
camp dogs for security, and they went wild now.
Those with wolf in their blood snapped and
howled fiercely until their owners hurled rocks in
among them to quiet them down.

The leader of the pack train was wise in the
ways of the red man. He stopped his caravan well
outside of camp and sent a word-bringer ahead to
request permission to enter. It was granted.

Touch the Sky made eye contact with his men:
Little Horse, Two Twists, Tangle Hair, all strate-
gically placed. As the first heavily laden pack animals trudged to a halt, his men all sent the same
signal: No imminent signs of trouble. Touch the
Sky saw how things were too. No freighter carried
a weapon to hand, nor were any of them well-
supplied with spare cartridges.

The leader, who had made this run three years
in a row, raised one hand high in peace as he approached Touch the Sky. "Caleb Riley sends his
regards," the teamster called out in English. "Said
to tell you he added some of Gail Borden's new
canned milk to the load. Says you're to try it in
your coffee."

Touch the Sky could not help but grin as he
greeted the man. The rest of the bull-whackers
had entered the clearing and were hobbling their
animals. Touch the Sky nodded to the camp crier.

He tore off down the paths, calling the rest out to admire the goods.

Even the most disciplined warriors began exclaiming and getting caught up in the excitement as the goods were heaped for inspection. Touch the Sky smiled, watching Honey Eater's eyes widen as she inspected a bolt of blue cotton cloth. One of the freighters, a friendly half-breed who liked children, was passing out licorice drops.

The clearing was humming with activity, streaming with Indians and freighters and animals. Touch the Sky was aware, without giving it much thought, that one of the freighters wore a serape and a big flap hat that left his face in shadows. The man caught his eye because of the powerful-looking pony tied by a lead line to his loaded mule. Perhaps he traded something for it at the Sioux Camp at Medicine Bend.

Touch the Sky turned away to translate something between the head freighter and Chief River of Winds. Big Tree chose that moment to strike.

The Comanche shrugged off the serape in an eyeblink, freeing his arms and exposing the long, single-edged knife in his sash. No one even appeared to notice as he cocked his right arm back and hurled the deadly weapon with lethal accuracy straight toward Touch the Sky.

But one person had noticed. Just as the knife was released, Little Bear's warning roar rose above the din of camp. Hearing it, Honey Eater reacted instinctively.

Almost as if it were all just one long movement, Big Tree tossed the lead line free and leaped onto the spare pony—one he had selected for speed and stamina. Touch the Sky was just in time to recognize his enemy, even as, from the corner of his eye, he saw something hurtling toward him.

An eyeblink later, just as the well-thrown knife should have punctured Touch the Sky's vitals, Honey Eater flew between him and the blade. A feral cry of misery and fear rose from Touch the Sky when he heard the sickening sound of the blade slicing into Honey Eater. Even as the lightning-fast pony raced from camp, bearing Big Tree to freedom, Touch the Sky's wife collapsed in his arms.

Chapter Three

Near chaos still gripped the Powder River camp when Wolf Who Hunts Smiling slipped out unseen.

His usually cunning features were now a mask of grim foreboding. As the people pressed closer to the center of the trouble, he exchanged quick nods with several of his toadies. Then, with Bullwhips forming a screen, he hurried down to the huge stands of cattails and reeds near the water.

It was the custom to make secret escape trails in case of surprise attack. Wolf Who Hunts Smiling hurried along one now, casting nervous backward glances.

His woman! That fool Big Tree had knifed Touch the Sky's woman—the very light of his life, she and that puling brat of theirs.

There was no man in the world Wolf Who Hunts

Smiling would not face, including the tall one. Indeed, he *had* faced Touch the Sky, more than once. Each had failed to kill the other—savage equals in a savage land.

But even Wolf Who Hunts Smiling would not lightly draw blood from the tall one's woman or child. Now it was imperative, the fleeing brave realized, that all of Touch the Sky's enemies band together and think like one man. Otherwise, they would all feel the deadly sting of his bottomless rage and *die* like one man.

He knew where Big Tree had ridden to—the prearranged spot where Big Tree, Wolf Who Hunts Smiling, and Sis-ki-dee were to meet after the killing of Touch the Sky. But that plan was smoke behind them now.

Wolf Who Hunts Smiling knew that Touch the Sky would not ride out immediately—his woman would come first.

But one of his deadly band might ride out. So now the Wolf hurried, fording the river once he was out of sight of camp and bearing toward the common corral from the west.

He gave a little whistle, and a pinto with a roached mane trotted over to him. Wolf Who Hunts Smiling grabbed a handful of mane stubble, swung onto his mount, and hunkered low over its neck. He urged the stallion northwest toward the tall, windswept pinnacle whites called Lookout Rock.

Sis-ki-dee, tears of amusement still streaming down his scar-pocked face, looked at Big Tree with mocking contempt.

"What, Quohada? Another dead woman on your string, and no hair to prove it? Perhaps you should ride back and ask Touch the Sky if you may scalp her before the funeral?"

Wolf Who Hunts Smiling, despite his apprehension, almost laughed outright at this. But Big Tree's scowl of rage checked him.

"Laugh, Red Peril. But up in Bloody Bones Canyon, you begged like a white man. Begged the tall shaman to spare your life. And he did, out of pure contempt, for his honor would not let him kill a coward."

The mirth fled from Sis-ki-dee's insane eyes, and for a moment Wolf Who Hunts Smiling was sure these two would kill each other. All three of them had sheltered in the lee of Lookout Rock. From here, a man could see anything approaching from any direction while it was still a long ride off.

"You two jays," the Wolf scoffed. "Are you women, trading insults in your sewing lodge? Have you eyes to see what has happened? Even now the woman of White Man Runs Him is dead or dying. I tell you now, and this place hears me, he saw Big Tree's face. And he will move heaven and earth to kill not only him, but anyone else involved in this."

These words sobered the other two like sharp slaps to the face.

"I will have to ride," Big Tree said. "And none can call me coward. Any man fool enough to face him now will die a dog's death."

Sis-ki-dee nodded. "The custom is clear. As the Wolf says, he will come for all of us. But he must start with the man who drew blood, and that is you, Quohada."

"It was Hiram Steele," Big Tree fumed. He shot an accusing stare at Wolf Who Hunts Smiling. "Every time you parley with hair-faces, we end up doing their donkey work. Now only look. Steele's trickery and bribes got me into that pack train—now he will stay back in the shadows while we fight the battle."

"So what?" Wolf Who Hunts Smiling shot back. "Why lick old wounds when it's time for action?"

"Is his she-bitch whore dead?" Sis-ki-dee demanded.

"She looked dead when I left," Wolf Who Hunts Smiling replied. "I could not see if it was a gut stab or higher in a lung. But the blood was copious."

"I will ride south to Blanco Canyon," Big Tree decided.

He meant the desolate spot, deep in the dead heart of the Llano Estacado or Staked Plains, that marked the homeland of the Quohada Comanches. It was many sleeps' hard ride from here, in the land of red rock canyons and burning alkali flats.

Wolf Who Hunts Smiling shook his head. "Good, but not good enough. He routed you out of the Blanco before. You must ride farther. Deep into the country of the Brown Ones. You speak their tongue, know their land. Touch the Sky does not."

By "the Brown Ones," Wolf Who Hunts Smiling meant the Mexicans. Big Tree did not argue, for his Cheyenne ally was right.

"I know a Mexican in Sonora," Big Tree said.

"His name is Poco Loco. He has a band of *pistoleros* who have defeated even the famous Texas Rangers. I used to sell Indian slaves to him. He has a stronghold deep in the sierras. I will ride there."

Wolf Who Hunts Smiling approved this with a nod.

"What if his precious woman does not die?" Siski-dee suggested.

"It matters not," the Wolf said. "I have already heard Touch the Sky make his vow publicly, with the Council of Forty as his witnesses. Any man who hurts his woman or whelp is marked for worm fodder. Ride, Big Tree, and lure him into Mexico. You are no second-line warrior, buck! He fears you, and rightly. Lure him into Mexico, and leave him there as carrion!"

Old Knobby looked about as miserable as Touch the Sky had ever seen him—perhaps almost as miserable as Touch the Sky himself felt, though that hardly seemed possible to the grief-stricken Cheyenne.

"Tarnal hell, Matthew," Knobby said awkwardly around the clay stem of Touch the Sky's best calumet, "I tried to get here in time. My hand to God! But them damned Diggers stripped me of everything I had. They boosted my hoss, too. But Fireaway was broke to hate the Injun smell, no offense. She bolted first chance, and somehow she found me. All they ended up gittin' was the clothes off my back."

Indeed, Knobby had ridden into a tense camp a short time ago wrapped in his own saddle blanket.

Desert Manhunt

Now, thanks to Little Horse, who was about his size, Knobby had been outfitted with a leather shirt and a pair of blue kersey trousers taken from a dead soldier. Double-soled, knee-length elkskin moccasins covered his legs.

His mouth a grim, determined slit, Touch the Sky accepted the pipe from his old friend and set it on the ground between them. Both men sat over a glowing firepit in Touch the Sky's now-lonely tipi. By custom, the seriously wounded Honey Eater had been rushed to the women's sick lodge. No men would be allowed in while her clan grandmothers chanted the old cure songs. Little Bear was safe for the moment with the women of Honey Eater's clan.

"You don't have to make excuses to me, oldtimer," Touch the Sky said. "Those bruises on your face are the color of grapes. I wish to God you could have gotten through, Knobby."

Again worry stabbed through him, and Touch the Sky fell silent, brooding. The only word he could obtain on Honey Eater came from her aunt Sharp Nosed Woman—and all she would do was shake her head sadly, muttering that it was up to the High Holy Ones now. The bleeding had been stemmed, and the wound packed with gentian and gunpowder.

"She gonna come sassy agin, tadpole?" Knobby asked quietly.

Touch the Sky's face was a study in abject misery. "There was so much blood lost," he said, his voice heavy with grief. "She took that knife for me, Knobby."

"H'ar now!" Knobby rebuked him, not liking the

dangerous, reckless gleam in the youth's eyes. "You got to hold the line now, boy. Your woman needs you, and you got you a pup on the robes now, too. Plenty of time later to settle the books with that red bastard Big Tree."

Touch the Sky nodded. "I don't set foot from this camp until . . . until I know about Honey Eater. One way or the other."

Knobby cut a strip from the hump steak he had cooked on the tripod outside the tipi entrance. His arrival had already occasioned slanted glances and hushed remarks from some of the others— remarks about Touch the Sky's loyalty to the hair-faces who were stealing their ranges. Others, however, had been impressed by the old trapper's obvious familiarity with Plains customs. His sign talk was proficient, and he knew quite a few Lakota words, a language understood by most Cheyennes.

Both men fell silent, watching orange spear-tips of flame dance in the pit. Touch the Sky sat with his Sharps carbine across his lap. One of his many enemies might well try to catch him off guard in his grief. Not that Touch the Sky feared death— but he was determined to live at least long enough to punish Big Tree and whoever else schemed with him in this.

"Brother!" came Little Horse's voice from outside. "I would speak with you."

Touch the Sky threw back the entrance flap and bade his friend enter.

"Well?" Touch the Sky demanded the moment Little Horse came in. This was proof the situation was serious, for no Cheyenne ever opened serious conversation without smoking to the directions and making inconsequential talk first.

"Big Tree rode toward Lookout Rock. I followed his trail long enough to verify it."

"And Wolf Who Hunts Smiling?"

"No one saw him ride out," Little Horse said. "Nor return. But his favorite pinto is lathered—I checked. He rode out, also."

"He was in on it," Touch the Sky said. "And Hiram Steele."

Knobby understood none of this except Hiram Steele's name. Touch the Sky translated.

"Wolf Who Hunts Smiling," Knobby repeated. "Ain't he the shifty-eyed one? That tough little buck what was on Wes Munro's keelboat with us?"

Touch the Sky nodded. "A low-crawling pig's afterbirth who sheds tribal blood."

"Ain't nobody lower than Big Tree," Knobby muttered. "Son of a bitch shot your ma in the back, and now he's hurt your wife. We've left that bastard off his leash too long already, Matthew."

While Knobby spoke, Little Horse watched his best friend rummage in a pile of buffalo robes near the center pole of the tipi. Little Horse frowned deeply when he saw what Touch the Sky drew out: a simple leather harness attached to several sharp steel hooks.

Old Knobby, who had spent years among the red men, recognized it too. His face paled behind his beard.

"Hell 'n' furies, sprout! You fixin' to set up a pole?"

Touch the Sky nodded. "I will hang from it through the night," he said in Cheyenne to Little

Horse. "Will you come cut me down at sunrise?"

With evident reluctance, Little Horse nodded. He had seen Touch the Sky go through this grueling voluntary ordeal before. "Setting up a pole" was a penance designed to propitiate the Holy Ones and sway them toward mercy on their red children. Touch the Sky would drive those steel hooks through his chest muscles—deep into the muscles. Then, his weight suspended in the harness, he would hang from a tall pole set up on a hill overlooking camp. The ordeal could kill even a strong man.

But neither Little Horse nor Knobby foolishly tried to talk Touch the Sky out of this move. His wife lay dying, her lifeblood drained from her. The look in Touch the Sky's eyes was a warning: He would brook interference from no man, not where his wife was concerned.

"Not only will I cut you down, shaman," Little Horse promised. "I will be out there with you on the hill through the night. There is nothing your enemies would like better than to gut you while you hang helpless."

Chapter Four

It was one of the longest, most agonizing nights of his hard life.

Touch the Sky had withstood the fiery pain in silence as he gouged the sharp hooks deep into his muscles. His face pouring sweat, he maintained that silence as Little Horse and Knobby rigged him to the pole and lowered it into its hole.

The pain of his weight pulling against those strained and tortured muscles verged on unbearable. All through the long night, Touch the Sky drifted in and out of consciousness like a man riding through a patchy fog.

By strict custom, his friends could gather near, but they could do nothing whatsoever to help alleviate his suffering. While he hung in that painful state, his mind drifting free, Touch the Sky saw many faces, heard many voices.

But one face kept returning to mock him, a grinning, ugly face streaked with the yellow and green war paint of the Comanches. Big Tree. The Red Raider of the Plains. Terrorizer of white settlers in Texas, now a nemesis of the red men on the Northern Plains. A brave man but without honor, a superb warrior but one without the compassion of all true warriors—and thus, one who counted women and children as "kills" along with the men he had slaughtered.

And while Touch the Sky hung there, balanced between life and death, Arrow Keeper's words returned from the hinterland of memory: *The worst hurt in the world is coming.*

Brother?

Touch the Sky?

Wake up, Matthew, wake

"—up, boy! Matthew! You hear me, tadpole?"

Slowly, like a sluggish snake after a cold night, Touch the Sky's mind returned to awareness.

He lay in the dew-tinted grass. Pain exploded in his chest with each heartbeat. Clean cloths had been tied over his bleeding wounds.

His friends circled him: Little Horse, Tangle Hair, Two Twists, Old Knobby. Worry was starched into their features. Two Twists made him drink a little hot tea from a clay bowl.

Golden splashes of morning sunlight dotted the grass. Touch the Sky tried to sit up, but it felt as if six-inch spikes were being kicked into his chest.

"Easy, buck," Little Horse cautioned him.

Touch the Sky tried to speak, but failed. He drank a little more of the tea. Then he licked his cracked lips and tried again. "Honey Eater?" he managed.

Little Horse shook his head. "We have waited with you, shaman. We will learn her fate at your side."

It took infinite effort for Touch the Sky to rise, even with the help of his friends.

"We will stop at Hawk Woman's tipi first," he said wearily. "I will get my son, too. Whatever the truth, he too will face it like a man."

Slowly, with many in camp looking on in sympathy, others with contempt, Touch the Sky's friends helped him down the hill and back into camp. Little Bear, who had been up almost all night worrying about his hurt mother, was sound asleep.

Tangle Hair picked up the mite from his robes, still asleep, and laid him over his shoulder. Then, with Little Horse and Two Twists supporting Touch the Sky, the group headed for the sick lodge.

It was the longest walk Touch the Sky could ever remember making. He could not tell, in this early-morning stillness, what the word was. It was quiet around the sick lodge, a small structure made from skins stretched over a frame of bent poles.

Touch the Sky paused with one hand gripping the buffalo-hide entrance flap. For a moment, all strength deserted him. He had faced down bullet, bow, and grizzly. But if Honey Eater had crossed over, Touch the Sky was not sure he was strong enough to endure the blow.

"H'ar now," Knobby said with false gruffness,

for in fact the old man was on the verge of tears himself. "Toss that flap back like the man you are, Matthew, and grasp the nettle!"

But at that moment, the decision was taken out of the young Cheyenne's hands.

"Will you men wake up the entire camp?" came a weak but recognizable voice from within, scolding them. "I can hear you in here! Will someone feed a hungry woman?"

With a shout of joy, Touch the Sky limped inside, the rest on his heels. Honey Eater lay propped up in a pile of robes, Sharp Nosed Woman at her side, tears of joy streaming down her face.

For a long moment, Touch the Sky and Honey Eater exchanged a glance—one whose meaning had become familiar for them. A glance that said: *Once again we have defeated the Black Warrior.* Then he was kneeling at her side, placing the sleeping Little Bear with her.

Sharp Nosed Woman had been casting suspicious glances at Old Knobby. But when he pointed at her and made the blossom sign—telling her she was as pretty as a flower—she blushed.

"Now you have all seen her," Sharp Nosed Woman fussed. "And you see she is still a pretty one. Now go, bring her a tender elk steak! I want it dripping in marrow fat, do you hear?"

It was understood that women were the masters in the sick lodge, and no brave ever took offense at being ordered about like a child if it was for the welfare of the sick and wounded. Even a chief could be put to work if an old grandmother demanded it from the lodge. Touch the Sky cleared out at Sharp Nosed Woman's command, though Little Bear was permitted to stay.

Immediately, seeing the joy in Touch the Sky's face, the camp crier began his rounds, shouting the news that Honey Eater had survived. Many, still half asleep, nonetheless came outside to sing the song to the new sun rising, joyous at her recovery.

"The Holy Ones smiled on you, buck," Little Horse told his friend as they prepared Honey Eater's meal. They knew she had lost much blood, so they also made a nourishing soup of calf brains and rose hips.

"They did," Touch the Sky agreed. In truth he was letting his friend do most of the work, for he was still too sore and weak from his overnight vigil. "But what Big Tree did cannot—*will* not—stand."

Little Horse nodded. "As you say. Our Medicine Arrows are still stained with dirty blood from Sis-ki-dee's murder of he who may not be mentioned."

Little Horse meant their former peace chief, Gray Thunder. By custom his name could not be spoken, for it was believed the dead might hear it and answer.

"This time," Little Horse continued, "the renegades were not content to shoot at us from afar, as Sis-ki-dee did when he killed our chief. Never mind that it was your woman. They violated our very camp itself!"

"You have seized this matter firmly by the tail," Touch the Sky said. "They are like daring children testing their elders. If this crime goes unavenged, they will be even more emboldened."

Besides all that, Touch the Sky thought, Big Tree hurt the Cheyenne's best reason for living. Now the Comanche would die a hard death. Touch the Sky had failed to kill Sis-ki-dee in Bloody Bones Canyon. That failure, in part, had encouraged Big Tree's bold attack. There could be no failure this time.

When Big Tree set out from Lookout Rock, he took five good ponies on his string.

White men divided time up into odd things called hours and minutes and seconds. But Big Tree knew that time was a bird, and now that bird was on the wing.

Touch the Sky, being a "noble red man," would remain in camp so long as his woman's life lay in the balance. But once she died—and she might already be dead—the tall one would move like wings of swift lightning.

So Big Tree rode his ponies hard, rode them right into the ground. He would hold one at a full, or near, gallop until it lathered, then switch to another at full speed. These moves were effortless for a Comanche, a tribe who were ungainly on foot but gracious as eagles in flight when on horseback.

He had stuffed his legging sash with jerked buffalo and dried fruit and did not need to stop to hunt or prepare food. Steadily south he fled, leaving the brown, rolling plains of the north behind him as he entered the sandstone country of the southern Colorado Territory. Deeper, through the opening whites called Raton Pass, into the land of the Pueblo tribes and the scant-grass deserts.

Desert Manhunt

Big Tree had run his horses ragged by the time he reached Navajo country. The southwest tribes were rich in horses this year, so it was an easy matter to steal a new string. Deeper he fled, through the desolate no-man's-land of the Staked Plain, across the great alkali pan of southern New Mexico.

Deeper, across the wide, shallow, muddy-brown river whites called the Rio Grande, Mexicans the Río Bravo. Deeper, always deeper, for he knew the tall one would be coming. It had finally come down to this time and this country.

For many winters now the two of them had played their deadly game of cat and mouse. Now the playing was over. Now one of them would die, and it would be a hard death.

Touch the Sky knew he could count on the moccasin telegraph to track Big Tree's movements even before he left camp. The brave did not ride out for several sleeps, for he knew better than to track Big Tree when his strength was down.

Smoke signals, mirror flashes, runners—every means was used as each tribe let the others know what this important and deadly renegade was up to. Touch the Sky was not surprised to learn that, as he expected, Big Tree had fled due south at a breakneck pace.

"He means to hole up in the Blanco Canyon," the tall brave informed his band. Knobby, too, sat around the fire, for he had been invited to remain in camp until Touch the Sky rode out. That way the two friends could ride together as far as Bighorn Falls.

"He can be flushed," Two Twists said confidently. None of Touch the Sky's companions had mounted a serious argument when Touch the Sky announced he was going after Big Tree alone. They understood that the real danger lay right here in camp. With Touch the Sky gone, Wolf Who Hunts Smiling and his lickspittles could rebel at any moment.

"Our shaman knows that canyon," Little Horse agreed. "If any of us can trap Big Tree in his own burrow, it is Touch the Sky."

And so the brave set out. He cleaned and oiled his Sharps and crimped a pouch full of shells; he made a new bow of green oak and strung it with tough buffalo sinew; he filled his foxskin quiver with new, fire-hardened arrows. He selected his favorite coyote dun and three other ponies; then, Old Knobby at his side, he rode out for the south country.

It was during this leg of the journey, the stretch between Powder River and Bighorn Falls, that Touch the Sky learned some disturbing news through the moccasin telegraph.

He and Knobby were just clearing the last series of razorback ridges north of Bighorn Falls when Touch the Sky saw smoke lines rising on the southern horizon: a message from the Southern Cheyenne camp at Washita Creek.

"Heap big doin's down south," Knobby observed, craning his withered neck to watch the dark puffs rise against a seamless blue sky the color of a gas flame. "What're they sayin', colt?"

A deep frown settled over Touch the Sky's weather-rawed features. "Big Tree did not hole up in the Blanco. He has fled into Old Mexico."

This was troubling news. Touch the Sky had counted on familiarity with the Blanco Canyon country to work in his favor. Big Tree was a formidable opponent on any battleground. But to fight him in new country was a daunting prospect—and whereas Big Tree was intimate with Mexico, Touch the Sky had never once crossed the border.

"He has allies there," the Cheyenne said glumly. "He is fluent in the tongue, knows the country like beavers know the timberline. It is a good choice on his part. And as for me, I have no choice but to follow him there."

"Well, I reckon that tears it," Knobby announced. "Looks like you 'n' me'll be ridin' together agin'. Just like when we whipped ol' Wes Munro and his land-grabbers."

Touch the Sky squinted at him. "You been chewing peyote, old codger?"

"You're the one what's soft in the brain," the trapper retorted, "iffen you think you kin just waltz into beaner country and flush Big Tree! *Puedes entenderme ahora?*"

At Touch the Sky's puzzled glance, the old man translated, "I just asked you in Mexer talk iffen you kin savvy what I said. I spent damn near five years with the Taos Trappers, learned Mexer talk real good. I made three, four pack-train runs down the King's Highway, too, between Santa Fe and Durango, Mexico. I may be all tied up with the rheumatick, boy. But I can still make my beaver. C'mon, Matthew, wha'd'ya say, boy? I can send a note to your ma and pa by a runner, tell 'em I got unexpected business down to the south country. It won't even be a lie."

Touch the Sky did not really debate it very long. He was an equal match for Big Tree, but not under unequal terms. Old Knobby was right—the savvy old mountain man might be slower in body these days, but his mind was sharp as a steel trap. This old frontiersman had taught Touch the Sky everything he knew about nighttime movement and survival, among other things. He'd be a good companion on this daunting mission.

"Good chance you might get killed," he warned the old-timer.

"Damn right," Knobby replied happily, chucking up his horse. "Wouldn't be no fun otherwise."

Chapter Five

In the hardscrabble years following the war with the United States in 1846–47, Old Mexico had become a country laid waste by road bandits and raiding Indians. The corruption of Santa Anna and other so-called generals had left the Mexican Army with beautiful uniforms, but demoralized, corrupt, and woefully inadequate to protect the vast frontier. Ambitious *jefes*, or "bosses," formed their own private armies and roamed virtually unchallenged—until another gang of thieves clashed with them over control of a region.

No *jefe* ruled with such total control, or inspired as much total fear, as the cruel Pablo Morales, known to friend and foe alike as Poco Loco because he was indeed "a little crazy."

Poco Loco and his gang of ten *pistoleros* ruled northern Sonora state. They operated out of a remote mountain bastion, the "lost pueblo" of Santa Rosa high in the snowcapped sierras. With Santa Rosa as a base, they struck with impunity at government caravans, private pack trains, border-survey teams, anything that moved along the nearly deserted roads.

Between raids, Poco Loco made his headquarters in Santa Rosa's only cantina, a little adobe hovel called Las Tres Hermanas, The Three Sisters. Normally it was dead as last Christmas in the cantina, especially since all locals knew who holed up there and either stayed away or behaved very carefully indeed when they went in. Pablo Morales was not always mean, and could in fact be quite generous when Captain Whiskey had him in tow. But like a half-wild mustang, he was totally unpredictable, and in an eyeblink could kill a man for snoring.

But on this night, his mood was jolly. A party of *ciboleros*, Mexican buffalo hunters, was passing through from Chihuahua. They brought the latest gossip from the Internal Provinces, and were quite diverting. The hunters knew of Poco Loco only by reputation, not sight, and did not hesitate when the squat, serape-draped, free-spending stranger challenged them to an arm-wrestling contest.

Most of Poco Loco's men were hanging around in the cantina, nursing bottles of tequila and forty-rod, and placed bets on their *jefe*. One by one, Poco Loco defeated the young, strong hunters. After four hard matches, he had not even broken a sweat.

"Amigo," said the leader of the *ciboleros* at one point, pointing to a man sprawled in the back corner. "That man there, he has been asleep for hours. Should someone wake him and send him home? His wife will worry all night."

Several of Poco Loco's men laughed outright.

"You hear this, *'manos*?" Poco Loco's man Esteban shouted to the rest. "Wake Senor Ramirez up and send him home to his woman!"

This occasioned another roar of laughter.

Poco Loco, still busy pocketing his winnings, looked up at the hunter, his cruel mouth tilting into a grin. The broad, bluff face was dusky with beard stubble, and a livid scar ran from his left temple down below the point of his jaw. A sawed-off scattergun hung in a special rig at his side.

"Friend," Poco Loco told the hunter, "that man has gone home permanently. I killed him several hours ago. You see, he was angry at me. Something about his sister and the loss of her honor."

The hunter traded uncomfortable glances with his companions.

"Shouldn't someone at least drag him out?" the leader asked hesitantly.

Poco Loco shrugged beefy shoulders under his serape. "Right now he is only drawing flies. Drag him out when he begins to stink."

The *ciboleros* finally realized who the strong stranger was. They left shortly after this, thanking Jesus for sparing them. But before long the batwings sprang open again and a huge figure moved into the cantina. A wide-brimmed plainsman's hat was pulled low, leaving his face in shadow in the dark interior. He ordered a cup of the local wine, then turned to the rest.

"Tengo cien dolares en oro," he announced. "I

have one hundred dollars in gold. My money says I can whip the king of the arm wrestlers."

Absolute silence greeted these words. Esteban and the rest watched, hands inching toward their weapons, as the huge stranger moved closer. His boot heels thumped on the floor, and the canny Poco Loco noticed that he walked as one unused to wearing shoe leather.

Poco Loco watched him, his swarthy face impassive, while he poured himself another shot of tequila. "Put your gold on the table, stranger," he invited.

The new arrival stacked ten American quarter eagles before the Mexican. Then he scraped a chair close, sat down, rolled up his sleeve. Still his face was obscured by shadow and the dim light from a single argand lamp. Poco Loco stared closer, recognizing that mocking grin.

"Just to make things interesting," the challenger said, placing an old coffee can on the table. He drew out two scorpions, handling them carefully, and placed them on their backs on the table, the deadly tails pointing up.

He arranged them so that the hand of whoever lost would come down right on top of one of them.

A buzz of excited talk swept through the cantina. Poco Loco's men gathered closer. The Mexican *jefe* grinned, revealing yellow teeth like two rows of crooked gravestones.

"This stranger," he said to his men. "I like him. He has a set on him. Maybe this one will live."

The two men gripped each other's hand and commenced their struggle. First Poco Loco started to win, then the challenger. The veins in their necks stood out like fat night crawlers, their muscles strained like taut cables.

The stranger gave a mighty shout, and then there was a loud thump as Poco Loco's hand smashed to the table, right on top of one of the scorpions, so hard the insect was instantly crushed.

Esteban's gun was halfway out of its holster when Poco Loco called out, "Lower your hammer, Esteban, and look closer! He pulled the stingers out of their tails. This is an old *compadre* of ours."

Big Tree whipped the hat aside. At the same time, he slid the gold across to his old friend.

"Keep it," he said. "Consider it your first payment."

Poco Loco had in fact already recognized Big Tree—one of the few men strong enough to beat him at arm wrestling. They had shared a virtual reign of terror many years earlier, before the Comanche moved on to the north country.

Gold was extremely rare in Mexico. Poco Loco stared at the coins, and his tongue brushed across his upper lip.

"The first payment on what?" he demanded.

"On the head of a Northern Cheyenne named Touch the Sky," Big Tree answered. "Also known as Matthew Hanchon of Bighorn Falls in the Wyoming Territory."

It was true that there was a reward on Touch the Sky's head. Years before, Hiram Steele had announced that he would pay three thousand in gold, no questions asked, to the man who could deliver him the head of Matthew Hanchon. That offer still stood.

"Wyoming?" Poco Loco asked. "Big Tree, I never knew you for a fool. That is thousands of miles from here. You know me, red one. I have made too many gringo enemies. I will not cross the border—the Americans have a better record of tracking down their outlaws."

"You will need to go nowhere," the renegade assured him. "Hanchon is coming to us."

"Why?"

Big Tree grinned. "I tried to stab him. I missed. I hit his woman instead. He is a 'noble' warrior who will never let this crime stand. He is coming to kill me."

"And you fear him?" Poco Loco said incredulously. "You? One of the few men I consider an equal?"

"I fear him," Big Tree admitted. "And I feel no shame admitting it. This is the warrior who killed Iron Eyes."

This news forced new respect from Poco Loco. Iron Eyes, once Big Tree's bosom companion in crime, had been the leader of the Kaitsenko—the most elite group of Kiowa warriors.

Poco Loco nodded. "You are right to fear him, and only a fool would not. But, Big Tree, it takes an even bigger fool to come into Sonora with blood in his eyes."

Poco Loco glanced toward the dead man in the corner, then at the room full of well-armed, battle-scarred hard cases. "How many men is he bringing with him?" he demanded.

"He is alone."

Poco Loco poured out a shot for Big Tree. "That is sad indeed, for no man should die alone."

* * *

"There she is, sprout," Old Knobby announced as the two riders topped a low bluff. "The Río Bravo. Look at her. Damn near four hundred yards across right here, but she won't wet the horses' knees."

The great river marking the international border wound through the valley below them, creating narrow green strips of growth in the vast, arid expanse surrounding them.

"Watch," said Knobby as they let their horses set their own pace toward the water. "She looks muddy brown from here, but that water'll be clear as spring runoff when we're close."

He was right, Touch the Sky noticed. The water was so clear, and the current so slow, you could almost miss it when your face was close. Both men threw their bridles, Knobby loosing the claybank's girth, before they let the tired, hot mounts plunge their noses into the river.

Both men flopped onto their bellies and drank, then plunged their heads into the water. Touch the Sky shook his eyes clear and made a careful check in all directions. Even up north it was common news that Mexico, exasperated by Indian raids into their country from the United States, had stepped up patrols along the border. And they were dealing summarily with any illegals caught in their country—especially red illegals, for no one despised Indians more than the Mexicans.

Knobby, too, scouted the terrain as he gnawed on a strip of jerked buffalo. The hard pace showed around his haggard eyes, and the old-timer mounted and dismounted with noticeable grunts.

But Touch the Sky had been impressed with Knobby's trail skills and still-sharp senses.

"See anything?" Knobby demanded.

"Dust puffs," Touch the Sky said. "South by southeast. Still too far away to tell anything, though. Could be a herd of antelope."

"Could be," Knobby agreed. "But we had us a smooth trip down. Too smooth. Trouble never leaves either one of us alone that long. Get set for more, you red son of the plains."

Touch the Sky's shaman sense—a slight prickling in his nape—told him the same thing. But there was nothing else for it: They must ride toward those puffs. All signs and all reports pointed in that direction, for it was the path taken by Big Tree.

They rested briefly, mainly to let the horses graze the grass near the river. Knobby had told Touch the Sky that graze would soon be scarce to nonexistent. For this reason, the two men had swapped two steel knives and a fine buffalo robe for two sacks of corn at a Navajo village near Winrock. It would be rationed sparingly to their mounts.

An hour south of the Río Bravo, Knobby halted them and broke out his brass Cavalry binoculars. After studying the dust puffs for a full minute, he announced, "God-in-whirlwinds, boy! Here comes the fight! It's *federales*, I can tell from the brass plates on their kepis. Mebbe fifty of 'em, and they've got us in their sights! They'll be in range quicker 'n scat. We best pull foot."

"Hold on," Touch the Sky said. "You're the one

who always told me it's best to take trouble by the horns."

Knobby removed his flap hat and scratched the bald hide at his pate. "Fifty agin two? You damn Cheyennes have got fightin' fettle, I'll give you that any day. But, pup, they'll cut us to stew meat! A Mexer is a poor shot, but look around. We got no cover here."

"Won't need it," Touch the Sky insisted, pulling his Sharps out of its boot. "Doctor me up some cartridges, old coot. Buffalo loads. I want double loads of black powder, at least two hundred grains per load."

Knobby caught on instantly when his companion said buffalo loads. Even as the old trapper began to uncrimp some cartridges, he said, "Double load will give you range, for sure. But you'll lose accuracy. Raise your muzzle. I'll try to spot your shots."

Touch the Sky prepared his Sharps, loading one of the double-charged shots and placing a primer cap on the nib behind the hammer. Then he hastily leveled a spot in the sand and took up a prone position, laying his muzzle across a low, flat rock to steady it.

He sighted down the barrel toward the advancing dust puffs and fired.

"Good range!" Knobby shouted behind him. "But you got windage drift to your left."

Touch the Sky reloaded and adjusted his muzzle angle. At his next shot, Knobby loosed a whoop.

"*That*'ll learn the stupid sons a bitches to cluster up!" the old-timer gloated. "You dropped a horse,

Matthew! That's holdin' 'n' squeezin', boy!"

Several more shots did it. The advancing party, still stuck out of effective range of their weapons, would not risk death in this open terrain. They veered due east.

"You done 'er, Matthew," Knobby said as they secured their gear to resume the trek. "But that red devil Big Tree won't rabbit as easy as them federals just done."

"I hope you're right, old friend," Touch the Sky replied. "I didn't come down here to make Big Tree run. I came down here to kill him."

Chapter Six

Captain Salvador de la Fuentes was worried.

He rode at the head of two small columns of dragoons and lancers. Between the columns, each made up of ten soldiers, rumbled a big Mexican-made freight wagon known as a wheeled tarantula. The civilian teamster glanced all around them, sweat pouring from under his straw Sonora.

Captain de la Fuentes could not blame the driver for his nervous fidgeting. To their left rose the sawtooth peaks of the sierra known as the Bad Death Mountains. On their right was a series of basalt turrets, each capable of hiding a rider.

And the whole world knew that this was Poco Loco's territory.

It was hard enough duty, being stuck for years at a time at a godforsaken frontier outpost, chasing the shadows of Indians and fighting dysentery and boredom. But these road bandits . . . well, at least this time the military supply wagon was well-protected, the captain reminded himself. Double the usual number of men. And his lancers were the pride of the Mexican Army, having proved themselves again and again in hard campaigns against a tough American army. Any of them would die before they would retreat, never mind the odds.

They were coming to the worst stretch, a sandy wash that made it difficult for the horses to run.

De la Fuentes slewed around in his saddle and raised his fist. "Take up wide intervals!" he shouted down the line to his *teniente*. "Dragoons, fix bayonets!"

The officer eased his heavy French revolver from its stiff holster and laid it on his right thigh at the ready.

"Maldito!" Esteban cursed. "They have doubled their manpower, *jefe*. And look! Lancers. No men to fool with."

Poco Loco took the glasses from his lackey and studied the formation below. He, Esteban, and Big Tree were crouched behind a basalt formation. The rest of Poco Loco's men were spaced about them behind other formations.

"It looks bad," the bandit leader agreed. "I have never been one to earn my breakfast if I can get it by some easy way. This is no easy way. We had better let it be this time."

Big Tree, a mocking grin playing at his lips, didn't bother taking the glasses. "Amigo, you have lost your fire! Time was, you would drive Texas Rangers out of breastworks just for sport! But never mind. I will make it easy for you to steal your breakfast. Watch me, and see how a Comanche can take the fight to an enemy!"

Big Tree stripped his cayuse of all rigging, leaving his rifle with Poco Loco. He took only his osage-wood bow and two quivers stuffed with arrows. And what he did next left the Mexican thieves struck dumb with wonder.

The soldiers saw Big Tree approaching, his pony running a defensive zigzag pattern, while he was still out of easy range. Bouncing freely on the back of his galloping pony, holding on only with his powerful legs, the renegade grabbed a handful of arrows and strung them so fast that no one could count the shots.

His first lightning volley dropped horses and caused shrieks of human and animal pain. The lancers formed a skirmish line and charged. Big Tree dropped them like clay targets, not discriminating between man and horse.

This still left him one full quiver. By the time that, too, was emptied into the main formation, Poco Loco knew the odds were in his favor.

The battle was brief, more of a massacre than a fight. Poco Loco himself killed the officer, using his shotgun to turn the man's face into a red smear as the soldier lay wounded on the ground. Esteban went around to all the bodies, putting a finishing shot in each man's brain.

"Big Tree," Poco Loco declared, "having you around is like having a second gang."

However, his jubilation was short-lived, for the

pickings turned out to be slim. Yes, they could certainly use the food and coffee, as well as the medical supplies. But this shipment included no payroll cash and no liquor rations—the real reason for the strike.

Poco Loco stared at all the dead men, sprawled just as they had fallen. Soon the carrion birds would be picking their bones clean.

"This is the way it is," he complained to Big Tree. "I strike, I kill, I go away with spider leavings for my trouble. I need gold. Are you sure this noble Cheyenne is coming? This red man whose plew is worth three thousand?"

Big Tree was a long time answering. He studied the shimmering haze over the sierra, then looked at his old companion. "Am I sure he is coming? No, mad one. I am sure he is *here.*"

After diverting the advancing *federales*, Touch the Sky and Old Knobby veered to the southwest, keeping the Río Bravo always over their right shoulders. Through a combination of trail signs and careful questioning, they had determined Big Tree's general direction.

But there were many possible strongholds here at the vast frontier dividing the two young nations. Reaching some of them would entail laborious climbs up steep headlands, time-consuming treks through countless canyons.

"The moccasin telegraph does not end at the border," Touch the Sky told Knobby. "It can't because the tribes don't end. Which Indians live around here besides the Kiowas and Comanches and Navajos?"

"Papagos," Knobby said. "Some Pimas, Tewas, Yaquis. Some of 'em is Pueblo peoples, others've come up from the jungles down in Mex or even farther down, way the hell down."

Touch the Sky had heard of these tribes, but never met any of them. But Knobby had already told him, in the long hours they spent in the saddle and in camp at night, something about these southern tribes. Most of them were not as warlike as the northern tribes, and riding in this blazing sun, Touch the Sky could understand that. The year-round heat down here sapped a man of his fighting fettle.

He soon had his chance to meet a Mexican tribe. Toward midday on their third day past the border, the two friends rose up out of a long, deep arroyo. Before them sprawled an unwalled complex of adobe huts, crude pole corrals, and neatly cultivated fields irrigated with an *acequia madre*, or mother ditch, run off the nearby Río Bravo.

"Papago village," Knobby announced, pointing to the fine horseflesh in a corral. "The Papagos're natural-born horsemen, damn near as good as a Comanche."

"They friendly?" Touch the Sky asked.

"I wouldn't 'xactly say that. Cortez and the rest of them fish-eaters have left 'em leery of visitors, if you catch my drift. But they live and let live. We should be safe riding in under the peace sign."

Knobby was right. Several sun-coppered Indians working in the fields watched the two men suspiciously as they approached a group of men conferring over a broken wagon wheel they were repairing.

Judd Cole

Knobby greeted them in Spanish, and they nodded, greeting him back. Though the two men were not invited to dismount, a goatskin of cool well water was passed up to them. Both men drank. The Papagos looked curiously at Touch the Sky while he watched them. They were especially fascinated by the enemy scalps hanging from his sash. A few had obviously come from white men.

"Ask them," Touch the Sky told Knobby, "if they have heard anything about a stranger riding into this area. A big, fearsome Comanche. The one who commands the Wendigo Mountain stronghold."

Knobby spoke in rapid Spanish. The men seemed to understand him, but no one offered to speak.

"Tell them," Touch the Sky said, "that he is a murderer of women and children. Tell them he shoved cold steel into my woman's vitals. Tell them he has come to their land to kill their women and children. Tell them I have come from the land of the short white days, all this way to kill him. To make sure he never hurts another woman or child."

The Papagos were silent for a long time after Knobby translated all this, watching Touch the Sky. Finally, one of them spoke to Knobby. When he finished, the old trailsman turned to Touch the Sky.

"This one says they have nothing to go on but your word. But he says he has looked deep into your eyes and seen the soul of an honorable man. He believes you. He also tells me you have strong medicine, and that if he defies it, bad dreams will

68

be placed over his eyes. He asked if you are called a shaman."

Touch the Sky met the man's eyes and nodded.

"He says," Knobby continued, "that the man you want is said to be in Santa Rosa. That's ten miles past here, a little *pueblito* way the hell up a mountainside. Says Big Tree has thrown in with a hardcase *jefe* by the name of Poco Loco."

Touch the Sky nodded again. He reached into his pannier, drew out a pouch filled with rich white man's tobacco, and gave it to the Indian who had spoken. Before they rode off, the man added something else.

"What'd he say?" Touch the Sky asked.

Knobby scowled. "Said to tell you, best cover your ass. The *gobernador* of Sonora has offered a two-hundred-peso bounty on the scalps of wild Indians. That's how come these is all wearin' their hair so short—so's scalpers can't get holt of it."

"I appreciate the warning," Touch the Sky said. "Maybe I'll even cut my hair. But for right now, let's make tracks toward Santa Rosa. I want to get the lay of the place. Then I mean to strike right off. We have to let Big Tree know, right from the jump, that he's got no place to hide. And that goes for anybody who tries to help him."

Poco Loco's mood improved considerably as the day advanced and the level in his tequila bottle steadily went down.

"I say it now, compadres," he called out to his men, most of whom surrounded him at the little deal tables of the Three Sisters cantina. "We did not become rich men today. But did you see this red killing machine? *Qué destreza!* What skill in the killing arts! Big Tree, I have seen the gringo circus in Texas. Their trick shooters on trained ponies could not stand in your shadow."

Big Tree nodded slightly, acknowledging the praise. But he kept a careful eye on Poco Loco. The man was like the Spaniards—one hand extended in friendship while the other always hid a knife.

However, the canny renegade had indeed figured one thing right: Poco Loco might be treacherous, but he was also cunning. Big Tree wanted him to appreciate his warrior skills—which were also, of course, a bandit's skills. If Poco Loco thought Big Tree might make him rich, he would protect him like the Virgin Mary.

And protection was what Big Tree needed. He was sure, deep down in his bone marrow, that Touch the Sky was out there. Right now. Watching, waiting, biding his time until the perfect moment. Big Tree could kill him, but he must buy time.

A sudden scuffling of chairs, and abrupt female shrieking, made both men look toward the back corner. Esteban and several of the men had been drinking heavily since the raid on the army supply caravan. A flash of snow-white skin and red-lace petticoat told them what was happening to the young woman who served tables.

Poco Loco shouted to get their attention. "Esteban, I have told you before, this building was once a chapel. None of that inside. Take her out into the courtyard."

Big Tree grinned as the men dragged the protesting woman outside. "No one can say you lack a sense of propriety, my friend."

Poco Loco grinned. "There is very little I—we—will lack, my Comanche friend, once I unleash you on the Camino Real. Some of the merchant trains bound for Durango·and Aguascalientes have only five or six private guards. However, it takes money to make money. My men need weapons, new rigs, liquor. I am starting to believe you are waiting for a chimera. You said this Cheyenne is already among us, but what? Is he like God himself, everywhere felt but nowhere seen? I have neither seen him nor felt his presence."

Big Tree was about to reply when a sound like a shriek of the damned made both men flinch. Poco Loco even dropped his glass into his lap.

The hell-spawned scream was followed, after a brief, shocked silence, by a mad confusion of shouts and curses.

"Amigo," Big Tree said calmly. "You have not yet seen him, and it will be some time before you do. But one of your men has just felt him."

Poco Loco pushed away from the table and stumbled outside. Big Tree, still grinning, followed more slowly. He was not surprised by what they found.

A man, his trousers still tangled around his legs, lay dead in the *plaza mayor*, or main square. An arrow slanted at a forty-five-degree angle through his head, having entered behind the right ear and exited through the left eye socket.

"Look, Poco Loco," Big Tree called out merrily. "The arrow is fletched with crow feathers. Only one tribe fletches with crow feathers. Guess which tribe that is. And now some advice. Cover down, if you value life itself. From now on, keep a wall behind you and a tree on both sides."

Big Tree glanced up toward the grainy darkness of the mountains surrounding them. Then he looked at Poco Loco and noticed that the hardened killer was shocked sober.

"More will die," Big Tree said. "But we can kill him. And the gold for his head will outfit us for the King's Highway and a life of riches."

"We can kill him," Poco Loco agreed. "And we will. But much slower than Francisco here died. I will bury him under the sun up to his neck and then slice off his eyelids. An eye for an eye. Only then will your Senor Hiram Steele get the head."

Chapter Seven

"Look at them," Medicine Flute gloated, nodding across the wide central clearing. "Keeping vigil for their noble red man."

Wolf Who Hunts Smiling and the rest of the Bullwhips, gathered in a council circle just outside Medicine Flute's tipi, nodded at these words. But in fact, many of the people around Touch the Sky's tipi were merely visitors coming with little presents for Honey Eater and her child.

"With luck," Wolf Who Hunts Smiling chipped in, "their long vigil will finally be rewarded by the return of his bones. If I have reckoned Big Tree right, this time White Man Runs Him is riding to the last battle."

"I could only wish," Medicine Flute said, "that he might have suffered the agony of seeing his woman die before him."

"Never mind her," said Crow Killer, leader of the Bullwhip Soldiers. "We will have a free hand with her and their whelp after the tall one is gone under. I mean to take her out on the prairie."

Crow Killer was referring to the ancient custom frowned upon by many. Men in authority could declare a woman tainted and "take her out on the prairie"—that is, any man who wanted to was welcome to top her. After this, the shamed woman always killed herself, for there could be no place for her in the tribe. And an Indian without a tribe was a dead Indian.

"Look there," Wolf Who Hunts Smiling said. "Here comes Two Twists again, anxious to report the latest news about Touch the Sky learned from the moccasin telegraph. See? Even now he is running over to Little Horse with it. You can see from the glad light in his face that the tall one still has breath in his nostrils."

"Patience, Panther Clan," Crow Killer cautioned the Wolf. "Killing Touch the Sky will take time. How long have all of us been trying? How many times have we failed? Big Tree can do it, but give him some time."

Medicine Flute had been mulling something while the rest talked. Suddenly a canny glow came into his eyes. He had been absently blowing on his leg-bone flute while he thought. Now he laid his instrument aside and addressed the others.

"Brothers! Have ears. I am keen for a little sport. Why wait for Big Tree? How would you enjoy watching Honey Eater's face, not to mention the faces of Touch the Sky's men, when they learn he has been killed? And even better, how would you like to convince Touch the Sky, before he dies in the south country, that his woman is dead?"

Wolf Who Hunts Smiling frowned impatiently. "What, are we girls playing let's pretend in our sewing lodge? I call you shaman only to fool the fools, bone blower. Have you grown to believe in your own false magic?"

"Magic?" Medicine Flute scoffed. "Add magic to an empty gun, and you are a dead man. Never mind magic, Panther Clan. Only think. How do our enemies get their news about their noble champion?"

Wolf Who Hunts Smiling was impatient, with a hair-trigger temper. But he was also wily and quick. Almost immediately after Medicine Flute's question, the Wolf's lupine grin spread across his face.

"Of course," he said softly. "The moccasin telegraph."

Medicine Flute's fleshy lips formed a triumphant smirk. "As you say, buck. Crow Killer can pick one of his best soldiers. He can tell the Headmen he needs to send the man out for an extended scout. That man rides deep into the south country. Once there, he sends up false smoke."

"And false smoke blows both ways," Wolf Who Hunts Smiling said. "Our man down south sends up word of Touch the Sky's death. Meantime, up here, we send up smoke saying that Honey Eater died from her wound after all. And truly, she had not come sassy yet before he left. There is often a fatal fever after a false healing."

This was indeed a stroke of genius, and the rest congratulated Medicine Flute for his inventiveness. As for Wolf Who Hunts Smiling, in his secret heart of hearts, he was not at all convinced that Big Tree could indeed kill Touch the Sky. But something like this could. In his agony, Touch the Sky would lose focus, would let the red-hot emotions govern the cold killer. And against a foe like Big Tree, one mistake was all it took to send a man to sleep with the worms.

"Pick a good man," the Wolf ordered Crow Killer. "Tell him to take a good string of horses with him and to ride hard. Send him to my lodge before he rides out. I want to be sure he has the message right. Big Tree's knife did not kill Honey Eater. But we will watch her die inside when she hears her bull has been felled."

"As you say," Medicine Flute agreed. "And when our false smoke about her death blows south, the misery you see in her face will be reflected in his."

Touch the Sky and Knobby had made a fairly dry, if somewhat cool, camp in a cave high in the mountains above Santa Rosa. From the mouth of the cave, they could see the little pueblo spread out below in a teacup-shaped hollow. The night before, Touch the Sky had crawled down about five hundred feet from the cave to launch the deadly shot that killed one of Big Tree's companions.

Knowing their survival depended on staying in motion, the two friends had quit the cave the very next morning, moving to a well-hidden cleft in the caprock. Sure enough, Big Tree and one of the Mexicans—a bear of a man with a livid scar covering half of his face—had come searching the area and located the cave.

"I could draw a bead on them now," Touch the Sky said almost wishfully, watching them from behind a shoulder of lava rock.

"You could," Knobby agreed. "And then we'd be gone beaver on account it's flush of day and there ain't nothin' behind us but cliffs. They'd come up here to flush us, sure as hell's afire."

Reluctantly, Touch the Sky nodded. It was good to hold the high ground, but not when you had no escape trail. Besides, he wanted to make Big Tree sweat a little. A quick kill would let him off too light. He needed to see death happening all around him, closing in on him. Touch the Sky wanted him to suffer from night sweats, frazzled nerves, the kind of pressure that drove a man mad with worry. Only then would he grant him the dog's death he deserved.

Tell me how you die, Arrow Keeper had once said, *and I will tell you what you're worth.*

"Well begun is half done," Knobby assured his young companion. "That kill last night, Matthew, was a good start. But they're forted up down there. That must be Poco Loco with Big Tree, and he looks about half rough. Plus look at them houses— loopholed for rifles. Ten men could hold off a regiment. What we got to do, we got to make it hot for 'em around here. We got to make 'em break and run. We get 'em in a running fight, we got mebbe half a chance."

Touch the Sky nodded, watching the two men below as they began to return to Santa Rosa.

"You're right, old trooper. We have to make it

77

hot for them. Too hot to hang around here. We can't rush that town, but we can sure as hell sneak in after dark. We're going to pay Big Tree and his Mexican friends a friendly little visit tonight."

The night after Francisco's head was skewered by an arrow, the streets and plaza of Santa Rosa were deserted.

The local citizens, long subjugated by cut-throats and tyrants, knew only that yet another battle was being waged with their town as the site. They were used to staying indoors after darkness anyway, to avoid the depredations of Poco Loco's drunken men.

Poco Loco, however, fumed at the humiliation of being locked down in his own stronghold. He had the windows of the Three Sisters cantina re-inforced with stout boards and posted sentries on the rooftops of the town.

"I am glad to see you, 'mano," Poco Loco informed Big Tree over a hand of faro. "Truly glad you have returned to the country where we notched our first kills. But you have brought a smallpox blanket back with you in this Cheyenne cur."

Big Tree tossed down a card. "I spent much of this day looking for sign. I found very little. But we must continue to try flushing him out by day. That, and maintain absolute vigilance by night."

Even as Big Tree fell silent, one of the sentries called out the all clear. The rest followed suit.

"Full moon tonight," Poco Loco remarked. "And up here in the mountains, every night is brilliant with stars. Also, I have told my men to keep brush fires burning at both ends of the town. A mouse would have trouble entering this town unobserved."

Big Tree said nothing to this, only sliding his big, steel-framed .44 from its holster and checking the loads. Watching him, Poco Loco nervously slid his sawed-off scattergun from its hip sling and laid it across the table.

"You think he will sneak in anyway?" Poco Loco asked.

Big Tree thumbed his hammer to half-cock. "Do I think he *will*? No. I think he is already here."

A harsh bark of laughter was Poco Loco's only response. But in the long, unbroken silence that followed, the big Mexican's face began to sweat.

He glanced around the dimly lighted interior. The old man who owned the place cowered behind the short plank counter, wishing they would go away. An old local, almost toothless, sat nursing a bowl of beans and tortillas in the back corner. With men on sentry duty, the place was almost deserted.

Outside, an owl hooted. Slowly, Big Tree let his chair settle forward onto its front legs. Poco Loco watched his face.

"What?" the Mexican demanded. "It was only an owl."

"Was it, crazy one? And how many owls have you noticed making their nests up here in the mountains instead of down in the forested valleys?"

Poco Loco said nothing. Outside, the owl hoot sounded again, but it seemed to have moved slightly.

"Should we go outside?" he asked Big Tree.

The Comanche shook his head. "No need to go looking for your own grave."

Slowly, methodically, with the infinite patience of a warrior focused on nothing but victory, Touch the Sky made his way carefully down the side of the mountain.

He had left Knobby to the important task of caring for their ponies, which were hidden in a grassy barranca perhaps a mile across the nearest ridge. Touch the Sky had stripped down to his clout and his moccasins, taking no weapon but his obsidian knife.

The moonlight made vision easy, but also exposed him. He had darkened his body with mud first. Still, he stuck to cover as much as possible as he eased into the little pueblo.

He knew sentries would be posted and that he had to locate them. Luckily, the drunken scouts were undisciplined. Before long he had spotted the guards, for each of them carelessly skylighted himself.

Touch the Sky calculated which of the sentries would be easiest to reach from his present position. Before he set out, an image surfaced in his mind, the image of Honey Eater lying on the ground, her lifeblood seeping out around the haft of Big Tree's knife.

Big Tree. Why not make a nervous sweat break out all over that red tyrant?

Softly but clearly, Touch the Sky made the sound of the owl hoot. These debauched *pistoleros* would pay it little attention. But Big Tree would know exactly what it meant.

Again Touch the Sky watched the silhouetted figure atop the house just to his right. Then, after briefly touching the medicine pouch on his clout, the Cheyenne began low-crawling toward the house.

Chapter Eight

Chapter Eight

"Bless my ass," grumbled Victorio Robles, rolling out of the warm nest of his bedroll.

He had just been kicked awake so that he could begin his stint of guard duty on the roofs. *Maldito*, but it was cold up here in the mountains at night! He shivered as he stepped into his boots and buckled on his leather gunbelt.

Victorio and several other men had confiscated a little house a stone's throw away from the cantina in Santa Rosa. The rightful owners had been forced to move in with relatives across the plaza— Poco Loco was the only "law" in this territory, so whatever his deputies did was legal.

Victorio's head still throbbed from his drunk of the night before. But he took a hair off the dog, lifting a bottle of mescal to his lips and drinking his breakfast. Thus fortified for guard duty, he stumbled out into the grainy predawn darkness.

Santa Rosa was as still and quiet as a graveyard. Thin pockets of mist floated in the streets like silent ghosts, and behind the mountains in the east the first hint of sunrise lightened the sky. A dog howled mournfully at the edge of town, and Victorio could hear his boots scraping in the dirt.

Peaceful enough. All this panic over one Indian who made a lucky shot. Victorio shrugged. *Indios* were pissants. The priests claimed they did not have souls. Without a soul, one could not show courage or great skill as a warrior.

He arrived at an adobe house at the outskirts of the village.

"Roberto," he called to the man up on the roof. "Throw down the ladder."

There was no response.

Victorio raised his voice. "Roberto, you fool! If Poco Loco finds out you fell asleep on guard duty, he will flay your soles. *Eres un necio?* Are you a fool? Now, throw down the ladder!"

Still nothing. The fool wasn't just asleep, Victorio realized. He must also be drunk.

Cursing, Victorio went inside the deserted house and scrounged around until he found an old piece of rope. He went back outside and managed to toss the rope around one of the vigas, the logs that protruded from the top edge of the adobe.

"You son of a worthless whore, Roberto," he muttered as he hauled himself up the wall. Such exertion, with a hangover, made his stomach flutter with nausea.

"You stinking sot!" Victorio pulled himself up

onto the roof. He glanced around until he spotted Roberto, curled up in sleep at the far corner of the roof. "Wake up, you worthless dungheap," Victorio barked, crossing to the sentry and kicking him in the leg.

Nothing. Growling with irritation, Victorio reached down, gripped Roberto's jacket, and tugged him around onto his back.

"*¡Ay Dios!*"

Shock slammed into Victorio like a body blow, and he made the sign of the cross. He leaped backward, his breath snagging in his throat.

Roberto's head lolled back as if connected to his neck by only a string. His throat gaped open in a raw, red, obscene grin of death. The stench of death fouled the air.

Most shocking of all, however, was the gaping hole in Roberto's chest where the Cheyenne had quite literally ripped out his heart.

"But, *jefe*," complained an agitated Esteban, speaking for the rest of the men. "That red bastard tore Roberto's heart from his very chest! *Madre de Dios!* It is still missing. He is a demon from hell, and I say he ate that heart!"

"He did not eat it," Big Tree said quietly—so quietly that the rest gathered around the Tres Hermanas ignored him. They were busy staring at Poco Loco, waiting for his response.

The leader of the pistoleros was unsure how to handle this thing. Here it was, barely after sunrise. He *should* be sound asleep until at least noon. Then he would usually have a woman or a girl brought to his bed for some fun.

Instead, this flea-bitten blanket ass from up north had disrupted his life completely. Poco Loco was starting to feel the warmth of a slow-simmering rage.

"He has killed two of us in two days," Victorio chimed in, his face still drained of color after the discovery of Roberto's corpse. "I am no coward—I fixed bayonets against the gringos at Cerro Gordo! But this now, it is different. Tonight, when the sun goes down, who will be the next to die?"

"And why has he been able to kill again?" Poco Loco asked. "Are you by-God men or a bunch of *perfumados*? He never should have been allowed into town in the first place."

"Must we stop the wind from blowing, too?" Esteban demanded. "This *indio* moves like a shadow."

Poco Loco's deadly scattergun was up in a moment, both muzzles staring at Esteban.

"Is the cow bellowing to the bull?" the *jefe* asked, quiet menace marking his tone.

"Look at both of you," Big Tree scoffed. "Doing exactly what the Cheyenne wants you to do—acting like a bunch of panicked women."

Poco Loco frowned so deeply, his shaggy eyebrows met. "You are the one who brought this curse in among us, Big Tree."

"Yes, and I will kill him. And then you will profit from the kill, for the money is yours. But all of you must show your courage. He is deliberately working at us, driving a wedge between us. If we let him succeed, he will destroy us. But if we get into lockstep and stay there, he is worm fodder."

Poco Loco took heart at these words. "Big Tree

is right. This fight is ours to win. Today we will scour the hills around this town. If he is holed up anywhere near here, we will rout him!"

Esteban and the rest seemed to draw a little comfort from their *jefe*'s confidence.

"Now you're acting like men with stones on them," Poco Loco approved, throwing his fiber morral onto the table. "Good liquor for all! I have a bottle of officer's whiskey, taken from the saddlebags of that *capitán* we killed yesterday."

The men cheered, for everybody knew the best whiskey in Mexico was reserved for the army. Poco Loco pulled a bottle out, then immediately frowned.

The bottle felt greasy. He looked closer and saw that the dark brown glass was covered with blood! Only now did he notice that the sack, too, was stained with wetness. Poco Loco turned it over on the table, and something wet and solid plopped out. He glanced at it in curiosity for only a moment, then felt the gorge rise in his throat when he realized it was Roberto's missing heart!

About midmorning, with their shadows slanting slightly west, Knobby called out, "Here they come!"

Touch the Sky, busy rigging something over the narrow opening of their limestone cave, spoke without turning around.

"Let 'em. We won't bother to cover the sign we were here. I know Big Tree. He'll make sure one of the Mexicans goes in the cave first."

"Just mind your business there," Knobby warned him. "That-ere snake gets loose, you'll git

a heap more 'n just sick. That's a Sonora rattler—
twice the pizen as the American rattler. Saw a
feller up and bit by one near Copper Canyon. That
poor hoss swole up big as a hog 'fore he croaked."

"Shut your damn mouth," Touch the Sky
snapped, nervous sweat oozing at Knobby's vivid
description. Knobby had caught the snake by
crawling out into some sunny rocks just after daylight. It was trapped in a thin piece of hide that
had been quickly folded over on it and stitched
shut with an awl and sinew. Then, working
through the cloth, they clipped off the tiny rattler.
And several chunks of jerked meat had been
shoved into the pouch too, so whoever found it
would think it was a food cache and open it
quickly.

He hid it well enough to look like a cache, but
not so well that it would not be easy to find.

"There," he said, backing out of the cave. "With
a little luck, that's three men down."

"Ahuh," Knobby said, his voice grim. "And with
a little o' the wrong luck, we'll be looking up at
daisies! They're formin' into three search parties
right now. Big Tree and two Mexicans leading
'em."

"No more cold camps up here," Touch the Sky
decided as he gathered up his kit and rigging.
"We'll get the horses and keep them with us from
here on out."

Knobby watched him shrewdly. Below, some of
the men were already fanning into the foothills.

"I see which way the wind sets," Knobby finally
said. "You wouldn't be keeping the horses 'lessen

Judd Cole

you expected a running battle. You mean to drive them out of Santa Rosa?"

Touch the Sky nodded. "We can pick away at them, but you see how it is. With them forted up, we'll run out of camps around here. Put them on the run, they're bound to slip up."

The old trapper looked a little doubtful, but he nodded nonetheless. "Every major battle in history was won with either a quick slaughter or a running fight. I 'spect thissen won't be no different."

"No," Touch the Sky said quietly, jacking a round into the chamber of his rifle and watching the searchers move up from the valley. "No different at all."

"God-*damn* that whoreson Indian!" Poco Loco fumed, watching his man Benito writhe in the dirt like a man in a seizure.

"The poison is working on his brain already," Big Tree said casually, sliding his big .44 from the holster and thumbing it back to full cock. Esteban started to object, but Big Tree coolly blew a hole through Benito's pomaded head.

The snake had escaped into the cave when the men leaped back from the entrance.

"I noticed," Poco Loco said, his eyes slanting toward Big Tree, "how you fell back and let Benito go in first."

Big Tree grinned. "I'll send a priest to console his widow. Nor did I see you rush forward to save your man."

Poco Loco, despite his surly mood, could not help grinning at Big Tree's brutal honesty. This

88

was a man who gave it to you raw and real, with the bark still on it. That is why, despite their mutual animosity and distrust, they had always admired each other.

But the men . . . they had never tangled with Indians from the north country, proud Indians who perhaps knew too much of warfare.

"Big Tree," he said quietly while some of the others dug a grave for Benito. "We may have to flee this place. I have another stronghold. It is in a better position. I am for staying right here. But the men—once it reaches a certain point, they must either be given something to do or they will rebel. You know that?"

The Comanche thought about this. "And if we are in motion, he too must be in motion. That exposes us, but he must take more chances too."

"*Preciso*. However, this place—it is a hard climb to reach it. I will wait one more night here in Santa Rosa and see if our noble red man strikes again."

Chapter Nine

"The place is called San Sebastian," Poco Loco explained as he banged open the door of an iron stove and stirred the embers to life with an old broom handle. "I holed up there once during the war. So remote the place has never been sacked."

"Remote won't matter," Big Tree objected. "If an eagle can get to it, so can Touch the Sky."

"He can get to it, of course. But he will have to show himself to do it. He will have to cross a vast *jornada*, then climb through barren pinnacles. Unlike this place, which sets low and offers cover all around, San Sebastian is atop a long, barren spine of mountains."

Poco Loco lifted the lid from a blue-enameled coffeepot and tossed in a piece of eggshell to boil with the beans. He set it on the flat iron top of the stove. Both men had holed up in the reinforced cantina with a sentry outside all night long.

"San Sebastain was made from heavy stone," Poco Loco said. "Those buildings will be there when God retires."

"And the residents? They will not fight?"

Poco Loco, busy breaking open his scattergun to check the loads, looked at the Comanche and smiled. "There is the beauty of it, compadre. There are no residents. The people who lived there were inordinately fond of dogs. Kept hundreds of them around. Then rabies swept through the region, and the people were either killed or driven off. The place is so remote, no one has settled there again."

Big Tree considered all this as he huddled under his sleeping robe, waiting for the stove's warmth to penetrate the chill. "It might do," he finally agreed. "But it would be better if we could kill the Cheyenne right here."

"If pigs had wings, they could fly, amigo." Poco Loco snapped closed the breech of his gun and dropped it into its special sling over his hip. "I told you yesterday, I do not look forward to this flight. I would rather kill him here, too. But you see how it is with the men. They will rebel if I simply force them to sit here in this hollow while we are picked off like beef cattle."

A sudden scuffing of gravel outside made Big Tree swing up from his robes, big-framed .44 in his fist.

Poco Loco laughed. "Lower your hammer, Quohada! It is only Esteban. He is calling out the men for roll call. I want to be sure our sneaky friend did not come calling in the night."

Poco Loco poured coffee into a pottery mug.

"Three men he has killed so far, Big Tree. You are right that a run to San Sebastian will expose us. But we are clearly vulnerable anyway, yet the Cheyenne is not. The effort will be worth it if his head is truly worth so much gold."

Outside, Esteban called out, "Lupe!"

"Yo!"

"Ernesto!"

"Present!"

"You know," Big Tree said quietly, "the Cheyenne is not alone? There is one other man with him."

Poco Loco stopped his cup halfway to his lips and stared at the other man. "Amigo, you are like the whores in Mexico City, you know that? You name one price when you show your tits, another when you remove your skirts. You did not tell me all this at once, for you knew I would tell you to pull stakes and keep riding. So, what about this second man?"

"I know only that he wears leather boots and his feet slew outward when he walks, like a hair-face, not an Indian. I found prints they did not bother to hide."

As he heard the men answer to roll call outside, Poco Loco's somber face began to relax. "Well, we will take what good news we can. At least it sounds like the men are all accounted for—he did not strike in the night. Perhaps we will not have to flee this place after all."

Outside, Esteban shouted, "Manuel?"

Dead silence.

"Manuel? Manuel Torres?"

Silence, as thick and deep as the folds around a

country graveyard. Poco Loco and Big Tree exchanged a long glance.

"Is Manuel a heavy sleeper?" Big Tree asked.

Poco Loco frowned. "The man is always up with the birds."

Big Tree nodded, seeing how things stood. "He will not be getting up this morning," he said quietly. "And we will be riding for San Sebastian."

Touch the Sky and Knobby did not risk another camp after the discovery of their previous one. Instead, they simply stayed in motion, keeping their horses immediately to hand and taking turns sleeping in two-hour shifts while one of them stayed on guard. This way the horses continued to graze fresh grass and get plenty of rest for the ordeal both men knew was coming.

"They know about victim number four by now," Knobby said. "That'll tear it, you watch. You'll get your wish. They'll be pulling foot today."

Touch the Sky nodded. The two of them sat behind the cover of a sandstone shoulder well above Santa Rosa. They could see, in the gathering sunlight, men milling about in the plaza below.

"They'll ride," he agreed. "Big Tree won't just sit and wait. He's smart enough to know he has to use natural advantages. They'll ride to some spot where we can't use ground cover and high ground against them."

"Ain't just Big Tree," Knobby said. "We got to worry about the pepper-gut, too, the one called Poco Loco. You saw them Injuns' eyes when they said his name. I got a good look at his ugly, scarred pan yestiddy. 'At sumbich is crazy as dogs in the hot moon."

Knobby lapsed into a moody silence for a spell, gnawing on a cold biscuit he'd been saving in his possibles bag. Both men looked rough. The need to stay in motion kept them exhausted, yet old Knobby steadfastly refused to do less than a man's share. If Touch the Sky tried to let him sleep more than two hours, the old man would come awake on his own, grumbling about ignorant savages who couldn't keep white man's time. Like all mountain men, he believed a man had to pull his own freight so long as he walked the earth.

"Sprout," he said now, cautiously. "You 'member a saying your pa likes? One about the pitcher and the well?"

Touch the Sky thought for a minute, running through a list of John Hanchon's favorite sayings. Then he grinned. "Sure. 'The pitcher can go once too often to the well.'"

Knobby nodded. "That's the one. I just wunner— you think maybe you're doin' that now? I mean, by killin' off them Mexers one by one before you do for Big Tree? Ain't the point to kill him, not these others?"

Touch the Sky said nothing, mulling the old man's words. After all, the point *was* to rid the world of Big Tree. He was letting his rage over Honey Eater's ordeal color his motives. But what if he did go once too often to the well? What if he was killed hacking at a branch, while the root— Big Tree—escaped damage?

"A warrior," Knobby added, "is 'sposed to stay

frosty and shoot plumb. You kill from the head, not the gut."

Finally, Touch the Sky nodded. "You're right, old-timer. Revenge shouldn't even enter the mix. Never mind tormenting Big Tree. Let's kill that red son of the Wendigo and get the hell out of here."

But even Knobby, who had spent plenty of time south of the Rio Grande, had forgotten what the country to the west of them was like. Touch the Sky's new resolve to kill Big Tree without delay was rendered meaningless by the more immediate problem of staying alive themselves.

The Jornada del Muerto, or Desert of Death, stretched for an unrelenting eighty miles. Old Knobby had wisely made crude sunshades for men and horses, fashioning them out of rawhide flaps with eye slits in them. These proved indispensable, for the white alkali sand and broad gypsum flats reflected an unrelenting glare, one that could drive men and beasts mad if unprotected.

The terrain was hard on the horses. Loose sand taxed their ankles and drifted over sharp-edged rocks and shale that could trip them up and cut them. Water was scarce, and only the survival skills of a hard life spent on the frontier saved the two friends. Old streambeds that seemed bone dry could yield a little water if you dug into them a few feet; the hollow tops of boulders that never saw sunlight often held pools of rainwater.

There was also the problem of visibility.

Finding sign was no problem, for their enemies were not trying to hide their movements. The pursuers had kept a respectful distance, following the boiling cloud of dust. But as they had feared, snipers were left behind in wallows to rise up and shoot at them. One bullet had sliced through Touch the Sky's rigging, spooking his coyote dun. About an hour later, a surprise sniper killed one of the ponies on Knobby's string.

"That does it," Touch the Sky announced. His lips were set in the tight line that foretold an enemy's death. "Time to play a trick I learned from Big Tree himself."

Working quickly, Touch the Sky and Knobby gathered enough wiry palomilla grass to stuff a crude buckskin suit. They put the fake rider up on the dun and tied it down.

"Just keep riding west," Touch the Sky directed, cutting a fast little roan off his string. He swung up onto its back and laid his Sharps across the withers. "I'll be back."

First he rode due east, backtracking. Then he cut north, pushing the spirited mustang to a powerful gallop. When he guessed he might be somewhere behind the next sniper's position, Touch the Sky reined in his pony and hobbled it behind a craggy mound of rocks.

He did not bother with concealed movement. Others out ahead might spot him, so he concentrated only on speed as his eyes desperately swept the deep browns and parched yellows of the arid terrain.

There! He had just spotted a glint of reflection off to his left. A moment later he grinned, thanking the Mexican male's love of hammered silver: A man was hunkered in a wallow, drawing a bead on the distant figures approaching. It was the silver conchos on his sombrero that gave him away.

Touch the Sky had no idea if the sniper was dropping a bead on the dummy rider or Old Knobby. The Cheyenne didn't waste a moment. First, he unleashed a shrill war cry to interrupt the Mexican's shot.

The man whirled, bringing the muzzle of a carbine with him. Touch the Sky squeezed his trigger, then heard the most sickening sound in the world, bad powder fizzling in his primer load!

The Mexican's carbine barked at the same moment Touch the Sky twisted in midair, minimizing the target. The bullet burned across his chest like a white-hot wire of pain, opening a thin line of blood. The Mexican jacked in another round even as Touch the Sky leaped, swinging his rifle like a war club.

The solid wood stock caught him on the point of the jaw, rocking his head back hard and knocking his sombrero off. Touch the Sky wrenched the carbine from him, tapped the muzzle into his chest, and fired point blank. The Mexican's heels were still scratching the dirt as the Cheyenne raced back toward Knobby.

"That's five down," Knobby greeted him with a poker face. "But I'm guessing it wasn't Big Tree you done for?"

Touch the Sky shook his head, gazing ahead toward that roiling cloud of dust on the horizon.

"No," he answered. "I can make all the vows I want to. But Big Tree has his own plans, and mainly he plans to be the last one to die."

Chapter Ten

Meantime, far to the north in the Powder River country, Medicine Flute's treacherous plan was being carried out.

Crow Killer, leader of the Bullwhip soldier society, picked two good riders. One was sent far south to the red-rock country, the other about half that distance. Both were to send up false smoke messages—one intended to travel south for Touch the Sky, the other north for the Cheyenne camp.

Naturally, the lie was received up north first, for that rider had less distance to travel. Soon after the camp crier raced through the paths, shouting the news of Touch the Sky's death, his worst tribal enemies had gathered at Medicine Flute's tipi.

"Did you hear, brothers?" gloated a triumphant Wolf Who Hunts Smiling. "Did you hear it? When his she-bitch Honey Eater heard of it, the women of her clan were forced to surround her. Even now they are watching her. Only the constant reminder of her child has restrained her from falling on a knife."

"Even better," added Crow Killer, "is watching the stunned look on the faces of Little Horse, Two Twists, and Tangle Hair. His men look like drunks who have woken up in the wrong country! Even now they are huddled in Little Horse's tipi, crying in each other's arms."

"They are not crying," Wolf Who Hunts Smiling corrected him. "Not those three. They are laying plans. But let them. We are safe. Without their think-piece, Touch the Sky, they are helpless. Too, we are far away from the supposed crime, and they have no cause to draw blood in camp."

"It would be worth a little blood," Medicine Flute said. "The pleasure of seeing their faces, of hearing his whore cry out to the holy ones, has been worth it. I only hope our little trick turns out to be no fooling. That is up to Big Tree."

Wolf Who Hunts Smiling nodded. "Only one pleasure could be greater, and we must miss seeing it. I mean when White Man Runs Him reads sign that his woman is supposedly dead. Bucks, he will make a groan from his soul that could make a dead man weep with pity."

"I tell you, *'manos*," said the *pistolero* named Ernesto. "It was I who found Luis. I tell you this—whatever struck his jaw hit with such force it snapped the head back hard enough to break his neck!"

"This *indio*," Ricardo said, "cannot be a mere

mortal. Has anyone seen him? Five times he has come among us and killed, yet who has seen him?"

"Yes," said Juan. "He is invisible and he has supernatural strength—the strength of ten men! This Big Tree, he has brought a northern devil in among us!"

Five of the remaining *pistoleros* had gathered in a little circle during a brief rest. Earlier, a sandstorm from Mexico's interior plateau had pelted them in a yellow wall of fury. Now a hot sphere of merciless sun blazed overhead, relentlessly driving the temperature up into triple digits. Sweat poured through the grime on their faces, making little mud streaks.

Esteban had been passing close enough to hear the last remarks. *"Vaya!"* he exclaimed. "Don't be fools. Would a supernatural devil have to use Luis's own weapon against him? This Cheyenne, he is a good killer, yes. But he was born of woman, hombres, and he can die like any man."

"Perhaps," Ricardo responded. "But he can kill better than most."

Esteban shook his head like a man who had seen the big animal. He nodded across the barren flat to the place where Big Tree and Poco Loco were hunkered in parley.

"So can Big Tree," Esteban said. "I was with him and Poco Loco when that Comanche shot out the eye of a Texas Ranger with an arrow at five hundred yards. The left eye—he did it on a bet."

"That was a Texas Ranger," Juan said. "No men to fool with, yet men you can *see*. How do you shoot the eye out of a man who never shows himself?"

Desert Manhunt

Esteban turned to stare into the windswept wasteland behind them. "He will show himself," he predicted confidently. "And when he does, the readiness is all."

"He won't get another one of us," Poco Loco swore with grim determination as he mopped sweat from his face with a limp, filthy bandanna.

He pointed due west. "See those two pinnacles rising side by side? San Sebastian lies between them. We will be there by nightfall if we encounter no more sandstorms."

"It is not sandstorms that worry me," Big Tree replied, casting a sideways glance toward the little knot of men. "Are you sure of your men?"

Poco Loco scowled. "Esteban is a good man, he will keep them bunched. But I do not blame them for scheming. You rode in among us singing songs of easy gold. Now, five dead comrades later, we see the gold is not so easy."

"Your 'comrades,'" Big Tree said sarcastically, "are shiftless, down-at-the-heels criminals who would shoot their own mothers for a plugged peso. You don't think about the dead ones any more than you think about the beans you ate yesterday."

Despite his weariness, the leader of the Mexican gang laughed outright, flashing strong white teeth.

"You know me well, amigo," he said. "If I can't eat it, drink it, or rut on it, I throw it away! No, I don't care about the men, Big Tree. But I need their firepower. How can we hold off *federales* and other gangs without firepower?"

"Granted," Big Tree said. Then he grinned slyly and added, "But three thousand in gold, especially in this poor nation where men labor for thirty cents a day, is a tidy sum, is it not? That would help a man recruit new followers."

Poco Loco nodded, catching the renegade's drift. Either way, Big Tree was arguing, Poco Loco came out of this ahead—assuming, of course, that the Cheyenne finally tripped up and got himself killed. That reward money could either outfit this gang or recruit a new one.

"He will kill no more of us," Poco Loco said again, gauging the distance to those twin pinnacles. He rose with a grunt of protest and slapped his hat on his thigh to dislodge the dust.

"Vamanos!" he shouted across to the rest of the men. "Let's go, boys! And from here on out, keep your thoughts bloody!"

"I figured out where they're aimin' to," Knobby said, his voice rasping harshly from a throatful of dirt. He pointed toward two distant pinnacles of rock on the western horizon. "That's the Sangre de Cristo range. Blood of Christ mountains. I ain't never seed it, but talk has it there's a lost pueblo up there. A whole village what's been deserted. They're goin' for the high ground."

Touch the Sky said nothing, but his friend's words made sense. Too damn much sense, he thought. The idea of attacking high ground would worry an experienced warrior at any time. But especially now, when Touch the Sky and Knobby were already balanced on the verge of exhaustion.

It wasn't just the daunting odds. Their enemy

were able to sleep, take regular meals, relax their guard now and then by posting sentries. Touch the Sky and Knobby, in harsh contrast, had to face a grim reality—they simply couldn't keep this grueling contest up much longer. Grain for the ponies was dangerously low, and graze was virtually nonexistent out here on the *jornada*.

Yes, he had managed to kill five men. But look how many remained. More important, look *who* remained. Big Tree. And now, with his reserves of strength almost tapped out, Touch the Sky had to face the hardest phase of the battle.

Needs must when the devil drives. That was another favorite saying of John Hanchon. And Touch the Sky knew his white father was right. One way or another, it had to get done. Big Tree had left Honey Eater for dead, and for that he must die.

"Well," Knobby said, cutting into the Cheyenne's thoughts, "they're ridin' again, see their puffs? One thing for sure, they ain't sendin' any more snipers back. Looks like we won't be able to take out any more of 'em on the trail."

Touch the Sky started to reply. But at that moment something caught his eye—smoke sign, rising up from the headlands north of the Rio Grande. Kiowa Apache country, he guessed.

He watched the columns and puffs rise in a careful sequence, various shapes symbolizing specific tribes and warriors. His nape began to tingle when he saw that it was word from his own tribe.

Knobby, too, spotted the smoke. "What's the word, sprout?" he demanded in a dusty croak. "My sign's a little rusty."

"News from Powder River," the warrior replied tersely, his eyes squinting. Sweat broke out on his face when he saw the "cut-off cloud," an abruptly truncated smoke signal that symbolized a death.

"What news?" Knobby persisted.

Touch the Sky held silent, forgetting to take his next breath as he watched the long, thin column rise. The symbol for a woman.

"Well, what damn news?" Knobby demanded.

Touch the Sky's face drained cold as death when he read the last symbol—three quick puffs that symbolized the tribe's shaman.

Touch the Sky had no idea how long he sat there, his shocked mind simply shutting down in the face of this brutal news. When he finally came to awareness again, Knobby was gently shaking him. The old man's face was white as moonstone.

"Katy Christ, Matthew," he said softly. "You look like you just got a peek into hell itself. What is it, boy?"

"Honey Eater," Touch the Sky managed, the words coming up out of his throat like nails tearing at it. "She is dead."

Big Tree had no way of knowing about the newest conspiracy up north—the plan to make Touch the Sky believe his woman had died. So he felt his pulse thudding with dread when he, too, spotted that smoke sign north of the border.

So he had killed Touch the Sky's woman, after all? Big Tree felt the forbidden thrill of a child who has stolen a valuable object. Yes, it was his, and it was a thrill to have it. But surely he must pay for the crime.

Pay? If Touch the Sky saw that sign, the very Wendigo himself was about to be unleashed.

The Comanche let his cayuse slow until Poco Loco caught up with him.

"Amigo," Big Tree said, "tell the men to move their weapons to full cock. Trouble is coming, and soon."

Poco Loco laughed. *Vaya!* Look, this is the worst time to attack. The worst place."

The Mexican pointed at the ground, littered with loose lava rock and chunks of half-buried basalt, left centuries earlier by glacial action. It made riding treacherous.

"A horse can barely trot here, much less gallop," Poco Loco pointed out. "And look, no cover at all. We would have a clear shot at him from any direction."

"He is coming," Big Tree insisted, though he did not have the courage to add, he is coming for *me* because I snuffed out the very reason for his existence. The Comanche only hoped one thing, that the Cheyenne would have so much blood in his eyes, he could not see clearly the right course of action. Anger could block a man from his best movements. And a split second's mistake was all Big Tree required.

"Good, let him come," Poco Loco said confidently. "I have been wanting a look at this big Indian."

All too soon, however, Poco Loco got his wish.

Big Tree had noticed the dust spirals approaching from their right flank long before any of the others. It was Esteban who first raised a warning.

"Rider approaching!"

Poco Loco broke out his field glasses, then handed them to Big Tree. "Is this our man, Quohada?"

Big Tree took one swift look and nodded. "The very man."

"What is he doing?" Poco Loco asked. "Is he a fool? Surely he means to stop well out from us and take a shot?"

But soon it was clear that the Cheyenne approaching them had no interest in sniping from afar. His rifle, muzzle thrust toward the sky, rested butt-first on his thigh. His left hand clutched his red-streamered war lance. He used no hands to ride, merely clinging with his knees.

"Here comes my gold!" Poco Loco sang out as he leaped down from his horse and started shouting orders. "Esteban! Quickly! Have the men scoop out wallows. Jorges! You and Ricardo lead the horses farther back out of range. The rest, check your loads! More than one of us is going to air him out! Let's see who scores the fatal hit!"

Big Tree, however, looked far less sanguine. This magnificent warrior wasn't riding in, facing almost certain death, just to shoot at the first pop-up target. He had a purpose in coming.

Big Tree wasted no time. A wallow wouldn't be good enough. Giving it no thought, he shot one of his remuda and forted up behind the dead horse. The Comanche grabbed a handful of arrows and notched the first one on his bowstring, waiting.

Now the drumming hoofbeats could be heard. When Big Tree could see the determined set of Touch the Sky's face, he launched his first arrow. It streaked past just to the left of the approaching

Cheyenne, and that shot sent him into defensive action.

Touch the Sky slid forward and down, gripping the dun's neck. At the same time, his mount began running a zigzagging pattern. Big Tree unleashed more arrows as the first riflemen opened up. Geysers of dirt shot up all around the pony's pounding hooves, and arrows ripped past Touch the Sky so swiftly and close that the fletching burned his skin.

"The fool!" Poco Loco screamed. "If he keeps coming, he will be in range of my shotgun! Hit him, you blind fools!"

A bullet passed through Touch the Sky's rawhide shirt, tugging at it. Another ripped through his buffalo-hair halter. But now he could see the place where Big Tree was hunkered down, launching arrows from behind that dead horse.

"Jesus, Joseph, and Mary, *hit* him!" Poco Loco screamed. Ricardo leaped up from his wallow, drawing a clear shot on the Cheyenne. Touch the Sky's rifle bucked, and a red smear replaced the Mexican's face. Big Tree stopped firing arrows, tensing his muscles for what was coming. He would have to be quick to avoid a hard death.

Jorges turned to leap out of the Indian's path, and a moment later the war lance punched through his chest from behind. And now the lethal maniac on that magnificent horse was bearing down on Big Tree, his obsidian eyes livid with hatred. One hand went to the knife in his belt even as he prepared to leap.

Big Tree sprang hard to the right just as Poco Loco's scattergun roared with a deafening explosion. Touch the Sky, on the verge of leaping, missed the main brunt of the buckshot. But a smattering of pellets slammed into his chest, tearing away skin and knocking him backward so that he almost fell off his horse.

The dun, too, took some of the pellets, staggering hard. But the well-trained mount doggedly charged on, clearing the group of men and heading off into the vastness behind them.

Touch the Sky managed to turn around once and meet Big Tree's frightened eyes. "You are dead, Quohada!" the Cheyenne yelled. "From where you stand now to the place where the sun goes down, there is no safe place for you! If you go into breastworks, I will drive you out! I swear it by the four directions, and the Holy Ones hear me. Before I ride north again, you will be dead!"

Chapter Eleven

Knobby definitely did not like his companion's grim, trancelike silence. They rode on in no particular hurry now, for Big Tree and the panicked Mexicans had broken for the slope after Touch the Sky's bold assault. But the Cheyenne, Knobby told himself, now appeared like a dead man with his eyes open.

At one point, Knobby saw Matthew's leg brush hard against a sharp-spined prickly pear, ripping deep gashes—yet the warrior never even glanced down! It might as well have been a gnat landing on him, for all that he even knew of it.

A dead man with his eyes open . . . that's what Matthew was, all right, Knobby thought. He was too exhausted to complete this mission in high country. I'm the one with snow in the eaves,

Knobby told himself. But that young buck has done all the fighting.

"That was a nice piece o' horsemanship back there," Knobby said quietly. "You trimmed 'em by two more, sprout. That leaves only five Mexers, countin' the *jefe* and that shotgun of his. But it also leaves Big Tree."

Knobby waited. Their tired mounts stopped now and then to blow as they began the ascent into the mountains. Leather creaked, Knobby's bit ring chinked, but no sound from the Cheyenne. The old man wasn't even sure he'd heard him just now.

"We got Big Tree left," Knobby repeated, "and you goin' at him in the high country. It don't bode good, boy! I say you need rest. They ain't goin' nowhere in a hurry, you—"

"Whack the cork, old-timer," Touch the Sky cut him off. "I don't need rest. All I need is the hair of the mother-rutting son of a bitch who killed my wife."

Knobby scowled. "So to hell with common sense, huh? Well, looks like Big Tree has kilt your boy's ma—you gonna cost him his pa, too, with your bullheaded, cussed stubbornness? Don't take no Philadelphia lawyer to prove that we're both beat out."

Those words sank through somewhat, and Touch the Sky gave his friend a long look.

"What do you mean, 'looks like' Big Tree killed my wife?"

"Looks like," Knobby snapped. "That's what I said. What, did I switch to Chinee on you, boy?

110

Hell, you saw some smoke up in the clouds. Is that truth writ in blood?"

Knobby said no more. But the words he had just spoken fell on Touch the Sky's ears like rain to dry earth. Knobby wasn't saying the word about Honey Eater was not true—but he was saying it *could* be a lie. For a moment, hope surged inside Touch the Sky like a swelling bubble. But he refused to let himself grasp at this possibility—for then, the discovery that his woman was indeed in the Land of Ghosts would hit doubly hard. Finally Touch the Sky said:

"Straight words, Knobby. We'll make a cold camp when we hit the slope."

"Now you're talkin' like John Hanchon's boy. We need sleep, chuck in our bellies. This hoss'll tell you somethin' else, too."

Knobby used his left elbow to tap the walnut stock of the Kentucky rifle in his saddle boot. "So far I've let you take care of the killin' because this was your battle. I come along to be your guide. But you can't do it alone from here on out—not up there in them peaks. Either both of us bust caps, tadpole, or both of us will be lookin' up to see grass."

Touch the Sky raised his eyes to look at those two gray pinnacles prodding into the blue belly of the sky. Old Knobby had already done his job—but the old trapper was right. This was no time, the warrior cautioned himself, to let grief sway his decisions. He must put the grief away from his mind. His enemies would like nothing better than to see him swollen with rage, berserk, and thus

111

incapable of the cool decisions that often determine a battle.

"It's me and you, old campaigner," Touch the Sky finally said. "And I don't care how long in the tooth you are—a man couldn't ask for a better partner when his bacon is in the fire."

Touch the Sky's insane but effective charge had left Poco Loco's surviving men in the grip of panic. No one bothered to bury Ricardo or Jorges—indeed, no one even broke out a rosary and prayed over them. It had become every man for himself, and the devil take the hindmost. And the name of this devil was Touch the Sky.

"Big Tree," Poco Loco fumed when the two men could not be overheard, "I saw that savage's face! Man, I never saw the kill light in a man's eyes like that. He was possessed by a demon. Whatever you did to him, it was a mistake. I know this kind—hurt one of his, he kills two of yours."

Even as he spoke, Poco Loco craned around in the saddle to stare down the narrow, rocky trail behind them. Esteban, still loyal despite his abject fear, had wisely taken up the drag position—that way none of the four *pistoleros* could bolt back down the mountain.

Not that a wise man would, Poco Loco thought—not with that red killing machine trailing them. But men were seldom wise once their nerves frazzled like worn ropes.

Big Tree, unlike the Mexicans, showed nothing in his face. It remained an inscrutable stone mask. But he, too, had seen the preternatural hatred and need for vengeance in Touch the Sky's eyes. Yes, the Cheyenne had let Sis-ki-dee go, up in Bloody Bones Canyon, when the Blackfoot begged for mercy. But even begging for mercy—a humiliation Indians considered worse than outright defeat—was out of the question for the man who killed Honey Eater.

Therefore, Big Tree saw clearly how things stood. He must kill Touch the Sky before Touch the Sky killed him. And since there was no distance he could run to escape the Cheyenne, what better place than this sierra—and what better time than now?

A sudden snarl of rage abruptly interrupted Big Tree's thoughts. For a heartbeat, he thought one of the nervous men had finally gone mad with fear—or worse, that Touch the Sky had got the jump on him.

Then he saw it: the brindled fur of a dog watching them from a ledge of rock just overhead. A wild dog, at least half wolf, Big Tree thought—and a steady stream of saliva rolled off its lolling tongue, a sure sign of rabies. He had heard of it happening before: A virulent strain of rabies could haunt an area, infecting generations of dogs.

In one smooth, steady motion, he pulled the .44 from its holster and snapped off a round. It caught the dog in the chest and flipped him back off the ledge.

"There'll be more than one around here," Big Tree said. "Keep a red eye out."

"Best be careful when we reach San Sebastian," Poco Loco said. "We may have to clear the buildings of dogs."

Big Tree nodded. But looking up toward the

ledge, after he killed the dog, had given him an idea.

"This is the only way up?" he demanded of Poco Loco. "You are sure of it?"

"Does asparagus make your piss stink? Of course I am sure of it. The back of the range is all cliffs."

"Good." Big Tree grinned, his old fighting spirit returning. Was he not a Quohada Comanche, one of the feared Red Raiders of the Plains? Which tribe had cleared Texas and driven almost every white-eyed bastard from the Arizona Territory? Indeed, which tribe, according to the white man's newspapers, had killed more hair-face settlers than any other?

Big Tree said, "Our noble red man is distraught with grief. He will not be focused as a warrior must be. Why should his ride up the slope be uneventful?"

Poco Loco was too tired and snappish for girls' guessing games. "If you drift near a point, compadre, make it."

"Just keep riding," Big Tree said. "I'm going up to that ledge. I'll catch up with you later."

When they were well up the slope, the crude trail narrowed and forced Touch the Sky and Knobby to ride single file. The Cheyenne took the point position.

They had tethered their remounts at the bottom of the slope near a little runoff rill that provided some water and scant grass. Both men knew it would not be a horse battle up topside, but close-in fighting. Unlike their enemy, however, they had no exact idea of what lay above, the layout of the place, what natural cover it provided.

Both men were also veterans of frontier violence, and knew better than to expect an easy ride up. They kept their weapons at the ready as they ascended, scanning every nook and cranny for hidden marksmen.

Now more than ever Touch the Sky applied the skills of the warrior, skills taught in training and honed in the hard school of experience. He watched from his side vision as much as from his forward vision. Constantly he slid to the ground to place his fingertips against the sensitive rock, reading it for motion vibrations.

Nor did he ignore the coyote dun's sensitive nostrils. Cheyennes taught their horses to hate the smell of enemy tribes.

Even now, through his red waves of exhaustion, Touch the Sky was aware of it: that tiny prickling in the nape of his neck, the shaman's "third eye" warning him of danger. He turned around and met Knobby's eyes.

The old mountain man nodded. He, too, felt it coming—felt it deep in his old, aching bones. Touch the Sky watched Knobby's thumb reach up and pull the over-and-under's twin hammers back to full cock.

"Easy," Touch the Sky said soothingly into the dun's ear.

Slowly, inexorably, the two men followed the steep, tortuous trail as it wound steadily upward, taking them closer and closer to their meeting with the Black Warrior called Death.

* * *

Big Tree had worked quickly as the rest of his companions continued their ascent toward the deserted pueblo above.

It took coaxing, but his sure-footed cayuse finally climbed over to the ledge beside the trail. As Big Tree had hoped, the opening behind the ledge, into which the dead dog had tumbled, was big enough to conceal his horse.

At one edge of the ledge balanced a massive boulder, perhaps the size of a small pony. Big Tree knew he could not possibly move it by himself, not even with his impressive strength—not on level ground. But the ledge under the boulder was dirt.

Working quickly, keeping a constant eye on the trail below, Big Tree used his knife and his hands to scoop out a little trough in front of the huge boulder. The ledge was not quite level—it tilted a little forward. That angle, plus the rock's formidable weight, should send it plunging straight down if a strong man got his back behind it.

There was just enough space behind it for the Comanche to wedge himself in. He braced his muscle-corded back against the boulder, then slapped both hands against the stone face of the mountain.

Big Tree gave it one little test push, straining hard. He felt the satisfying sensation of the boulder yielding behind him. Grinning, the Comanche relaxed again, letting it return to its normal resting place.

Now it was a question of vigilance and careful timing. Big Tree settled in for the wait, his cold-as-flint eyes watching the trail with unwavering attention.

Desert Manhunt

*   *   *

Touch the Sky was slowly coaxing the dun around a dogleg bend in the trail when he saw his pony's nostrils suddenly quiver—quivers that led to a snort as the dun recognized the enemy smell.

Touch the Sky's mistake, however, was to first glance right—after all, that was the direction of the sun, and Big Tree always attacked from out of the sun.

That brief mistake made him miss the first shuddering movements of that huge boulder just above them and to their left. By the time Touch the Sky heard Knobby's warning cry, it was too late. His head snapped left just in time to see a huge gray mass blocking out the sky as it plunged downward.

Knobby, right behind his friend, had spotted the rock's motion a split second before Matthew did. He reflexively raised his Kentucky long rifle and swung the muzzle hard, catching the Cheyenne in his left ribs and sweeping him hard off his pony.

But Knobby didn't think he moved in time. And then his own horse was rearing in panic as a resounding crash just ahead of them made it seem like the entire mountain was coming down on them.

Chapter Twelve

"Look at them," Two Twists said, scorn heavy in his voice as he nodded toward the Bullwhips. "That is the second bladder of corn beer they have broached this day. You would think the death of he who may not be named is the Spring Festival to them."

By custom, Two Twists had avoided using Touch the Sky's name, especially since there was a very good chance that he had died an unclean death—killed before he could sing his death song.

Little Horse suddenly threw down the elk steak he had been trying to eat. It landed in the cooking fire outside his tipi and threw sparks on Two Twists and Tangle Hair. Both men flinched, watching him.

"His name is Touch the Sky," Little Horse said

boldly. "What proof do we have that he has gone under?"

The other two gaped. The great flywheel of habit had kept them from questioning smoke sign—especially sign that rose in the Sweetwater Creek region, home of their Sioux allies. But Little Horse was right. Their enemies had shown no respect for anything else. Why not corrupt the moccasin telegraph, too?

"I do not think he is dead," Little Horse added. "And neither does *she*."

All three looked at the lone tipi that sat separately from the others. Honey Eater had insisted on moving back into it. And Little Horse was right. After recovering from her initial grief, Honey Eater had drawn from her deep well of inner strength. She had said nothing about her new resolve to anyone. But Little Horse could see it—she would not believe in the death of Touch the Sky until she had incontrovertible proof.

"You are no shaman," Tangle Hair said slowly, "but you speak straight arrow. How many times have they lied about Touch the Sky? We were fooled because it came in smoke this time. He may indeed be dead. But I agree with you, buck. He is alive until *proven* dead."

Now Two Twists nodded, his young face easing into a grin. "Both of you are so ugly, you shame your mothers. But you are right this time. It is the same with Arrow Keeper. When he disappeared, most ceased to speak his name. But Touch the Sky convinced us we could still name him, for none had seen him die. And truly, has Arrow Keeper left this world? How many times has he warned

Touch the Sky of trouble since his supposed death?"

While Two Twists spoke this last, a group of merrymakers had broken away from the big knot of braves gathered near the Bullwhip lodge.

"Here comes a trouble cloud blowing our way," Tangle Hair said, nodding as the Bullwhips approached them. "Look to your weapons."

"Never mind weapons," Little Horse said. "They are unarmed and led by Medicine Flute. Anything he leads will not involve weapons, only mouth."

The group halted well back from the firepit: Medicine Flute, Wolf Who Hunts Smiling, Crow Killer, Swift Canoe, and several others.

"Bucks," Medicine Flute called out, his voice drunken from long hours of imbibing corn beer, "we wish to console you on the loss of your noble leader, Scrape the Clouds."

This deliberate distortion of Touch the Sky's name drew gales of laughter from the rest. Swift Canoe, stupid as dead wood, did not get the pun at first. When he finally did, he laughed so hard he fell upon the ground in convulsions.

"No, shaman," Crow Killer corrected Medicine Flute, deliberately using Touch the Sky's title to rub it in. "His name was Hit the Heavens!"

More laughter.

"At any rate," Medicine Flute went on, "his name now is In the Ground. And such a tasty bit of a squaw going to waste! Perhaps—"

Medicine Flute never finished his gibe. Indeed, it was some time after that night before he could talk coherently again. Little Horse, who had a deadly throwing aim, always kept a few good-size rocks in his parfleche—when a man was out of bullets in a frenzied fight, they could mean the margin of victory.

Little Horse drew one out, rose up onto his knees, and used his free left hand to aim along as he fired a rock hard at Medicine Flute. It whopped into his mouth with audible force, smashing several teeth, ripping lips and cheeks as they tore into teeth. The force of it knocked Medicine Flute to the ground and evoked a womanish shriek of pain.

"The next two-legged worm among you," Little Horse announced hotly, "who speaks of Touch the Sky in my hearing will die hard!"

Since all Indians respected actions more than words, Little Horse gave still more force to his talk. He stood up and walked between his enemies and the campfire—a symbol that sent the rest of them back to their lodge, dragging the whimpering Medicine Flute with them. When a man crossed the fire like that, all fooling was past. The next word meant sure death for someone.

"Good work, brother," Tangle Hair said when they had left. "But we had best circle our robes with dried pods this night. And even if Touch the Sky really is still among the living, you don't need to be a shaman to know that he is up against the fight of his life."

"You took a nasty gash," Knobby said. "But by God, you come sassy! Boy, I swan, you'd wade into hell and come out with a land grant!"

"I sure as hell don't feel so damn sassy," Touch the Sky said, wincing as he touched the huge puff in front of his left ear. "I feel like death warmed over."

The two men had made a cold camp just past the site of the boulder strike. "Camp" was overstating the case—it was merely a protected nest among some boulders, more than half the space taken up by their horses.

"It was definitely Big Tree," Knobby confirmed. "I saw him jump down into that holler behind the ledge and get his horse. I shoulda busted a cap at him, but I was scramblin' to pull your raggedy ass out."

The last of the day's sunlight was bleeding from the sky. It was cold up here, and when the wind picked up it cut into their skin like knife blades.

"They're up there by now," Knobby said. "Waitin' on us."

Touch the Sky nodded glumly. Killing Big Tree down here would have saved them a lot of grief— not to mention, possibly their lives. But when had it ever been anything *but* hard against that red son of the Wendigo?

A sudden noise of rocks scraping sent both men into firing position. But it was only Knobby's claybank, shifting around.

"We goin' up tonight?" Knobby asked.

Touch the Sky shook his head. "No. You're right. We'll rest the whole night. I go up there now, I might as well hand them my weapons. Besides, Big Tree can see in the dark like a damn cat. I like dawn better. We set out an hour before sunrise, that should put us topside as the sun comes up. We'll need to get the lay of the place, figure out where we're going to stage out from. We can't make plans until we see what we've got to work with."

"Boy, either you're gettin' wiser, or my brain's gone soft and I can't tell shit from apple butter. Sounds like you're talkin' sense."

"I better be," Touch the Sky said as another spasm of pain washed over him. "Because luck and guts won't do it—not against Big Tree."

Before the glowing, blood-orange sun had dropped below the horizon, Big Tree and Poco Loco made a good mind map of San Sebastian.

The place was indeed made mostly of solid stone, huge blocks of fieldstone that must have been dragged into place by slave labor—probably Indian slaves. It was not really a town—just a small central plaza, its flagstones cracked and weed-infested now, surrounded by perhaps a dozen small stone dwellings.

"You were right," Big Tree confirmed, returning from a quick survey of the north face of the mountain. "Nothing but straight cliff. And so much scree at the base, even a mountain goat would need two days to climb it."

"What did I tell you?" Poco Loco boasted. "And you saw how the south face is. One narrow, twisting trail. It is the quarter of the full moon. If he comes up this night, our sentry will see him. Besides all that, he may be dead, for all you know. You said it looked like your trick killed him."

"Looked like," Big Tree repeated, "means nothing where that one is involved. When I hold his head over the bag, then I will believe he is dead. Who is watching the trail now?"

"Esteban himself. I wanted the best man there. Esteban is scared, but the rest are pissing themselves."

Big Tree nodded. "Esteban has a mouth on him, but I noticed he stays cold when the gunfire begins. Like you, Poco Loco. Both of you are too crazy to truly respect death."

The Mexican grinned, gold teeth gleaming in the setting sun. "Oh, I am no hero, amigo. There are women I wish to top, liquor to drink, men to kill—I am not eager to die yet. But this Cheyenne, he has challenged his tether too often and must reach the end of it. We are two of the best killers on God's green earth, Quohada! This is no Chapultepec Castle we have here, it is a natural fortress! The fight is ours to win."

Big Tree nodded. "You are right. But more will die."

He nodded down the little slope behind him. Besides Esteban, who was out of sight from here on guard duty, only three men remained alive: Lupe, Ernesto, and Juan. Each man now was on sentry duty atop one of the stone buildings.

"Should we leave the men out all night?" Poco Loco asked.

Big Tree shook his head. "Each by himself is a mere toy for Touch the Sky. At dark, we call in Esteban. Then all six of us fort up in the house we already fixed up. However, I suggest sending Esteban back out before dawn."

By "fixed up" Big Tree meant the solid rock walls they had built to block off the windows, whose wooden shutters had rotted long ago. They had been forced to kill two more dogs—wild, but not rabid this time—that had claimed the place.

Thinking of the dogs, Big Tree said, "There are too many droppings around here. We have not seen nearly all the dogs we are going to encounter."

Poco Loco raised the muzzle of his scattergun. "Why do you think my girl is out of her sling? But, amigo, it is an ill wind indeed that does not blow harm to someone—dogs are sunrise hunters. If our noble red man attacks at dawn as I feel he might, we will have one more ally on our side."

"Perhaps," Big Tree said. "But when it comes to killing that one, only a fool would bank on someone else doing the job. Sleep on your weapon. Better yet, do not sleep."

Chapter Thirteen

During the cold, fitful hours of rest, Touch the Sky could not always separate facts from dreaming.

Night had settled over the remote sierra called Blood of Christ like a change of climate. Rocks that, by day, had collected sun warmth now turned cold and miserable to the touch. Though bright moonlight kept them from total darkness, a powerful north wind shrieked down off the Colorado Plateau and continually blew rafts of clouds in front of the moon.

In his fitful sleep, Touch the Sky heard that wind howling. But he could not always tell it from the battle cries, from the cries of dying men and ponies, as dream images were placed over his eyes. Honey Eater appeared to him, and even in sleep he reached out to grasp the elusive image that always disappeared like snowflakes melting on a river.

And then there were the dogs.

Throughout the night Touch the Sky heard them, not sure if they were part of the dreams or part of the night: dogs howling, dogs barking, dogs growling and snapping.

When he finally came awake, it was sudden and all of a moment. Touch the Sky simply blinked once, and the moment his eyes opened, he knew where he was and what had to be done.

It had ever been so, for him. Other men might drift through life and follow the forks in the trail as they appeared; they could sleep late in the mornings, bounce their children on their knees, spend the warm mornings visiting with their clan and soldier troops. For him, however, the cycle was sure and relentless: The end of one battle meant only the beginning of the next. Born in one world, raised in another, now neither world accepted him.

Touch the Sky shook off his pensive mood even as he sat up and began rolling his buffalo robe. His experienced eye could tell, from the grain of the light, that perhaps an hour remained before sunrise.

"You awake, Knobby?" he said softly.

In fact the old man was sound asleep, for exhaustion had seeped into every pore of his aching, worn body. But at the sound of Touch the Sky's voice, Knobby sat up. Old reflexes made him reach for his Kentucky rifle even before he came fully awake.

"Course I'm awake," he groused. "Hell, I was only restin' my eyes."

Touch the Sky fed the remaining grain to the horses.

"We're going up without them," he decided. "It's not that far, and they'll just be sure targets. We can find cover better without them. That's not riding country up there, anyway."

"That's dyin' country up there," Knobby said. "Let's just hope it ain't us doin' the dyin'."

" 'Hope' your ass, old-timer. Let's make *sure* we don't do the dying."

Knobby grinned. "Well, cuss my coup! The pup is barkin' like a full-growed dog this morning."

Their moods slightly better now, both men quickly fell to on a final inspection of their weapons. Touch the Sky tied a short sling on his Sharps and strung it over one shoulder, his bow over the other.

They shared a few stale corn dodgers and a long drink of cool mountain water.

"Ready?" Touch the Sky asked.

Somewhere nearby a dog howled. Both men listened to the mournful sound as the ululating noise echoed from peak to peak in the morning darkness.

"Ready, goddammit," the mountain man replied. "Let's go make our beaver."

Esteban started violently when a hand touched his shoulder.

A shout of fear got stuck in his throat like a suppressed cough. He sat up, throwing his blankets aside, and groped for his big dragoon pistol.

"Easy, *'mano*," Poco Loco's voice calmed him. "I'm just telling you it is time for guard duty."

Esteban stared around the dimly lighted room. Big Tree was wide awake and probably had been all night. He sat, pistol in hand, watching the dwelling's only door. Lupe and Juan were fast asleep.

"*Jefe*," Esteban protested. "Do we truly need a sentry out there? We are impregnable here."

"Here, yes. But tell me, brother. Do we never leave this place? We must go outside sooner or later, and it is crucial to know if that red devil has made it up here to this level."

"What if he came up during the night? What if he is already out there?"

Poco Loco, growing impatient, shook his head. "Big Tree knows him. He says no, he will come now. And you know how many dogs are holed up along the slope as you near the top. We would have heard a racket from them had he tried to slip by."

"Send Lupe," Esteban protested, trying to keep the whine out of his tone. "Chief, I have a bad feeling about going out there. Send Lupe or Juan."

"I *thought* you were a man," Poco Loco snapped. "That is why I want you out there."

Esteban, who could not stand a challenge to his manhood, forced himself to rise and wrestle on his boots, spurs jangling. He spun the cylinder of his gun, checking the loads.

"Position yourself just past the end of the trail," Poco Loco instructed him. "There is a jumble of rocks there that will provide good cover. You can't miss it if he comes up, amigo. A cockroach could not hide on that trail. It is pressed in on both sides by solid walls of stone. We will all take turns, two hours at a time."

"What if I see him?" Esteban asked.

"Most important is to fire a shot to warn us. I promise: From the time you fire a bullet until the time we appear will not be enough time to chew a biscuit."

For a moment, Esteban looked a little heartened. He was not a timid man, and the life of a pistolero had not left near-death scrapes remote from his experience.

But he recalled how Manuel's neck had been broken by the force of whatever struck his jaw, how Jorge's heart had come tumbling out of Poco Loco's fiber morral.

"I have a bad feeling about going out there," he repeated. But all he got for his protests were cold stares from Big Tree and Poco Loco—stares that said, take your chances out there like a man or we kill you for sure in here.

Esteban held his pistol at the ready as he lifted the heavy beam from the door and pushed it open, expecting death even as he did. But there was nothing outside, just a broad, gray, moonlit expanse of bare rock and stunted trees.

The wind rose to a howling shriek that sounded like all the devils in hell crying out at once. Esteban stepped out into the darkness, and Big Tree slammed the door shut behind him.

Touch the Sky had not realized, from farther down the slope, how constricted the only trail would grow as it neared its terminus in the caprock.

He had hoped to emerge on one of the flanks, sneaking around the sentry he was sure would be posted. But soon he realized that would prove impossible. The piles of scree and glacial moraine that crowded the narrow trail became solid walls of stone, so precipitous they were nearly vertical.

At most, Touch the Sky calculated with a sinking feeling of doom, the two men would have an area perhaps forty feet across from which they would be forced to debouch in the open. That wasn't very wide, and made things easy for a sentry in good position.

He and Knobby made good time while the last vestiges of night provided cover. They leapfrogged from boulder to boulder, one covering the other. Soon, they had angled around the last turn. Now the final, rock-strewn slope rose ahead of them.

Touch the Sky, pressing behind a jumble of rocks, spoke close to Knobby's ear.

"If you had to guard this trail, where would you dig in?"

Knobby nodded just to the left. "That cleft right there in that granite. Man could draw a bead on a pissant from there and hardly show himself."

Touch the Sky nodded, for his thoughts drifted the same way. The key to survival up here was to first clear that sentry post. From there the next priority would be shelter, some spot from which to operate while getting the lay of the place topside.

But rushing it was out of the question—ten men could not dislodge a coolheaded marksman from that opening, much less two. They could, of course, wait one entire day and try to ease past at night. But they were exposed here, vulnerable should anyone come down the trail.

Touch the Sky's warrior experience told him that only one strategy might work here: a distraction. Something the sentry wasn't expecting, something that would disrupt, just for a moment, his normal vigilance.

There still remained about forty yards of slope before they reached the vulnerable open stretch. As they set out to cover this final expanse, Touch the Sky again reminded old Knobby:

"Try like hell to avoid burning powder. One shot will bring Big Tree and the rest all over us like ugly on a buzzard."

The old man nodded. However, they had moved only a few feet before all hell suddenly broke loose.

With a savage snarl of rage, a yellow streak of fur leaped on Touch the Sky. His first thought, even as he reflexively tucked and rolled away from the leap, was that a mountain cat was about to kill him.

Claws raked his back, causing an explosion of fiery pain. Then he saw that his attacker was a dog as it missed him by inches and thumped into the rocks beside the trail.

Touch the Sky was at an awkward angle to defend himself, having been twisted off balance when he ducked from the dog. Desperately, as the fervid animal scrambled up with amazing dexterity and prepared to leap on him, fangs bared, the Cheyenne fumbled his knife from its beaded sheath and tried to set himself on the balls of his feet for balance.

The dog leaped, but Touch the Sky did not quite have time to get the knife up at the ready. A heartbeat later, Old Knobby flashed into view, giving a mighty swing to Old Patsy Plumb. The rifle's heavy stock slammed into the dog's skull even as it cleared the ground. The blow did not kill it, but as the stunned animal gathered itself, Touch the Sky drove his blade deep into its vitals.

Both men leaped for cover again, fearful that the racket had alerted the sentry above. But no one showed himself, and there were no warning shouts or shots.

"Good work, old-timer," Touch the Sky whispered. "You pulled my bacon out of the fire again."

Even as he spoke, Touch the Sky slid a flint-tipped arrow from his quiver. Knobby watched him notch it on his bowstring.

"The hell you doin'?" Knobby whispered hoarsely.

"I'm going to shoot a cloud," Touch the Sky answered.

Knobby, squinting as if the Cheyenne were a half-wit, glanced up into a sooty morning sky. The sun was still only a promise in the east, and any clouds were certainly invisible right now.

But it was true—the Cheyenne was aiming almost straight overhead. Knobby still hadn't caught his friend's drift, but a nervy little grin twitched the old man's lips.

"Good mornin' for cloud huntin'," Knobby agreed affably. "Make you a deal, sprout. You shoot one, and I'll skin the son of a bitch!"

*   *   *

Esteban had settled down since coming out to begin his stint on sentry duty.

Yes, he had indeed had bad forebodings about this day. But he felt safer here in the cleft than he did down below in the house. After all, it was an arduous climb just to reach this little pocket in the solid rock. Only one way up, and he could see every inch of it—as well as the end of the trail below.

He had heard a quick burst of snarls below, but Esteban hardly gave it a thought. The dogs were always fighting and snapping at each other. It hadn't been loud enough, or long enough, to signal intruders.

Esteban had finally settled down enough to build himself a cigarette with steady fingers. He had just put away his makings and was licking the paper when he heard it: a sudden clattering sound in the rocks.

Only—the noise came from *behind* him!

Panic held the Mexican immobile for perhaps ten heartbeats.

The last thing he had expected was noise from behind him. That must mean the intruders had already made it up here during the night.

He knew he had to look. Just a quick peek. If he poked his head out just for a moment . . .

No! No, he told himself. It was some kind of a trap. No one could be up there. Do *not* show yourself.

But again—another clattering noise. Definitely from behind this position.

He had to look. Taking a deep breath to steady

his resolve, Esteban nudged his head around the edge of the cleft and studied the terrain behind him.

Nothing. No one. Perhaps, after all, it was just—

He lost the thought when he saw it: An arrow lay broken among the rocks where it had landed.

A trick. He realized exactly what was happening, but just as he moved to duck back, a white-hot spike of pain replaced his throat. The arrow punched through his neck so hard it cracked into the rock face behind him. But Esteban was in no position to notice this as he hurled out of his safe nest and crashed into the rocks far below—the scream deep in his throat lost in a bubbling gurgle of frothy blood.

Chapter Fourteen

"*That* kissed the mistress!" Knobby gloated as he watched the Mexican come tumbling down out of the rocks, his neck skewered by Touch the Sky's arrow.

"Yeah, well, a kiss won't impress Big Tree. Let's recite our coups later," the Cheyenne said, breaking at a run for the end of the trail.

His rifle at a high port, Touch the Sky leaped over the dead sentry, stopping just long enough to grab the big dragoon pistol and stuff it in his sash. Then he raced for cover farther back in the caprock. Knobby followed him at a slower pace.

"You can just see San Sebastian from here," Touch the Sky said from behind the cover of a traprock shelf. He nodded toward the east. Perhaps two hundred yards away, the stone buildings could be glimpsed in a tight cluster.

"Look," Knobby said. "They got the other two Mexers up on the roofs. They ain't got a good angle on us here, but we won't get close by daylight. See how open it is around the buildings? Why, Katy Christ! You could have a Wild West show in that space."

Touch the Sky grunted affirmation, not liking the lay of things up here. Movement would not be impossible, but it would be risky. There were piles of rocks and some stunted scrub trees at this end. Closer to the little village, everything had been cleared off.

"I'd say trying to kill Big Tree in a built-up area is suicide," Touch the Sky decided.

"And I'd say that's about as wise as anything you ever spat out your feeding hole."

"And that Mexican boss with him—you saw his sawed-off. That's a man with experience at close-in killing."

"Uh-huh. So what do we do, tadpole? We ain't goin' to burn them out, that's for damn sure."

Touch the Sky was watching the body of the dead sentry. "No," he agreed. "So I think I'd better sneak back down there and hide that body a little better. His relief will be coming soon. I don't want him to be warned too early."

Knobby understood and approved with a nod. "When you can't bring Mahomet to the mountain, you bring the mountain to Mahomet. That'll be one more Mexer down."

If it works, Touch the Sky thought. If it works. But how often could the pitcher keep going to the well before it finally went dry? Besides, even with one more Mexican down, Big Tree was still alive.

Killing these Mexican bandits was still only hacking at the branches of the tree of evil. Killing a man like Big Tree, however, was like digging up the roots.

Touch the Sky put all thoughts away from his mind. Then, making sure he stayed out of sight of those guards, he slipped down to hide the dead man.

"I don't like it," Poco Loco said quietly to Big Tree.

Under cover of daylight and the sentries, the two old comrades had come outside to reconnoiter. Now they stood at the edge of the plaza, staring toward Esteban's sentry post.

"I told him to use his mirror," Poco Loco said. "I told him to flash the all clear every hour to Juan and Lupe. But there has been nothing since the sun came up."

"Nothing? You are sure of this?"

Poco Loco frowned at this challenge to his capabilities. "Am I sure? Does a big-titted woman sleep on her back? Of course I am sure. I have watched every minute."

"Could he be asleep?" Big Tree asked.

Poco Loco shook his head. "Not Esteban. He is a good man. Besides, he was too scared to sleep."

Big Tree definitely did not like what he was hearing. His eyes squinting, deep in speculation, he scanned the rugged terrain to their west. If a man paid him to describe his idea of what the moon must be like, Big Tree would describe that godforsaken waste of scree and twisted growth.

"You think he is up here?" Poco Loco said,

dread clear in his voice. "You think he killed Esteban?"

That was precisely what Big Tree thought. But he could see that even Poco Loco, tough as jerked leather, was on the verge of panic. And in fact, Big Tree himself was beginning to taste the bitter bile of fear.

"We will know soon enough," the Comanche said evasively. "It is time to send Esteban's relief."

Poco Loco's obsidian eyes goaded Big Tree. "Care to go yourself, war leader?"

Big Tree refused to rise to the bait. He merely replied calmly, "You go, *jefe*."

"I never miss breakfast," the Mexican replied tersely before turning and cupping his hands around his mouth.

Poco Loco shouted up toward the nearest roof. "Lupe! Time to relieve Esteban!"

Lupe, a feckless-looking man with a drooping teamster's mustache, shook his head. "Send Juan," he said.

"Fuck your mother!" Juan shouted from a nearby roof. "Esteban has not shown his hide since sunup! I am not going out there!"

Big Tree's .44 fairly flew into his fist. He snapped off a round, and Lupe's sombrero fluttered to the ground. The scared Mexican scrambled down.

"All right!" he shouted. "I am going. But I have a wife and children in Saltillo. Juan should go!"

Juan *will* go, Big Tree thought. All in good time. Juan, Lupe, and the rest were merely bones being thrown to the wolf. Bait to make that wolf show himself, just once . . .

*   *   *

Lupe did not feel so frightened so long as he was in clear sight of San Sebastian. But as the deserted settlement dropped from view, his pulse began to thud in his ears.

Death stalked this place, palpable as wet fog to the skin. Lupe's grandfather swore that, just before a man's appointment with the Grim Reaper, he would see an image of himself, his second self, as it said good-bye. And Lupe had indeed seen himself in a dream last night, standing beside his bedroll and gazing at himself with the saddest expression.

Slowly he picked his way through the scattered rocks, his carbine clutched tight against his right hip in case he had to snap-shoot.

A sudden skittering sound sent him to his knees, weapon pointed toward the noise. But it was only a windblown leaf tumbling over the rocks.

Santísima Maria, he said softly, crossing himself as he again cautiously rose to his feet and resumed his journey toward the pinnacle with the cleft in it, a natural sentry post. It did not seem likely, he thought, that a man as sharp as Esteban could be killed in such a secure post.

Perhaps, after all, Esteban was just asleep?

Lupe kept his gaze in constant motion, scanning the terrain around him, as he moved closer and closer to that cleft pinnacle.

"Esteban?" he called out. "Esteban, are you up there?"

"Where the hell else would I be?" answered a grumpy voice in Spanish.

Relief surged through Lupe. He was so glad to

hear his comrade answer that he hardly noticed how different Esteban sounded—but perhaps a long stint out here in the raw night wind would work on any man's throat.

"You fool," Lupe upbraided him even as he scrambled up the rock toward the cleft. "You were supposed to send mirror flashes back. Did you fall aslee—?"

His voice trailed off when Lupe got his first glimpse into the cleft. Then, all in one confused moment, several things happened simultaneously.

It had been old Knobby whose voice he heard answering in Spanish. And it was to have been Touch the Sky's job to kill the new arrival—a routine and silent kill with an arrow the moment he showed himself.

But just as Touch the Sky released his bowstring, Lupe's careless left foot came down on a loose stone, not solid rock ledge. The Mexican tumbled back roughly but harmlessly to the flat below even as Touch the Sky's arrow sliced past his face.

Touch the Sky cursed, groping for his knife and hoping to get one clear toss at the sentry before he could gain his feet again.

But Lupe instinctively squeezed off a warning round, and Touch the Sky realized it was too late now—Big Tree and the other two were warned.

Cursing again in English, Touch the Sky pressured the dragoon pistol's trigger and the big gun bucked in his hand, a round punching into Lupe's vitals. One more down, Touch the Sky told himself, but now the element of surprise was lost.

141

"I'll get his weapon," Touch the Sky told Knobby. "You climb down the other side and start looking for a good place for us to hole up. The odds are down to three to two now, so I doubt they'll try to flush us."

"Big Tree ain't no hero," Knobby said. "You think he might just run?"

Touch the Sky nodded. "That's exactly what I think. So wherever we hole up, let's make sure we're in sight of the trail. That's the only way down from here. And I'll tell you right now, Big Tree won't leave this mountain alive unless I'm dead."

"Unless *we're* dead," Knobby corrected him. "I'm tired of that red bastard's ugly face. That sumbitch needs killin', and he needs it bad."

Touch the Sky knew they could see the pinnacle from San Sebastian with field glasses. Since his presence up here was no longer a secret, he didn't bother to sneak as he climbed down to Lupe's body and confiscated his weapon and bandolier.

Indeed, he even stared toward the houses and grinned his mocking, defiant grin as he knelt with one knee on Lupe's neck to hold the head in place. He made a quick outline cut around the scalp, then snapped it loose with one powerful tug and held it aloft.

"That stinking, flea-bitten, gut-eating savage!" Poco Loco fumed, handing the glasses to Big Tree. But the Comanche only waved them off—his sharp eyes had seen the mocking demonstration out in the rocks.

"*Jefe!*" Juan called out from the roof. "What do

we do now? That red devil is up here!"

"I have a remarkable grasp for the obvious, numbskull," Poco Loco shouted up to his man. "Stop blubbering like a woman and be a man!"

But in a quieter tone, the Mexican gang leader said with malevolent fury to Big Tree, "I should kill you, Quohada. When you rode in among us, I had ten men. Now look up there on the roof! That is the scrag end of my gang! And we are trapped here between the sap and the bark with a killing machine!"

"You could try to kill me," Big Tree agreed calmly. "And perhaps you could do it. You are no man to take lightly, Poco Loco. But there is also a very good chance that I would kill you first, true?"

Poco Loco said nothing. Some truths were too obvious for comment.

"But only think," Big Tree continued. "With me dead, you lose your best chance for survival against the Cheyenne."

"Why?" Poco Loco retorted. "It is you he is after."

"Are you so sure, amigo? If that is so, then why am I still alive while all of your men except one is carrion?"

Poco Loco met this with a gloomy silence.

"We two stand our best chance," Big Tree continued, "if we stand back to back against Touch the Sky. As for your men. You yourself admitted such as they are easily replaced. Keep your courage in your parfleche, Poco Loco, and we will soon be three thousand dollars richer."

Poco Loco considered all of this for some time before he finally nodded. "But what can we do?"

he protested. "We are low on food, supplies. We can't stay up here forever, hiding."

"No," Big Tree agreed, nodding. His weathered face was inscrutable as he turned and slowly stared up toward Juan.

"What we need," Big Tree said, "is to lay a trap with our remaining piece of bait."

Poco Loco was still distracted by his own worries and did not see where the other man was looking. "What bait?" he snapped peevishly.

"The bait up on the roof pissing himself in fright like a squaw woman."

Poco Loco met his eyes. "You mean—deliberately sacrifice Juan?"

Big Tree's lips twitched in the beginning of a grin. "You sound horrified. The tall one has killed your men anyway. Why should we not exact a profit from his killing? Besides—consider the alternative."

After some time, Poco Loco nodded. "As you say, Quohada. It is him or us."

Big Tree noticed the slight emphasis on the word "us," but kept a straight face. He knew Poco Loco as well as he knew himself. So he knew full well the Mexican would look out for his own hide and no one else's—exactly as Big Tree meant to do.

Both men fell silent, and in the distance rose the lone, mournful howl of a dog.

Chapter Fifteen

"Anyhow," Knobby said, gnawing on the last of his jerked meat, "they wa'n stupid enough to send another guard out."

A long day was almost behind them, and now Sister Sun sent their shadows slanting sharply toward the east. They had taken shelter behind a hastily erected breastwork of stone, almost certain that attempting to hide was a waste of time—the remaining trio were not likely to attack. Indeed, Touch the Sky thought—that would be preferable to the infinitely more dangerous job of routing them out.

Both men had taken turns snatching what sleep they could, for they were certain this night would bring trouble. Big Tree knew full well that a trapped man's chances for survival went down dramatically the longer he waited. Nor was the

Comanche one to let his enemy determine the battle plan.

"No, they sure as hell don't want to lose another gun," Touch the Sky said. "And that's the only reason they aren't sending a guard out. Big Tree and his Mexican friend with the scar are both two seeds from the same pod. They'd pick a baby up in a second if it would stop a bullet from hitting them."

Touch the Sky paused, listening to it: another long, drawn-out howl from the pack of wild dogs that obviously lived around here. Sometimes he could hear them snarling and fighting among themselves; other times he saw their eyes glowing furtively in the dark, watching him and Knobby.

"Them sons a bitchen dogs might go for the horses," Knobby said. "If we leave 'em alone too long."

Touch the Sky knew the old-timer was right. But this whole mission was a fool's venture, and the horses were just one more reckless chance that had to be taken. Besides, he was worn out from fretting all the things that might go wrong.

All day long, and during his fitful naps, Touch the Sky had been haunted by the pretty face of Honey Eater. Did the mother of his child still live, in spite of that smoke signal? Hope was a waking dream, and Touch the Sky clung to hope like a drowning man in a raging river, clinging to driftwood.

The wind, cooling rapidly now as the sun went down, suddenly rose with a howling shriek, slicing through their inadequate clothing.

"Colder 'n a landlord's heart," Knobby muttered.

Touch the Sky knew the old trapper was suffering bad, though Knobby said nothing. Touch the Sky was only one third his age, yet his bones were weary. What must it be like for Knobby? Despite his guilt at Knobby's suffering, however, Touch the Sky was glad the old man had insisted on coming along. That wild dog might well have gotten its fangs into his throat if Knobby hadn't knocked it ass over apple cart. It felt good to have a veteran frontiersman riding shotgun.

And besides—weariness didn't matter. This mission had to be completed. In one sense, it didn't matter if Honey Eater was dead or alive. Big Tree had to die. Touch the Sky knew that, knew it down deep in his bones the way a Baptist knew Jesus.

Again Touch the Sky examined the darkling sky, calculating how much time remained before the Red Raider of the Plains made his next move.

"Won't be long," Knobby assured him. "What's come so far has just been pee doodles. Before this night is over, boy, me 'n' you are gonna stir up a Fandango!"

"Juan," Poco Loco said casually, "go feed the horses before it gets too dark."

Juan, nursing the last of his mescal in the corner, looked up sullenly. Now that so many of his comrades were dead, he blamed Poco Loco and that savage Big Tree. But this was no time to mutiny—the two he hated were also his only hope for survival.

147

"Can't it wait until morning?" Juan said.

"No," Poco Loco added, "because we might be making our break tonight, and we'll need rested mounts."

This news seemed to hearten Juan. He set his bottle aside, grabbed his rifle, and moved to the front door. He waited until the other two were covering him, then threw the door open.

Nothing outside except the gray-black, barren twilight. Wind howled, making Juan grab to save his Sonora hat. But the prospect of leaving this hellhole heartened him. He went on outside and aimed for the corner of the plaza where the horses were tethered.

It had been Big Tree's idea to lure one of the wild dogs with meat, then tie it up as a sentry near the horses. Any attempt to approach them set the dog yapping like it was right now.

"I didn't think we'd ever get rid of him," Poco Loco said the moment the door shut behind the departing man. Poco Loco was glad now that they could talk. "What is the plan?"

"It won't be fancy," Big Tree assured him. "There isn't enough time to get creative. I think the best plan is to make the Cheyenne think we're making a break down the trail under cover of darkness. We'll wait until Juan comes back, then we'll act like we're planning it all out with him."

Big Tree interrupted himself for a moment when he heard it: a snarling clamor of dogs. Either fighting among themselves, or angry at the human intruders up here. Hearing the noise made him nervously recall the odd prophecy of a Kiowa medicine man: *Keep the dog far hence that is foe to Big Tree!*

"We will pretend," Big Tree continued, "that our best chance is to escape down the trail one at a time."

Big Tree tapped the deck of cards Poco Loco always carried in his vest pocket. "We will draw cards to see what order we ride out in. And, of course, you will stack the deck so that Juan rides first."

Poco Loco grinned, revealing yellow teeth like two rows of crooked gravestones. "*Claro*. The Cheyenne will strike at Juan, and when he reveals himself, we will strike at the Cheyenne."

Big Tree nodded. "As I said, nothing fancy. But at least it is a plan."

Poco Loco nudged the door open. He could see Juan hurrying back across the plaza, head bent into the wind.

"It is," he agreed. "This has been a hard bargain for me so far, Quohada. I have traded nine men for a chance at that Cheyenne, and still I have not had my opportunity. Let us hope number ten will be the charm."

It had better be, Poco Loco thought. Because if the Cheyenne kills number ten, he will turn to numbers eleven and twelve. And one of those numbers is mine.

Shortly after sunset, Knobby shook Touch the Sky from a light doze.

"Heigh-up, sprout! They're movin' out on us!"

Touch the Sky sat up quickly and glanced around the protective wall of the stone breastwork. It was true: There was enough moonlight to see that the trio in the house were cinching up.

"Only one way they can be going," the Cheyenne said quietly. "And that's down the mountain."

" 'Lessen it's a trap," Knobby remarked.

"Of course it's a trap," Touch the Sky said. "I know Big Tree like I know the Bighorn country. It's a trap. They were hoping we'd attack by now. They didn't provision themselves for a siege. So now they're drawing us out for a clear shot at us."

"Should we hang back and drop their horses?" Knobby suggested.

Touch the Sky shook his head. "Bad idea. What if ours are dead or gone when we get below?"

Knobby grunted affirmation. Something else occurred to him. It wasn't just dogs that posed a threat to their horses.

Knobby said, "They *will* be dead if them bastards ride down—they'll make sure they're dead. And us trapped on foot in the middle of goddamn nowhere."

"Check your powder," Touch the Sky told his partner. "We'll play it like this. We need to see what they've got planned before we move. But we don't dare let even one of them very far down that trail, or we can kiss our horses good-bye. You'll go back to that cleft in the pinnacle and watch them from there. I'm going down the trail a ways before they get started."

Knobby frowned. All his warrior instincts warned him against the folly of dividing their force, small as it was. But Touch the Sky's next words made good sense and showed he was thinking like his enemy.

"My hunch goes like this. They'll send the last member of the gang down the trail, hoping to draw me out for a shot. If that doesn't happen soon after their man hits the trail, they'll figure it's safe, and they'll hit it too. That's where you come in, Knobby. You can't get a plumb bead in this light. But you can shoot close enough to scare Big Tree back off that trail. I don't care about either of the Mexicans. It's Big Tree I want."

The old trapper nodded, clicking back the Kentucky rifle's mule-ear hammers. "Then it's Big Tree we'll get. Let's get 'er done, boy."

Juan didn't really mind it when he drew the low card and had to ride first down that trail. That way, at least, his back trail would be covered. Of course, the prospect of hitting that trail left him with a sickening loss-of-gravity tickle in his stomach. But he would rather harrow hell than sit up there in that stone coffin, waiting for death to strike.

"Give your mount his head and let him set the pace," Poco Loco informed him. "I will ride down behind you, about five minutes after you set out. Keep a good eye to the shadows—that is where he will lurk."

Poco Loco and Big Tree had taken up positions among the boulders heaped at the head of the mountain trail. Each man took advantage of what moonlight there was, scouring the surrounding terrain.

Juan made sure he had a primer cap on the nib of his rifle. "See you down below," he called out bravely, swinging up into the saddle and nudging his mount toward the trail.

Touch the Sky heard the Mexican descending long before he came into view.

As the exhausted Cheyenne crouched there in the darkness beside the narrow trail, his optimism began to grow. For it had occurred to him: If he killed the next man silently and efficiently enough, he might simply be able to wait right here for Big Tree, too, to come down.

He left his knife in its sheath. A knife was excellent in a grappling struggle or for ground fighting—and most fights quickly ended up on the ground. But a stabbed man often cried out. In Touch the Sky's experience, clubbing a man to death was the most silent way to kill.

His Sharps was solid, with a good length. He took off his leather shirt and wrapped it around the barrel, using it to get a good grip.

The steady clip-clop of approaching hooves grew gradually louder. The Cheyenne touched his medicine pouch as he sent a silent prayer to Maiyun, God of the red man, asking him once again to make him worthy to be a warrior.

Big Tree waited, in the first minutes after Juan rode down, for the crack of a rifle, the shriek as an arrow pierced Juan's lights, the frenzied nickering of a panicked horse. But down below all was silent—ominously silent, like the dead calm before a gully washer.

Maybe, just maybe, it's clear, Big Tree thought. A hard little nubbin of hope began to grow inside him. The Cheyenne could be asleep or holed up.

Think that way, a sudden inner voice warned him, *and you'd best sing your death song.*

Big Tree glanced through the darkness toward Poco Loco's rock. Best to stick to the plan, the Comanche thought. Let Poco Loco go next. He didn't want that crazy bastard behind him anyway—not now, with the Mexican nursing a grudge against him.

Besides, if Touch the Sky was down that trail, as Big Tree believed, then it was best to have two men go first—that was two chances Touch the Sky would be killed before Big Tree got to him.

Sometimes the balance of opportunity could shift in an eyeblink. Touch the Sky had been in enough battles to realize that. Seldom did raw power or pure attrition bring on a victory—almost always, one side or the other got a sudden break.

These thoughts, however, were very remote from his mind as the Cheyenne raised his rifle like a club in the darkness, preparing to strike at the descending enemy.

At that moment, a heavy bank of cirrus clouds blew away from the moon. Unnoticed by Touch the Sky, a tiny piece of silver trim on his rifle stock glinted for a moment in the moonlight.

Juan, descending with his head swiveling from side to side, felt his heart skip a beat when he saw something flash beside the trail—up ahead, just to the right: Had there been enough time, he might have ruined the opportunity by halting his horse and thus warning the bushwhacker.

Instead, with the reflexive quickness of a cat, he

nudged his rifle off his saddle tree and let the barrel swing right and down. At the same moment a shadowy figure loomed up, Juan pressured his trigger, and an orange spear-tip of muzzle flash illuminated—point blank—the war face of the Cheyenne!

Chapter Sixteen

That shot, Poco Loco told himself the moment he heard a rifle speak its piece down the trail, that was Juan's old British trade rifle. He recognized its distinctive, high-pitched crack.

He waited for more shots, but none came. There was only a long, suspenseful pause, then the recognizable clatter of iron-shod hooves on rock as Juan's pony made its escape down the trail.

Quickly, knowing his life depended on the right decision, Poco Loco tried to read these clues.

If the Cheyenne had struck first, silently as usual, then it was unlikely Juan would have gotten off a shot. On the other hand, if Juan got lucky first, it would make sense that his rifle was the only one Poco Loco heard.

Hope sounded its notes in his breast as Poco Loco continued to mine this vein of thought. After

Judd Cole

all, Juan could indeed have gotten lucky. Though a bit of a coward, he was intelligent and careful; more important, that red killer had to be getting careless by now. This ruthless pace, the exhausting ride, the lack of sleep or good shelter—even the best men courted death once they got careless on *la frontera*.

But if Juan had killed the Cheyenne, why would he escape down the trail instead of coming back up here to gloat and brag with his comrades? It didn't make—

Christ Jesus!

All of an instant, Poco Loco understood: It was the Cheyenne's head! That was why Juan was running like a bat out of hell. Every one of the men knew the head was worth three thousand in gold to some gringo named Hiram Steele.

That pause after the shot: Juan must have taken just enough time to decapitate the corpse.

Originally, Poco Loco had meant to wait until Big Tree went down first, knowing that was his best protection against the Cheyenne killing machine. Now, however, it was suddenly more important than life itself to get down that trail first and lay hands on that treacherous son of a bitch Juan.

Big Tree struck a lode when he said it: A man in Mexico toiled for thirty cents a day. To hell with any gang—Poco Loco could take that head himself and live in comfort down in Guadalajara.

Poco Loco slid his scattergun from its sling on his side and broke open the breech to make sure both bores were loaded. Then, his face urgent with the need to hurry, he raced for his mount.

*   *   *

Big Tree, who knew Touch the Sky far better than did his Mexican companion, interpreted events quite differently.

The Comanche, too, hunkered behind his boulder, had been surprised to hear Juan's British rifle crack first. It was not Touch the Sky's way to allow his prey a shot.

However, the pause after the shot, then the clopping of escaping hooves, answered the mystery for him.

Big Tree's ear was trained for survival. He recognized immediately, from the sound, that the escaping horse was riderless. A riderless horse sent up a different pattern, less rhythmic.

And if Juan's horse was riderless, the best conclusion was that Touch the Sky had killed the rider.

Big Tree saw Poco Loco break for the trail, and a cynical grin tugged at his lips. Let the Mexican run to the trap. Big Tree had other ideas.

There was a chance Poco Loco would succeed where Juan had not. He was a steady man in a crisis, never getting so agitated that he forgot to make every shot count—one bullet, one enemy.

If a shotgun roared, Big Tree thought, that might be a hopeful sign. But he didn't count on it. Instead, he meant to take a leaf out of the Cheyenne's own book. He was going to take cover behind the very rock breastwork that Touch the Sky had used. Big Tree had one chance, and he knew it. That was to make the Cheyenne come to him, not the other way around.

If Poco Loco did kill the Cheyenne, all well and

Judd Cole

good. Big Tree would be out nothing except an unnecessary vigil.

Big Tree glanced around uneasily, wondering about the second man with Touch the Sky. He hadn't seen any sign of him up here, but that didn't mean he wasn't there.

For a moment the big renegade flinched when a sudden howl sounded, very nearby this time. Those damned dogs were obviously moving in.

Moving quickly from boulder to boulder, Big Tree raced west toward the breastwork.

Shit-oh-dear, Knobby thought as he watched all the action below. What the hell's going on?

He could not see well enough from his position in the cleft pinnacle to draw a bead on anybody. If he could have, he'd have been happy to backshoot Big Tree. But when that gun went off down the trail, the old man had watched the Mexican *jefe* take off for below. Soon after that, Big Tree broke for the rocks to the left of the trail.

Tarnal hell, Knobby thought. Talk about being trapped between a rock and a hard place! He had to make a decision. Stay right here and wait for Matthew, thus keeping an eye on Big Tree, or break for below and see if Matthew was still alive but perhaps injured.

If Matthew came up soon enough, that would be best, Knobby thought. Then he could simply warn the Cheyenne, as he broke up from the trail, that Big Tree was waiting in their old hiding place.

But although Knobby forced himself to wait patiently, Matthew didn't show.

"Katy Christ," he muttered out loud. Much as

158

he hated to make the wrong move, he had to check on the sprout. If he was lying down there bleeding to death . . .

His tired old bones flaring in protest, Knobby clutched Patsy Plumb close to his chest and began climbing down from his post.

Touch the Sky had no idea that the Mexican named Juan had seen him. Only the reflexive instincts of a honed warrior made him tuck and roll just as that rifle went off.

The Cheyenne had no time for grace or to plan his leap. Even as a bullet creased his skull, thumping it like a mule kick, he simply threw himself down and forward—right into the forelegs of Juan's pinto.

Already the Mexican was squaring around for a second shot, and Touch the Sky knew it. Desperate, he relied on an offensive move perfected by beleaguered Cheyenne warriors in the days before they rode horses but their enemies did.

A horse was very vulnerable in its thin forelegs. Touch the Sky wrapped himself around these as he fell, twisting hard left to topple the horse, then immediately hard right to avoid its falling weight.

He succeeded in making the horse crash down hard, snapping Juan's spine as it did. But the tired brave could not quite roll completely clear himself. The horse's big head cracked down hard on Touch the Sky's, and though he fought against it, the darkness of oblivion washed over him even as the horse struggled to its feet and escaped down the trail.

* * *

Judd Cole

Poco Loco had not bothered with discretion, coming down the trail after that thieving bastard Juan. All the Mexican gang leader could think about was laying hands on that valuable Cheyenne head.

But he reined in abruptly, heart leaping into his throat, when he saw the tangled mass of limbs in the trail just below him.

Startled, he slid to the ground and moved his horse between himself and the two men who lay sprawled ahead. Thus protected, Poco Loco stared at the inert forms while he cautiously waited and assembled all the details.

What he saw made his scarred visage divide itself in an ear-to-ear smile.

Juan was dead as a Paiute grave—that was clear from the impossible angle of his spine. The Cheyenne, however, was merely unconscious. Poco Loco could see the steady, strong rising of his muscle-corded chest.

"Juan, old chum," Poco Loco said softly, chuckling, "I owe you an apology. Good work, hombre! Your death has handed me three thousand *yanqui* dollars in gold."

Poco Loco quickly hobbled his horse foreleg to rear. Then he walked closer, lining the muzzle of his scattergun up with the unconscious Cheyenne's heart. It was essential not to mar the face. Poco Loco wanted this Hiram Steele to see exactly whom he was paying for.

Poco Loco took up the trigger slack, squeezed harder, and then came a booming roar. A heartbeat later, the back of Poco Loco's skull lifted off like the lid of a cookie jar, and the Mexican folded to the ground dead.

Desert Manhunt

"Kiss for ya, you ugly beaner bastard," Knobby said out loud from his position about twenty yards farther up the trail. Patsy's top muzzle still gave off curls of smoke.

Then, his fingers crossed, Knobby moved forward to see if Matthew still belonged to the world of the living.

Matthew did indeed belong to the living. But he had also cracked his head hard under the impact of the falling horse. When Knobby asked the groggy Cheyenne what tribe he belonged to, he answered with a straight face, "Coyotero Apache."

Any other time, Knobby might have laughed out loud. But it wasn't particularly funny right now— not with Big Tree prowling the area and Touch the Sky too stove up to be moved.

Knobby did what he had been doing all his life— made the best of a bad situation.

Moving very carefully and slowly, he dragged his friend as far off the trail as he could. Then the old man, grunting and cursing, kneecaps popping, gathered up rocks and built another breastwork for defense. At least, Knobby consoled himself, they knew Big Tree had only one direction from which to approach them.

That done, Knobby managed to shoot a mountain goat. He butchered out the hindquarters, the only part that made good eating. He built a fire under some rocks and cooked the meat on it.

By daylight Touch the Sky had come to, though his head throbbed in painful explosions every time he tried to move. Knobby, who had guarded the trail during the long hours, took a turn at sleeping. Off and on they relieved each other, sleeping and fortifying their strength with fresh meat.

Knobby had already informed Touch the Sky that Big Tree was holed up behind their old breastwork. Touch the Sky considered it for some time. Finally, he saw how things stood.

"Big Tree would have come down by now," he told Knobby, "if he wanted to force my hand against him. But he's not. He's deliberately holding back. He's giving me the choice."

The old man nodded. "I figgered it by now, too. He's putting it to you as straight as it could be put. You can ride out now and live out your days. Or you can go up topside and maybe dig your own grave. Been almost a whole day now he's been waiting. It's time to post the pony or pull stakes."

Touch the Sky nodded. Neither one of them doubted what Touch the Sky intended to do.

"I'm going up there at sundown," Touch the Sky said. "This has dragged out too long, and I'm sick of it. But there's no good reason for you to wait here. If you do, he could kill you if—well, if he whips me. And there's a good chance he can. I hate that bastard, but I'm the first to say he fights like five men."

"Ahh, t' hell with you," Knobby said with exaggerated nonchalance. "I ain't goin' nowheres. Get your blanket ass up that slope and kill that red son, wouldja, boy? Pretty quick I got to get—your ma and pa would like to brand the year-old colts *some* goddamn time. Used to was, you didn't take so damn long to kill a worthless varmit!"

Touch the Sky rallied at this show of bravado,

for it was exactly the kind of show that his own band would have put on at a time like this. When death breathed down a man's neck, that was the time to joke and make light of it with companions. Otherwise terror might defeat him even before the battle.

But bravado was to make a man feel courage. It would not kill Big Tree. Touch the Sky settled into his robe, watching the light in the sky, waiting.

Although Knobby had recruited their ponies safely, Touch the Sky chose to go up that slope silently on foot.

The sun had settled behind the horizon, leaving the mountains shrouded in their customary cloaks of cold darkness. But a three-quarter moon and a star-spattered sky provided ample, if ghostly, light.

Touch the Sky's double-soled moccasins were silent on the sharp-edged rocks. He ascended the trail like a shadow, gliding silently, making progress without appearing to be moving.

Sweat broke out on his back, causing the sharp gusts of wind to slice into him. He could feel the reassuring weight of his Sharps in his hands, the knife tucked into his sash. Though he was aware that Big Tree was any man's equal, Touch the Sky did not feel great fear—only a calm, fierce determination to rid the world once and for all of this Comanche menace.

Staying behind rocks, he eased up off the trail onto the flat above. He glanced left and immediately spotted them in the moonlight: dead dogs.

Several of them, scattered around in front of the breastwork. Two more living dogs, evidently scavenging carrion, skulked off as the Cheyenne appeared.

Looks like Big Tree had himself a night of it, Touch the Sky thought absently. But was he still behind that breastwork? Or had he moved east and reoccupied the town itself?

Cautiously, moving from boulder to boulder, Touch the Sky began to ease across the barren expanse. He was just moving past the lookout pinnacle, the one with the cleft in it, when Touch the Sky heard it: a low, simmering growl that originated from overhead.

Dog close by, he thought, glancing overhead. But when he did, a shock slammed into him like a body blow.

Big Tree stood crouched in the cleft, ready to spring on him! But the shock of seeing the Comanche in his present condition completely stunned Touch the Sky and blunted his instincts to react.

Big Tree had torn all of his clothes off, and his naked body was savaged by tooth marks. Obviously he had been attacked by a pack of wild dogs. Just as obviously, judging from the white foam pouring down his chin, at least one of the dogs that bit him was rabid.

It was not a man who hurled himself down onto Touch the Sky, but a wild and savage animal. The Cheyenne was slow to move, and the big Comanche's weight threw him hard to the ground.

Touch the Sky's rifle was useless, close in like this. He threw it aside, even as he fought to avoid

Big Tree's gnashing teeth, and wrestled his knife from its sheath.

Big Tree didn't need a weapon. Rabid as he now was, his teeth had become all the weapons he needed. Touch the Sky knew that he was worm fodder if he let his enemy bite him.

Like all insane men, Big Tree's prodigious strength was nearly doubled. He easily trapped the Cheyenne under him, though Touch the Sky had managed to get a hand under his chin so he could keep Big Tree's mouth rammed shut.

Thus they struggled, Big Tree wearing him down, Touch the Sky unable to get his knife hand around for a killing blow. Slowly, inexorably, the Cheyenne's left arm weakened. With an abrupt snarl of triumphant rage, Big Tree threw his head back and bared his dripping fangs for the final plunge.

Touch the Sky's last image was of his beautiful wife, drained pale as moonstone from loss of blood. And then Arrow Keeper's voice came back to him from the hinterland of memory: *Tell me how you die, and I'll tell you what you're worth.*

And all of a moment, Touch the Sky knew that he could not let his adversary triumph—could not let this miserable, literal dog's death be the final statement on his own worth as a man.

With a howl of rage that drowned out Big Tree, the Cheyenne arched his back hard and threw the Comanche aside. In a heartbeat his knife hand was free, Touch the Sky leaped, and then heat flooded his hand when he shoved the obsidian blade deep into the renegade's warm and beating heart.

*   *   *

Many sleeps later, as twilight glittered to life over the Powder River Cheyenne camp, a lone rider on a coyote dun appeared on the final ridge overlooking the camp.

"Hii-ya!" he shouted to the rest, announcing his arrival with the war cry. "Hii-*ya!*"

Touch the Sky, who had no way of knowing that false word of his death had been sent north, could not understand the look of overwhelming joy on the faces of his men as they raced up the slope to greet him.

He knew only, with no shame in his heart, that he was crying hot, copious tears when he saw her: Honey Eater, walking, then running, out of their tipi to greet him. Little Bear ran out behind her, shouting for his father.

Honey Eater still walked among the living. In that moment Touch the Sky forgot everything else except his gratitude to the Holy Ones who had kept her alive. He raised his lance toward the heavens, and he found himself saying the same words his friend Little Horse had said at the beginning of this epic journey: *There is hope*.

TROUBLE MAN

ED GORMAN

Ray Coyle used to be a gunfighter. And when he gets word his boy has been killed in a gunfight in Coopersville, he has to go there—to bring the body home. But when the old gunfighter steps off the train, he brings his gun with him, along with something else . . . trouble.

___4440-4 $4.99 US/$5.99 CAN

KIT CARSON

BLOOD RENDEZVOUS
DOUG HAWKINS

The high point of any trapper's year is the summer rendezvous, the annual gathering where mountain men from all over the frontier meet to trade the pelts they risked their lives for. But for Kit Carson, the real danger lies in getting to the rendezvous. He is leading a party of trappers, all of them weighed down with a year's worth of furs. That is enough to make them a tempting target for any killer on the trail—especially when the trail leads through Blackfoot territory.

___4499-4 $3.99 US/$4.99 CAN

CHEYENNE

RENEGADE NATION
ORPHAN TRAIN
JUDD COLE

Renegade Nation. Born the son of a great chief, raised by frontier settlers, Touch the Sky will never forsake his pioneer friends in their time of need. Then Touch the Sky's enemies join forces against all his people—both Indian and white. If the fearless brave's magic is not strong enough, he will be powerless to stop the annihilation of the two worlds he loves. *And in the same action-packed volume . . .*

Orphan Train. When his enemies kidnap a train full of orphans heading west, the young shaman finds himself torn between the white men and the Indians. To save the children, the mighty warrior will have to risk his life, his home, and his dreams of leading his tribe to glory.

___4511-7 $4.99 US/$5.99 CAN

Dorchester Publishing Co., Inc.
P.O. Box 6640
Wayne, PA 19087-8640

Please add $1.75 for shipping and handling for the first book and $.50 for each book thereafter. NY, NYC, and PA residents, please add appropriate sales tax. No cash, stamps, or C.O.D.s. All orders shipped within 6 weeks via postal service book rate. Canadian orders require $2.00 extra postage and must be paid in U.S. dollars through a U.S. banking facility.

Name_____
Address_____
City_____State_____Zip_____
I have enclosed $_____ in payment for the checked book(s).
Payment <u>must</u> accompany all orders. ❏ Please send a free catalog.
    CHECK OUT OUR WEBSITE! www.dorchesterpub.com

Last Chance

DEE MARVINE

Mattie Hamil is on a frantic journey west. On her own, with only her grit and determination to see her through, she has to find her charming gambler of a fiancé, and she has to do it fast—before her pregnancy shows. From a steamboat along the Missouri River to the rough-and-tumble post-gold-rush town of Last Chance, Montana, Mattie's trek leads her through danger and sorrow, friendship and joy. But even after she finds her fiancé, no bend in the trail leads to what she expected.

___4475-7 $4.99 US/$5.99 CAN

DAVY CROCKETT

BLOOD HUNT

David Thompson

With only his oldest friend and his trusty long rifle for company, Davy Crockett explores the wild frontier looking for adventure, and has the strength and cunning to face any enemy. But even he may have met his match when he gets caught between two warring tribes on one side and a dangerous band of white men on the other—all of them willing to die—and kill—for a group of stolen women. It is up to Crockett to save the women, his friend and his own hide if he wants to live to explore another day.

_4229-0 $3.99 US/$4.99 CAN

The Dark Brand

H. A. DeRosso

Driscoll made a mistake and he's paying for it. They stuck him in a cell—with a man condemned to hang the next morning. Driscoll learns how his cellmate robbed a bank and killed a man...and how the money was never recovered. But he never learns where the money is. After Driscoll serves his time and drifts back into town, he learns that the loot is still hidden, and that just about everyone thinks the condemned man told Driscoll where it is buried before he died. Suddenly it seems everybody wants that money— enough to kill for it.

___4412-9 $4.50 US/$5.50 CAN

LAST OF
THE DUANES

Buck Duane's father was a gunfighter who died by the gun, and, in accepting a drunken bully's challenge, Duane finds himself forced into the life of an outlaw. He roams the dark trails of southwestern Texas, living in outlaw camps, until he meets the one woman who can help him overcome his past—a girl named Jennie Lee.

___4430-7 $4.99 US/$5.99 CAN

Dorchester Publishing Co., Inc.
P.O. Box 6640
Wayne, PA 19087-8640

Please add $1.75 for shipping and handling for the first book and $.50 for each book thereafter. NY, NYC, and PA residents, please add appropriate sales tax. No cash, stamps, or C.O.D.s. All orders shipped within 6 weeks via postal service book rate. Canadian orders require $2.00 extra postage and must be paid in U.S. dollars through a U.S. banking facility.

Name_____

Address_____

City_____State_____Zip_____

I have enclosed $_____ in payment for the checked book(s).

Payment <u>must</u> accompany all orders. ❑ Please send a free catalog.

CHECK OUT OUR WEBSITE! www.dorchesterpub.com

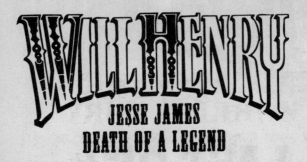

WILL HENRY

JESSE JAMES
DEATH OF A LEGEND

Beneath the bandanna, underneath the legend, Jesse James was a wild and wicked man: a sinister and brutal outlaw who blazed a trail of crime and violence through the lawless West. Ripping the mask off the mysterious Jesse James, Will Henry's *Death Of A Legend* is a novel as tough and savage as the man himself. Only a great Western writer like Henry could tell the real story of the infamous bandit Jesse James.

_3990-7 $4.99 US/$6.99 CAN

Dorchester Publishing Co., Inc.
P.O. Box 6640
Wayne, PA 19087-8640

Please add $1.75 for shipping and handling for the first book and $.50 for each book thereafter. NY, NYC, and PA residents, please add appropriate sales tax. No cash, stamps, or C.O.D.s. All orders shipped within 6 weeks via postal service book rate. Canadian orders require $2.00 extra postage and must be paid in U.S. dollars through a U.S. banking facility.

Name_____

Address_____

City_____ State_____ Zip_____

I have enclosed $_____ in payment for the checked book(s).

Payment <u>must</u> accompany all orders. ☐ Please send a free catalog.

CHEYENNE

JUDD COLE

Follow the adventures of Touch the Sky as he searches for a world he can call his own!

#3: Renegade Justice. When his adopted white parents fall victim to a gang of ruthless outlaws, Touch the Sky swears to save them—even if it means losing the trust he has risked his life to win from the Cheyenne.
__3385-2 $3.50 US/$4.50 CAN

#4: Vision Quest. While seeking a mystical sign from the Great Spirit, Touch the Sky is relentlessly pursued by his enemies. But the young brave will battle any peril that stands between him and the vision of his destiny.
__3411-5 $3.50 US/$4.50 CAN

CHEYENNE

Double Edition:
Pathfinder/ Buffalo Hiders
JUDD COLE

Pathfinder. Touch the Sky never forgot the kindness of the settlers, and tried to help them whenever possible. But an old friend's request to negotiate a treaty between the Cheyenne and gold miners brings the young brave face-to-face with a cunning warrior. If Touch the Sky can't defeat his new enemy, the territory will never again be safe for pioneers.
And in the same action-packed volume...
Buffalo Hiders. Once, mighty herds of buffalo provided the Cheyenne with food, clothing and skins for shelter. Then the white hunters appeared and the slaughter began. Still, few herds remain, and Touch the Sky swears he will protect them. But two hundred veteran mountain men and Indian killers are bent on wiping out the remaining buffalo—and anyone who stands in their way.

___4413-7 $4.99 US/$5.99 CAN

CHEYENNE
WENDIGO MOUNTAIN
DEATH CAMP
JUDD COLE

Wendigo Mountain. A Cheyenne warrior raised by white settlers, Touch the Sky is blessed with strong medicine. Yet his powers as a shaman cannot help him foretell that his tribe's sacred arrows will be stolen—or that his enemies will demand his head for their return. To save his tribe from utter destruction, the young brave will wage a battle like none he's ever fought.

And in the same action-packed volume . . .

Death Camp. Touch the Sky will gladly give his life to protect his tribe. Yet not even he can save them from an outbreak of deadly disease. Racing against time and brutal enemies, Touch the Sky has to either forsake his heritage and trust the white man's medicine—or prove his loyalty even as he watches his proud people die.

___4479-X $4.99 US/$5.99 CAN

A BALLAD FOR SALLIE

JUDY ALTER

Longhair Jim Courtright has been both a marshal and a desperado—and in Hell's Half Acre, the roughest part of Fort Worth, he is a living legend. His skill with a gun has made him a hero in some people's eyes . . . and a killer in others'. As soon as young widow Sallie McNutt steps off the stage from Tennessee, her refined manners and proper attire set her apart from the other women of the Half Acre. And it isn't long before something else sets her apart—someone wants her dead.

___4365-3 $4.50 US/$5.50 CAN

Dorchester Publishing Co., Inc.
P.O. Box 6640
Wayne, PA 19087-8640

Please add $1.75 for shipping and handling for the first book and $.50 for each book thereafter. NY, NYC, and PA residents, please add appropriate sales tax. No cash, stamps, or C.O.D.s. All orders shipped within 6 weeks via postal service book rate. Canadian orders require $2.00 extra postage and must be paid in U.S. dollars through a U.S. banking facility.

Name_____
Address_____
City_____ State_____ Zip_____
I have enclosed $_____ in payment for the checked book(s).
Payment <u>must</u> accompany all orders. ☐ Please send a free catalog.